ABOUT THIS BOOK

Welcome to Havenwood Falls, home to sexy men, strong women, and neighbors who bite. Discover supernatural mystery, thrills, and romance in a place where everyone has a deep, dark, and often deadly secret. This is only but one...

With her past memories mostly restored, Michaela Petran begins to pick up the pieces and resettle into life in Havenwood Falls. But resuming where she left off with the man she loves and the plans they'd made is no simple matter. Suddenly head of the family and leader of the moroi vampires, she faces an onslaught of unexpected obligations, making her feel like she has no choices in her own life. And even if she could have everything she wants, she can't help but fear it'll all be ripped away from her once again.

For five years, Xandru Roca ached for Michaela to return, but never believed it would actually happen. Now that he has a second chance with her, he's afraid he'll blow it by hanging on too tightly. But if he's not careful, she might again vanish from his life.

As they try to bridge the chasm between them, family matters demand their attention, pulling them apart. After all, there's still a strigoi curse, dictates of the supernatural Court, and dark magic wreaking havoc on their siblings. Family and love always come first, but while they try to save one, they risk losing the other.

HAVENWOOD FALLS BOOKS

Forget You Not by Kristie Cook

Old Wounds by Susan Burdorf

Fate, Love & Loyalty by E.J. Fechenda

The Winged & the Wicked by T.V. Hahn & Kristie Cook

Alpha's Queen by Lila Felix

Ink & Fire by R.K. Ryals

Lose You Not by Kristie Cook

Tragic Ink by Heather Hildenbrand

Nowhere to Hide by Belinda Boring

Flames Among the Frost by Amy Hale

Rock Me Gently by Susan Burdorf

From the Embers by Amy Miles

Defying Gravity by Kallie Ross

Break Me Not by Kristie Cook

How the Dead Lie by Stacey Rourke

The Lurkers Within by Danielle Bannister

The Collector: Awakening by Kristie Cook, R.K. Ryals, Belinda Boring & Nadirah Foxx

Addicted to You by Belinda Boring

Affliction Mine by C.J. Pinard

The Ward & the Wanderers by T.V. Hahn

Toil & Trouble by Melissa Wright

Of Salt and Stars by Seven Jane

Redefined by Morgan Wylie

Betrayal Among the Frost by Amy Hale

Forever Loyal by E.J. Fechenda

Fate's Demand by Emily Cyr

The Wu & the Wand by T.V. Hahn

A Demon's Redemption by JD Nelson

Also try the YA line, Havenwood Falls High; the historical paranormal line, Legends of Havenwood Falls; the darker, sexier side of town, Havenwood Falls Sin & Silk; and the local supernatural college, Sun & Moon Academy.

Stay up to date at www.HavenwoodFalls.com

BOOKS BY KRISTIE COOK

Savage Salvation (Sin & Silk)

Sun & Moon Academy Book One: Fall Semester

Sun & Moon Academy Book Two: Fall Semester

The Winged & the Wicked (with T.V. Hahn)

Havenwood Falls Short Story Anthology 2018

Havenwood Falls Short Story Anthology 2019

Havenwood Falls Short Story Anthology 2020

Havenwood Falls Short Story Anthology 2021

Havenwood Falls Spring Anthology 2022

Havenwood Falls Sunset Anthology 2022

BOOK OF PHOENIX

The Space Between

The Space Beyond

The Space Within

LOSE YOU NOT

A HAVENWOOD FALLS NOVEL

KRISTIE COOK

For the Havenwood Falls family
and my own

*The only people who truly know your story are the ones who help you
write it.*
~ Unknown

What is family? They were the people who claimed you, in good, in bad, in parts, or in whole. They were the ones who showed up, who stayed there regardless.

~ Unknown

CHAPTER 1

MICHAELA

"*B*adass vampire. I'm a badass vampire. I can do this."

Chanting the words out loud, I followed a horrendous stink down the third-floor hallway of Whisper Falls Inn, built by my father in 1854 and inherited by his twenty-four-year-old daughter, yours truly. Armored in elbow-length rubber gloves, an old hoodie, sweatpants, and shit-kicker boots, I pulled a scarf up over my nose and mouth, then held the broom upside down, ready to swing. I stopped at the end of the hall, in front of one of our two suites, this one in the uppermost turret of the Victorian mansion. Nobody had seen the guest since dusk last night, but the room key showed up on the front desk early this morning, and by noon, this odor had permeated all the way downstairs to the lobby. I had no idea what the guy had done in there, but judging by the putrid smell, it couldn't be good.

This was what my life had become.

"I swear to all, if there's a dead body in there, I'm going to be fucking pissed." I rolled my shoulders, then yelled, because I didn't know where in the building she was, "Mammie, I'm going in!"

Before I could lose my nerve, I slammed the door open and jumped back, just in case something pounced.

"Oh. My. *God!*" I screeched, bile rising into my mouth. I threw my arm across my face. "Oh god, oh god, oh god."

The only thing that pounced was the smell, a gazillion times worse now. My eyes watered, and my chest heaved as I fought the urge to puke. I tightened my grip on the broom handle and slowly made my way into the suite, my gaze sweeping the circular room. Blinking against the tears, I saw nothing out of the ordinary. The sitting area looked untouched. The bed was rumpled, obviously slept in last night—before the jerk took off without checking out—but nothing gross stained the bedding, despite the stench. Like feces. Or vomit. Or other bodily fluids.

The odor wafted strongest from the bathroom. Of course. I gave myself another pep talk as I inched my way there, which gave Madame Luiza, aka Mammie, plenty of time to find me and glide into the room.

"Oh, dear," she said. And considering she was a ghost, if she could smell it, it was bad. "Be careful, Michaela."

With her Romanian accent, my aunt said my name with its original pronunciation—Me-*hay*-la—rather than with the hard *k* everyone else gave it. Of course, everyone else tended to give me a nickname: Kaela, Kales, even Kaekae.

Because that was totally badass.

"How bad can it be?" I squared my shoulders and lifted my chin.

"I'll go in first," Mammie said. "Nothing can make me deader than I already am."

Before I could protest, she disappeared into the bathroom and returned only a heartbeat later. If ghosts could be green, she would have been. Her purple ball gown, in which she was perpetually dressed, appeared to be no worse for the wear, but that didn't really mean much, considering. Her cheeks puffed out, as though she fought a gag, and she clamped her hands over her mouth. She couldn't actually puke, but with that kind of reaction, whatever that bathroom harbored was way worse than I thought.

"Badass vampire," I repeated in a firm whisper before forcing myself through the bathroom doorway. And then I froze, staring at the scene in front of me. "What the fuck?"

"Language, dear," Mammie admonished, her voice muffled behind her hands.

"Really, Mammie? There's absolutely nothing else to say!"

A pinkish gelatinous goo stuck to nearly every surface, as though a giant troll had sneezed, spraying pink snot everywhere. It was splattered all over the faded and stained wallpaper, clung to the chipped porcelain sink and old-fashioned tub, and slid slimy trails down the warped mirror. Something large and plasma-y filled the toilet, pouring over the edge and slopping onto the yellowed tile floor.

I spun the broom and jabbed at it with the stick end. It shook like jelly. I lifted it with the broom handle, and my stomach lurched.

"He *molted*?" I shrieked. "That son of a bitch *molted* in my inn? And what the hell molts like *this*?"

The substance was not at all like a reptile skin. Not papery and dry. More like a big, bloodless placenta.

But mammals didn't molt.

"Skinwalker," Mammie whispered. "It must be. I *knew* he was no regular shifter."

"Skinwalker?" I echoed.

"They shed their skin to take on another—a whole different appearance. Sometimes a whole different life. They're very rare. I've only ever met one before, back in the 1920s."

"So what's all over the walls and everything else? Do these skinwalkers explode, too?"

Mammie patted her silver bun as she glanced around, then shrugged. "Maybe if their new body is larger than their old skin?"

"Ew! Gross." I shuddered at the image while trying to hold back the vomit that kept making its way up the back of my throat.

Groaning, I poked and prodded the gunk, working it out of the toilet, because it obviously was not going to flush through the pipes. Finally, the end of it flopped out of the bowl and onto the floor, splashing at my feet and sending Mammie out into the bedroom part of the suite. I tried pushing it out of the way with the broom handle. At first it jiggled, but barely moved. So I gave it a harder shove, and the handle slipped right through the substance like a knife through warm butter and drove into the wall. Little black things—and some not so little—poured out of the hole and scurried over the wall.

"Ahhhhh!"

I ran out of the bathroom screaming, with Mammie right on my heels, shrieking even louder. We flew through the hall, down the steps, rounding the flights, not stopping until we hit the lobby three floors down. I fell to my knees, panting and heaving, my whole body trembling as my hands pressed into my chest, as if they could slow my heart.

"Spiders," I choked out. "Fucking spiders."

Mammie burst out laughing.

Lifting my head, I glared at her with narrowed eyes.

She tried to rein herself in. "I'm sorry, dear. If you could have only seen your face. Are you sure you're moroi?"

"Hey!" I waggled a finger at her. "You were running and screaming, too."

"I was not running," she denied, but a smile twitched at her lips. "I can't run, dear. Ghosts fly."

And for some reason, that statement broke through my fear, and laughter consumed me until I was crying. Once I was able to compose myself, I pushed up to my feet.

"We're burning the whole place down," I declared as the front door opened.

A teen and a tween, both dark-haired, entered, the smell of an early summer evening carried in with them—pine, freshly mown grass, and wildflowers.

"You're *what*?" Gabe, my twelve-year-old brother, asked, his eyes wide in his thin face. They were still brown because he was still human, meaning his moroi gene hadn't been triggered. That usually happened at around twenty years old.

"Gabe decided he didn't want to hang out with Cody after all, so

I brought him home," Aurelia, our sixteen-year-old sister, also still human, whined as she followed behind him, both of their slender bodies clad in shorts and tanks.

What they called summer here in the mountains was a lot closer to the winters I'd grown used to during my five years in Atlanta. So while everyone else already wore summer attire, I was still comfortable in hoodies and jeans. And technically, summer didn't start until next week. Maybe by the end of July, I'd dare a pair of shorts.

"He could have walked," Aurelia continued. "It's not like it's all that far, but noooo, whiny baby insisted on a ride. Oh, well. Lena didn't want to do anything, and Laurel was being a snot anyway." Her nose wrinkled as she finally got over herself and noticed her surroundings. "What died?" Her eyes flew wide open, and she had the decency to throw a hand over her mouth in embarrassment as she looked at Mammie. "I didn't . . . I mean . . . what stinks?"

"Spiders. And gross stuff. You don't want to know," I answered.

"Spiders?" she and Gabe said at the same time. Except Aurelia sounded as freaked out as I was, while excitement colored Gabe's tone.

"Hey, don't you have a hot date tonight?" Aurelia asked me as her chocolate eyes gave me a once-over, her nose scrunching even more.

"As a matter of fact, I do," said a deep voice, preceding its owner from the front vestibule.

His tall, muscular frame emerged into the lobby, clothed in a dress shirt and black pants, rather than his usual T-shirt and jeans. The lavender color of his shirt, along with his dark hair and beard stubble, brought out the brightness of his gray-green eyes—the eyes that always got me. The eyes that had been the one aspect of Havenwood Falls I'd never been able to forget, even when the Luna Coven witches magically wiped my memory and replaced it with a false past. Something deep inside hadn't allowed me to completely forget Xandru Roca.

Like always, my heart went all trippy and my breath caught when I saw him.

The look he gave me in return was not quite as enamored. I glanced down at myself.

Oh, shit. "Is it that time already?"

"Rough day?" he asked.

"You could say that." I glanced upward, as though I could see through two floors to the third one. "We have a problem."

He gave me a small smile. "You go get cleaned up. I'll check it out."

"No, don't. You're all dressed up. You really don't want to deal with that." I turned to my brother. "Gabe, since you skipped out on your chores this morning, you get to take care of room 313. It's totally your kind of thing."

As I headed through the large dining room for one of the several pairs of French doors in the back, I heard footsteps ascending the grand staircase off the lobby—two pairs, one much heavier than the other—and Xandru saying, "No worries. I got your back."

Well, at least we'd both stink on our date tonight.

The sky was just beginning to darken as I strode across the rear lawn of the inn to the two-bedroom cottage the kids and I shared until we figured out . . . well, until we figured out life. We'd all been through a lot in the last several years and still weren't sure about our new normal.

Three months ago, I'd been tending bar at a club in downtown Atlanta and serving breakfast to drunks in the middle of the night, thinking I was some mutant form of vampire with a depressing past and no family. My true memories of growing up in Havenwood Falls, Colorado, population five thousand-ish, with a family who loved me and friends who still did, had mostly returned by now, although I still experienced some blank moments. But they were still just memories, not the life I'd stepped into when I came back. This new life was . . . I didn't know what it was yet.

Like I said, we were still figuring it all out.

Like what we wanted to do with the family estate. The mansion in Havenwood Heights provided a lot more space than the cottage at the inn, but without Mom, Dad, and Mammie, we all agreed it felt like *too much* room. Yet, at the same time, the memories there of when our family was whole made the walls feel like they closed in on us. I couldn't be there for more than an hour before the emotions became too much to bear—mostly sadness, but also a lot of anger.

Maybe not facing it all was a form of denial, but we chose to cram into the small cottage, the largest of the five that lined the back of the inn's property.

When they were even there, Aurelia usually slept in my bed and Gabe in the smaller bedroom, but they often took a room in the main house with Mammie to watch over them or spent the night with friends. Because of the nightmares, I tried not to sleep much at all, but when I did, it was rarely at night. The tattoo I received as my registry with the Court of the Sun and the Moon, a requirement for all supernaturals in Havenwood Falls, was infused with magic that allowed me to be outside in the sun, but after the novelty wore off, my biological clock reverted to my vampire ways. I favored the late afternoons and nights. I'd always been a night owl anyway, even before I'd been turned. So the arrangement was working for us. Sort of.

Considering everything, I felt like we were managing life quite well.

Just as I pushed the cottage's front door open, a loud splintering of wood followed by a scream came from behind me. I spun around just in time to see two bodies falling from a hole in the third-story turret and crashing through the glass ceiling of the conservatory just below it.

Screaming, I sprinted across the lawn and tried to open the outside door to the conservatory, but it was jammed. Much of the large, glass room's framework was made of copper piping, which they pumped steam through back in the day to heat the space, along with other metals for the fancy scroll work on the trim. Patina and tarnish had started to cover the metal, and rust had eaten some of it away, causing places to bend and deform, including around the door.

Focusing my mind on the metal, I bent it out of the way, allowing the door to swing open. When Xandru's brother Tase had triggered my moroi gene by giving me his blood, he'd passed on to me the Rocas' ability to control metal. It came in handy sometimes.

"Are you okay?" Xandru's voice came from the shadows.

I followed the sound, weaving around boxes, junk, and covered furniture stored in the conservatory to find him setting my little brother on his feet. They both stood in a broken hole in the wooden floor, next to a full-size replica of a knight holding his sword pointy end up—they'd missed it by mere inches.

"Yeah, I think so," Gabe said, his voice shaky.

"You're bleeding!" Pulling my hoodie off, I hurried over to him and pressed it to the gash in his head.

"Is everyone okay?" Aurelia asked from the doorway to the inn.

"Call an ambulance," I ordered.

"I said I'm okay," Gabe argued.

"You have blood gushing from your head!"

Unfortunately, neither Xandru nor I could give him our blood to heal him. Because we were both mature (turned) moroi, doing so would trigger Gabe's gene, and he was way too young for that. Thankfully, his blood didn't incite any kind of thirst from Xandru or me. We had control over that part of us. Now, if Tase were here, it might have been a whole different story—he'd cursed himself to excruciating bloodlust when he triggered my gene.

If I had any say, though, Atanase "Tase" Roca would never be around my brother or sister.

"It doesn't hurt." Gabe shrugged. "Xandru caught me. It was really cool! I can't wait until I'm turned."

I visually inspected the rest of his small-for-his-age body, but only found a couple of scratches. "I'd rather be safe than sorry." I looked up at Xandru to find his pants and shirt splattered with wet marks. "Are *you* okay?"

He shook his arms, pink gunk flying off his sleeve. "Besides whatever the hell this is? Yeah, I'm fine. I always land on my feet."

I ignored his cocky grin and grabbed Gabe by the shoulders,

walking him over to sit on the step that led inside to the inn. "What happened?"

He held his fist up and opened it to reveal a beaded bracelet. "I was trying to get this. It was inside the wall you put a hole in upstairs. But the wall broke more, and the next thing I knew, I was falling through it and down to the ground. Then Xandru was there, catching me right before we hit the ground. He's right. We landed on our feet!" He looked over at the hole in the floor. "Sort of."

"I hate to say it, Ms. Petran, but your inn needs some repairs," Xandru said, as he inspected what were obviously rotted floorboards.

"You think?" I squatted next to Gabe, re-inspecting him even as he pulled away. He was more interested in his newly found treasure than any injury.

He held the bracelet up in the waning light. "Do you think it's valuable?"

"Not as valuable as your life," I muttered.

A few moments later, the ambulance arrived. An EMT named Jordan took Gabe inside the truck to clean him up and do an evaluation. The wound wasn't nearly as bad as I'd thought it was.

"Heads bleed a lot," Jordan explained as he hopped off the end of the ambulance. My vampire senses picked up on his scent with a tinge similar to Mike McCabe's—mountain lion shifter. Mike was the local building contractor and had fixed the inn's roof last month. I supposed I'd need to call him again. "He should be fine. He's not showing any signs of a concussion, but it wouldn't be a bad idea to keep an eye on him throughout the night and tomorrow."

"Oh, thank god." I blew out a sigh of relief.

Gabe was fine. Thanks to Xandru. But what if he hadn't been there to catch him? What if it had been worse? This inn was a danger zone. Worse than I had believed.

Not long after the ambulance left, another visitor arrived.

"I called the Court," Xandru explained, wiping at a spot on his shirt. "So they could get a sample of this. Mammie told me it's from a skinwalker, but I'm sure they'll want to know more."

"I know *I* want to know more. Too bad it's not Addie," I said before we walked in to greet the male witch the Luna Coven had sent. "She would tell me everything."

The Luna Coven did all of the Court of the Sun and the Moon's magical bidding. At least, that's what many of the supes in town believed. Mammie, who'd sat on the Court for a short time, had let it slip once that there were some tasks the Luna Coven couldn't dirty their hands with. Not when their High Council leaders also sat on the Court, which ruled the supernaturals in Havenwood Falls, protecting the humans and our secret. The more unappealing tasks were passed on to other, lesser covens in town.

The middle-aged man was thorough in his inspection and collection of goo, which he stored in vials and dropped into his satchel, asking me questions I mostly didn't have answers for. I didn't think it possible for him to move any slower, but at least when he was done, he helped Xandru patch the hole in the turret with a flick of his wrist and a few chanted words.

"We'll test the samples and see what we can find out about this mystery person," he said as we finally headed back downstairs. "If anything, maybe there are traces of Adelaide's ink, which she can use to identify them. You all have a good evening now."

Yeah, right. I looked outside at the dark streets, and then at Xandru, and frowned.

"It must be past midnight if the twinkle lights in the square are off."

He pulled his phone out of his pants pocket. "Twelve-oh-four, to be exact."

"Another date ruined," I murmured as I scratched at a patch of dried skinwalker gunk on the back of my hand. I really needed a shower. We both did. "I'm so very sorry."

Giving me a smile, he shrugged. "Well, at least we were able to spend some time together, even if it wasn't the perfect date."

"Do you think we'll ever have a real second date?"

He stepped in front of me and brushed his thumb over my cheek. "That I promise you, Michaela Petran." He leaned down and brushed his full lips over mine. "But we don't have to call it a night yet . . ."

His mouth lingered on mine in a luscious kiss that I eventually had to pull away from before I collapsed from a lack of oxygen.

"I'm gross," I reminded him, taking a step back.

He moved forward, closing the space I'd just put between us. "Me, too. We could clean up together."

"Hmm . . . that is tempting."

His fingers skimmed over my cheek and down my neck, producing a shiver. "But? I hear a but coming."

"But Gabe is in the cottage. There's no privacy."

His hand cupped my chin, and I could tell by the look in his eyes that he was thinking what I was—there were plenty of other places we could have gone. Upstairs, in a guest room, for instance, since we had several vacancies. Or any of the other open cottages. But he didn't say it, and neither did I. We hadn't reached that place yet.

I'd begun to wonder if we ever would.

Instead, he kissed my forehead. "Try again tomorrow?"

I gave him a smile, which I didn't quite feel on the inside. "Yeah. Sure. Tomorrow."

But tomorrow didn't come. At least, not in that sense.

As had been the case for the last three months, every day brought new obstacles that kept us from having a real date . . . or any kind of relationship at all.

CHAPTER 2

XANDRU

"*D*idn't expect you to be home," Tase greeted as I trotted down the stairs after showering. "Date didn't go so well?"

"What are you doing here?" I headed for the bar cart in the sunken living room of the home we grew up in.

It was a large, two-story log cabin, built and added on to over the years by our father, once he had money, made with illicit business dealings. The walls showed off the natural logs, and Mom had always favored dark colors, so the interior felt a lot like a cave— a cave in a tree trunk. Maybe someday, when my sisters were older, Alina or Aurora could have the house and update the décor to brighten up the place. Well, Aurora might. Alina would likely paint everything black, to match her heart.

Tase stretched out on one of the leather sofas. "This is our home, bro."

I poured a glass of scotch. "You have your own place."

"So do you."

I snorted. I'd moved back here the day after our parents died and rented my place out. "We have a sister and brother still in high school. Someone has to be the adult around here."

He cocked his head. "Do you even know where they are?"

Pausing, I took a sip of my drink and listened for Andrei's and Aurora's heartbeats. "Yeah. They're in their rooms. Right where they're supposed to be. Even Alina is."

Only Adrian was out of the house, but he was twenty-two and always stayed at the condo he bought in Havenstone.

"What a good dad you are," Tase taunted as he slow clapped.

"Fuck off."

He pretended to be offended. "Is that any way to talk to your older brother?"

"What do you want?"

"I have to make a run to Montrose. Wanna ride with me?"

In Tase-speak, a run meant dropping off or picking up something probably illegal, or dropping off or picking up payment for something probably illegal. As a family, the Rocas had several business interests, a couple on the right side of the law, such as the metal works company I ran. Then we each had something of our own. Besides the ski resort he bought a few years ago, Tase's side interests tended to fall on the wrong side of the law. He, as well as our other siblings, liked to follow in our father's not-so-good footsteps.

Tase often made runs to Montrose. Located sixty miles away from Havenwood Falls on twisty mountain roads, it was the closest town with a population over a few thousand and a crossroads that led to Grand Junction and the closest interstate. I used to make the runs with him on occasion. Not my thing anymore.

I scrubbed a hand over my face. "Three hours in the car with you? Nah. I think I'll pass."

He leaned forward and peered up at me. We had the same dark hair and olive skin, and strangers often mistook us for twins. That was a little ridiculous, but there was no mistaking we were brothers. His eyes were now a little greener than mine, though. If he turned full-on strigoi, they'd glow a lime green. The Luna Coven High Council predicted he had about a year, eighteen months if their magic held. Perhaps enough time for Addie to find or create a counter-curse.

13

Perhaps not.

"What the hell's gotten into you, bro?" Tase asked. "You and I were a team."

"A team?" I scoffed. He was a distraction when Michaela was gone. Now he was trouble. "We haven't been a team since the moment you sold out to someone else and turned Michaela behind my back. You made me your unwilling sidekick. Someone to keep you company."

"Yeah, well, keep me company now. What else are you going to do? Sit in your room pining for Michaela and jerking off? That's not like you." He paused and glanced upward, as though he could see the upstairs bedrooms. "If you don't go, I'll ask Alina or Andrei. I know they'd love to come."

I growled. The last thing I needed was any of our younger siblings getting involved in his business, especially those who were still human and therefore a lot more breakable. If I had any say, Tase himself wouldn't be involved in his own business. Not this kind, anyway. He needed to focus on his legit shit, like the ski resort.

"You suck," I said, before throwing back the rest of the scotch and savoring the burn. "You know that's not happening."

"So you're going with me?"

"Will it get us arrested? Or in trouble with the Court? Because that's not an option." For a few different reasons.

Tase smirked. "Not if we don't get caught."

Against my better judgment, I acquiesced and went to my room to throw on jeans and a T-shirt. Ten minutes later, Tase's late-model Camaro SS turned onto Main Street toward the only highway out of town. As we passed the inn, I couldn't help but notice which lights were on in the cottage and the inn. Michaela was still up. I wasn't surprised. We were nocturnal creatures.

At one time, those lights would have been all the invitation I needed. At one time, she would have been happy to see me show up at her door unexpectedly. At one time, I knew exactly how she felt and how she'd react.

Now, though, I felt like I knew nothing.

And I didn't want to assume. Michaela had changed while she was gone, off in the big city on the far side of the country. Hell, I'd changed, and I hadn't gone anywhere. We were supposed to have grown and changed together, but that hadn't happened. Choices had been made for us, with no consideration for what we wanted. Especially for her. After everything she'd been through, I didn't want to push her into anything that I couldn't be sure she wanted.

So, instead of sitting on the couch with her, watching a movie or doing much more interesting things, here I was, making a run with my brother, smuggling only he knew what, because I wasn't about to ask. Some things were better left unknown.

When we pulled into a parking lot in front of a row of warehouses in Montrose and I smelled human blood, it became clear that it was a good thing I'd come.

As vampires, we craved blood. It sustained our bodies. Human blood tasted best—like heaven, actually—but animal blood served our needs just as well. As *moroi* vamps, we could still consume—and quite enjoy—regular food and drink, too. We were mortal, born human with a gene that made us prone to vampirism. When our gene was triggered, we turned. Although it was difficult to kill us, it wasn't impossible.

Human blood called to us louder than sirens called to their victims, and just one drop could send us into a frenzy. But unlike other vamps, we couldn't indulge in our true nature. Because each time we killed a human, the need for human flesh and blood escalated until it'd eventually drive us mad and turn us into strigoi. Strigoi were immortal predators. Nearly impossible to kill, they murdered for the thrill of it. Strigoi were true monsters.

The rulers of Havenwood Falls didn't tolerate strigoi. Any signs of a moroi becoming one meant death by execution.

This was why Tase had a death sentence hanging over his head. When he triggered Michaela's gene against her will, he caused a curse that had been on her family to jump to ours. The Luna Coven had managed to extricate the curse from the rest of us and instill it only in Tase—a curse meant to drive him to become strigoi. They also spelled him to suppress the urges, but that was a stop-gap, to buy time until they found a way to break the curse completely. If they didn't find one soon, though, it was only a matter of time before he lost all control.

We all grew up knowing about our heritage. Triggering our moroi gene was a ritual the Roca kids looked forward to for years, until we graduated high school and were finally old enough. Unlike the Petrans. While Michaela and her siblings knew what their parents were, the Petrans had always acted like their kids were too good to become vampires. Now we knew the curse on them was the reason, but my father had always mocked how they tried to deny what they were by drinking in secret. We grew up exposed to blood, all different kinds, human and animal. Even before I'd turned, I could smell the faintest traces on the air.

As soon as Tase parked the car in front of the warehouse in Montrose, the sweet scent slammed into me, making my mouth water.

He smelled it, too. A growl rumbled in his chest.

"I don't think you should go in," I said before he could open the door.

"I have to make the pickup."

"Just let me run in and grab it. Stay in the car."

"No!" he nearly shouted. "It has to be me. Just cover me, okay?"

Pausing, I gripped the door handle. "Who are these people? Do they know about you and the curse? Is this a game they're playing?"

His jaw muscle popped as he stared at the door, his leg bouncing up and down. "If it is, they lose."

"Tase—"

"Xandru, I smell a human female in there, bleeding out. And I'm *this* fucking close to finishing her off." He turned to look at me, his eyes glowing a brighter green than I'd seen them yet, his finger and thumb nearly touching. "You got my back or not?"

Then, in a blur, he was out of the car and throwing open the metal door with a flick of his hand before he'd even reached it. I shot out of the car and blurred inside, but I was still barely in time. A girl in her early twenties sat tied to a chair in the middle of the empty warehouse, blood pooled around her feet and Tase already at her throat, gulping like an animal.

"No!" I flew at him and yanked him off of her, throwing him several yards away. He landed in a crouch, glaring at me with those bright green eyes. "Control yourself, damn it!"

His nostrils flared, but he appeared to be holding his breath, the only way he'd be able to overcome the bloodlust. He *had* to overcome the bloodlust. If he gave in and killed her, it'd be that much easier to do it again the next time. And then the next, and then he'd be fast on his way to becoming strigoi and an unstoppable killing machine. The Court would be forced to kill him.

When I thought he'd regained some semblance of control, I let my fangs out and bit into my wrist, then fed the girl my blood, my eyes never leaving Tase, and his never leaving her throat.

I inhaled as I listened to our surroundings. Besides the girl, we were alone in the warehouse, but a faint scent of someone not human lingered on the air. They'd left only in the last few minutes.

"Find them," I ground out through a clenched jaw, needing Tase to leave before the blood he'd just drank gave him more strength than I could fend off. "Someone set you up, and you're letting them get away with it."

He glared at me for another moment, then nodded before becoming a blur as he ran outside. At least if he found them and killed them, it wouldn't affect the curse, since they weren't human.

When the girl had enough of my blood for her wounds to start healing, I untied her and carried her out to the car. Tase was nowhere to be seen, and I didn't want to stray too far from the girl, who might have been our only witness. Fifteen minutes later, there was still no sign of Tase, but the girl began to stir.

"Who are you?" she asked with wide brown eyes as she tried to sit up, her dark brown hair blood-crusted and matted to her face. Her gaze flitted around the cramped backseat and out the windows. "Where am I?"

I rushed over and squatted in between the door and the seats. "We're at the railroad warehouses in Montrose."

"Who the hell are you?" The smell of fear came off her in waves. She rubbed at her bloody neck, then looked at her hands and screamed.

"Shh, it's okay. You're okay," I tried to soothe. "I found you. You're okay now. It's not your blood," I lied to calm her down.

She blinked at me as her pulse quickened. Her eyes darted around, and then she tried to push past me and out the door, but I blocked her way.

"Please let me go," she cried. "Please don't hurt me again."

I placed my hands on her shoulders and held her in place. "I won't hurt you. I promise I didn't do this to you. But I have a few questions so I can find out who did."

Her eyes were wild as she looked around again, and then she swallowed, her gaze returning to me. Her whole body trembled under my grasp.

"Do you know who brought you here?" I asked. She shook her head. "What's the last thing you remember?"

Her brows came together, as if she struggled to recall. "I went hiking, and my foot slipped . . . I remember waking up in my motel, then going to Black Canyon. I started down the trailhead . . ." She paused. "But nothing after that."

"Were you alone?"

She frowned. "Yeah. My boyfriend doesn't like the outdoors. It's my sanctuary, though."

Not much of a sanctuary today. "Did you see anyone on the trail?"

She gave it more thought, then shook her head again. "No. Nobody."

"Isn't that odd? It's a busy time of season."

"Yeah. It is, isn't it? So tell me what happened." Her voice went from dazed and confused to angry and accusatory.

I held up my hands. "I didn't do anything. Remember? I found you. I saved you."

"From who? Or what?"

"That's what I'd like to find out." I leaned in closer and stared into her eyes, searching out the connection to compel her. When I felt it click in my mind, I asked her again, "What happened to you? Who did this?"

She stared at me with a vacant look. I probed harder through our connection. "I don't know. I went hiking and my foot slipped . . . I remember waking up in my motel . . ."

Fuck. She'd already been compelled. A magical blockade in her mind prevented her from remembering anything else. I just couldn't tell if it was done by another vampire or something else, such as a fae or a witch.

Footsteps sounded on concrete behind me, and I jumped and spun. Tase sauntered toward us.

"Did you find who did this?" I gestured toward the girl.

"Nah. No trace," he said. "No footprints. No scent to follow. Did she say what happened?"

I shook my head. "She's been compelled or glamoured."

Tase stopped in front of me and pushed a hand through his hair, his gaze bouncing around the darkened parking lot and warehouse. When he finally spoke, his voice came out low. "Does she know what I did?"

"No. She remembers nothing."

"Then let's make sure of that and get out of here."

I lifted a brow. "We're not going to leave her here. She has no idea where she is."

He blew out a harsh breath. "Damn it. Fine. What do we do with her then?"

The girl snorted. "Uh . . . hello? I'm right here, and I'm not some piece of trash you found on the side of the road."

Tase growled.

I dipped my head. "Is there somewhere we can take you?"

She started to get out. "I think I'll walk, thanks."

"Sounds good," Tase said, heading for the driver's side.

I grabbed his upper arm, stopping him. "You really think it's a good idea to just let her walk off?" I asked with sarcasm.

He rolled his eyes. "Fine."

"We're not leaving you here," I told the girl, pushing the front seat back, blocking her in. I slid into it as Tase went around to the driver's side.

We found her motel and parked in front of her door, then Tase slid out and waited impatiently as she climbed out from behind his seat. He leaned down until they were eye to eye, and he compelled her, changing her memory of everything that had happened.

"You were sick today, so you stayed in all day. You'll go hiking tomorrow. You just really want a shower and sleep, then everything will be okay in the morning," he told her. "And throw away those clothes. You never liked them anyway."

Hunching her shoulders and crossing her arms over her stomach, she went into her room, convinced that she didn't feel well.

We drove for miles in silence.

"This had to have been a set-up," I finally said, once we were well out of town and headed home. "Someone wants you to go strigoi."

"No shit," Tase agreed.

"Who?"

He shrugged. "I have enemies."

I turned to glare at him. "Are you kidding me right now?"

"Not at all. I've made a few enemies in my business dealings."

"That's not what I'm talking about." I gestured at him. "I mean this attitude. Like you don't give a fuck. This is serious shit, brother."

"Don't worry about it. I'll take care of it."

"How I would love to stop," I muttered. "It'd make my life so much easier."

"It's easy. Stop caring."

If only. "Unfortunately, you're my brother. Family. It's not so easy. Maybe for you, but not for me."

He didn't respond for a while. "Yeah, it's not easy, is it?"

We rode in silence again for a good thirty minutes.

"It has to be someone familiar with the curse," I said. "Who knows besides the Court and the family?"

"The Petrans."

"Michaela wouldn't do this."

"You sure about that, bro? She's pretty pissed."

"She has a right to be. You fucked everyone up. Killed her parents. Killed *our* parents. She's just as mad at you for that as she is for her own family."

He let out a sigh. "You're right. She has every right to be pissed," he said quietly. "I didn't know what would happen, though. Otherwise, I would have never turned . . ."

"And she knows that. Which is why she wouldn't be setting you up. She's pissed, but she's not out for murder. So who else? What about the witch who paid you to turn her? The one who so conveniently disappeared shortly after the Court found out about your arrangement?"

"Magda?" Tase's jaw popped. "She's not a problem. Trust me."

"She'd want you dead, especially if she wanted to come back to Havenwood Falls. Your word against hers, and with you gone . . ."

"I said she's not a problem."

Something in his tone pricked my ears. "Tase, man, don't tell me. You didn't kill her, did you?"

"No." He answered too quickly, though, and I could smell a lie on him.

"Fuck, bro."

"I didn't kill her," he insisted. "But she won't be a problem anymore. Just leave it at that."

"Well, if not her, then who?"

"I'm not worried about it. It won't happen again. I'll change some things up. I'd never met that contact before. I never will. I'll drop the whole line of connection, just in case."

Lies, lies, lies.

"I have an idea. Why don't you just drop the whole damn business? Get our family businesses back on the legal side of the line?"

Tase laughed. "Don't be stupid. You know as well as I do that most of Dad's businesses strayed far from that line. I'm just carrying on his legacy."

I scowled. For a long time, before Michaela left, I'd wanted to believe the Roca reputation was undeserved. Dad had always sworn it was when we were younger. He'd claimed the Old Families, and especially the Petrans, had been out to get us from the beginning. They'd let go of Mom, Dad, and our aunt and uncle as their servants, but according to Dad, they wanted to make sure we could never become equals, so they made up whatever lies they could to keep us down. That was also how he justified both families' behavior toward my and Michaela's relationship.

While she was gone, though, I'd become more involved in our family dealings and learned that our family really was as bad as everyone said. I just couldn't bring myself to care, though. Not after they sent her away. Now, I had a reason to care again. Sadly, the rest of the family didn't. Not even Tase, whose very life was at stake.

As we pulled into town, my phone went off with several missed text messages. All from Michaela.

Are you busy? I wouldn't mind some company.

Hey, did you get my last text? Do you want to come over?

I guess that's a no?

You could at least answer

Well, you're either busy or sleeping. I'll see you whenever I see you

"Son of a bitch," I muttered under my breath.

"Something wrong?" Tase asked as we turned onto our cul-de-sac.

I blew out a breath. "Nah. Just do what you said you'd do. Don't let this happen again."

I couldn't be mad at him or myself for going. If I hadn't, that girl would probably be dead and Tase would be one step closer to becoming strigoi . . . which meant one step closer to being put down by the Court.

As we walked up the drive toward the house, Tase snatched my phone out of my hand.

"Fuck, dude," he said after reading the texts. "Cock-blocked again. Sorry, man."

"The night was doomed from the start." I told him about the skinwalker and Gabe's fall through the wall.

Tase's eyes sparked when I told him about the worthless bracelet Gabe had discovered in the wall. I couldn't tell if he was amused . . . or something else. I would have almost said nostalgic, if I thought Tase had a nostalgic bone in his body.

"I'll make up for it," he said, handing my phone back to me, all humor gone. "Consider it taken care of."

Once inside, I followed him up the stairs to our rooms and watched as he paused to look in on our younger siblings. Before Mom and Dad died, Alina, Aurora, and I were the only ones Tase could tolerate—Aurora because she was the baby and he'd had a soft spot for her since before she was born, Alina because she was a girl, and me because we'd basically been best friends growing up. But something had changed since our parents' deaths. Since the curse. I was no empath, but my vampire senses picked up something new from my older brother. He hid so much of his life, but I realized for the first time what he'd been hiding the most—his feelings. Regret. Shame. Depression. I could practically smell them in his blood.

Who knew Atanase Roca, asshole extraordinaire, actually might have had a heart?

CHAPTER 3

MICHAELA

*T*hree weeks after what became known as the Day of the Goo, I awoke to the sound of saws and nail guns blasting outside my window. Stomping out, I found a McCabe & Sons Construction crew working on the inn.

"What the hell is going on?" I yelled at one of the guys.

"Ask the boss man," he yelled back, motioning toward Mike McCabe himself.

I strode across the green lawn to the inn's parking lot. Mike leaned over his work truck, his hands splayed out on the hood, a large document spread out in front of him.

"What is this, Mike?" I demanded before I was even halfway across the lawn, knowing he could hear me with his shifter senses.

He glanced over at me, then immediately dropped his gaze. I didn't care that I was dressed only in a tank and short sleep shorts. I'd worn less to work in Atlanta, and it had finally warmed up enough to at least be under the covers in them. But he was of a different generation, the gray sprinkled in his brown hair and the crinkles by his eyes evidence—although some of his weather-beaten look was a direct result of working outside for so many years.

"What is what?" he asked, his voice low as he continued studying what I realized were plans for the inn. The same plans

Everett Weston had asked Graysin to deliver to me months ago. Plans that I'd had to put to the side until I found a way to pay for them all.

"First of all, what are you doing here?" I asked, softening my voice. "You shouldn't be working. I'm really sorry about—"

"Work provides a distraction," he growled, and I could tell by his tone he didn't want to discuss his recent loss. My heart hurt for him. He'd been through so much lately with Braden, Reeve, and Aster, and although I didn't have kids of my own, I just couldn't imagine how he and his wife were coping. "Besides, the world doesn't stop turning, even when it feels like it ought to. We have jobs to do. I'm just checking in on this one, getting it going before I go back to the library site."

"But this isn't a job," I argued. "I haven't hired you for anything more than the roof, and you finished that a while ago."

Actually, I'd only hired him to *repair* the roof, but he'd gone and replaced the entire thing, saying it needed to be done. Of course, he'd been right. It'd needed a whole new roof pretty badly. I just hadn't had the money for it. He only charged me for the few patches I'd originally contracted for, though, saying the rest was covered.

"Well, let's see." He pulled out a stack of rolled up papers from his back jeans pocket. "I have a bid here. All of it based on Everett's plans. You remember that?"

I glanced at the paperwork. "Yeah. And I remember telling you that I couldn't do all of that right now. Only the absolute necessities."

"Well, see, right here I have a copy of full payment. It's all taken care of. Including the newly added tasks of a permanent repair to the hole in the turret and redoing all the glass in the conservatory."

I practically tore that piece of paper out of his hands. My jaw dropped at first. The bid had been to repair, replace, and/or restore any of the inn's exterior that needed it, from siding to the gingerbread trim to windows, as well as to prep and paint the entire outside. Nearly ten thousand dollars' worth of work. Except for the fairly recent issues with the turret, most of the work was cosmetic in nature and I couldn't yet afford to address it. But here was a copy of a cashier's check for the entire amount and then some.

"There's a deposit on there for interior work," Mike clarified. "Hear you have some issues inside your walls. We should inspect every wall. Spiders could be the least of your worries. And we can replace plumbing and electrical while we're in there, and bring it all up to code. According to what I'm told, it's all taken care of."

"How . . . ? Who . . . ?" My eyes narrowed. My nostrils flared. "Oh no, he didn't!"

"Yeah, he did," came an unmistakable voice from behind me.

I spun to find Xandru approaching with a cup bearing Coffee Haven's logo. Despite the indignation bursting at my seams, I couldn't help my smile. We hadn't seen each other for over a week, and even then, only a few minutes here and there since our last failed attempt at a date on the Day of the Goo.

He held the cup out to me. "Good morning."

Mike gave him a strange look before going back to work. He'd probably been up for many hours, like normal people. I wasn't normal. Of course, he wasn't either, but I supposed mountain lion shifters weren't nocturnal.

"Good morning," I said giddily, taking the cup.

Xandru walked back to the cottage with me as I sipped the delicious coffee.

"You know how I feel about this," I said.

"The coffee?"

"The money."

"Mmm."

"Mmm? That's all you can say?"

He shrugged.

"I can't take it. I wouldn't take yours, and I can't take any more of his. He's already paid off the inn's mortgages and everything else. He can't keep doing this," I ranted.

"You won't change his mind," he countered as we climbed the steps to the front door. "And stop trying. Tase has done a lot of bad shit, Kales. This is his way of making up for everything he's done to you and your whole family, and it's something to make him feel good about life. He needs that right now."

"Hmph," I grunted, opening the door.

"Do it for me?" He closed the door after we entered and leaned against it, lowering his chin and looking up at me through his thick, dark lashes. He surely knew by now what that look, those eyes, did to me.

I punched his arm lightly. "Stop it. That's not fair."

His gaze swept down my body, over my thin tank top and short shorts, lingering on my breasts and the tops of my thighs. His finger slid under the strap of my tank, the light touch sending goosebumps over my skin.

"And this is fair?" he asked, his voice husky. He tugged on the strap, pulling me up against him. He must have felt my hard nipples, because he gave me a cocky smirk. "I think you missed me."

I pressed my hips in, feeling him arouse under the pressure. "I think you missed me, too."

"Possibly." He leaned down, his full lips brushing over mine.

Morning breath.

Coffee.

I stepped back and clamped my hand over my mouth. "I need to brush my teeth."

He chuckled as I hurried for the bathroom. When I came back out, feeling more human—well, as human as a vampire can feel—I found him sound asleep on my couch. I sat beside him, about to wake him up, but stopped and studied his face. His sharp cheek bones and square jaw could have made him a pretty boy, especially with the stunning eyes now hidden behind closed lids, but he had a rugged look to him, rather than beautiful. Especially now. My thumb lightly caressed the purple circles under his eyes, then my fingers brushed over the dark beard that had grown beyond his usual summertime stubble over the last week. I hadn't seen him look so relaxed since I'd been back, and still, even in sleep, his forehead creased with worry.

I didn't know anything about the several one- and two-day trips out of town he'd been taking with Tase, only that it was absolutely necessary that his brother didn't go alone. Xandru refused to tell me more than that. But whatever the reasons had been, they obviously had not been mini-vacations. This wasn't the haggard face of too much partying. This was the gauntness of too much work, the wariness of constant and unending stress and worry. I wondered when he'd last slept and decided not to wake him.

He was still asleep after I showered—which said a lot. We'd tried to seize every opportunity that presented itself to be together, but they had been few and far between. Of course, for a while in the beginning, as my memories returned and everything about my parents—what they'd done, their deaths—had settled in, I'd been emotionally unavailable. Since then, we could hardly find more than a few moments at a time to be alone. It'd been four months now, and we still hadn't made love.

We'd done pretty much everything else, but we'd promised each other that our first time back together wouldn't be frantic, rushed, and meaningless. He wanted to do right by me, and I wanted it to be right, but that was in the beginning. We hadn't realized we'd be bogged down with work and family issues, and that days would turn into weeks and weeks into months. And now I didn't know if our expectations had been built up so high that we were afraid of disappointment . . . or if it just didn't matter enough anymore.

Don't think like that, Kaela, I reprimanded myself. But I couldn't help it, especially when he hadn't even stirred while I'd showered. We were like an old married couple, except we never got the engagement or the wedding or the honeymoon. And I was too young to be old, damn it.

I slipped outside and strode across the lawn to begin my day at the inn. When I took my place at the front desk, I noticed Mammie in front of the parlor picture window, watching all the hubbub of town square across the way.

"They're doing it all wrong," she said, a look of longing on her face as city workers and volunteers set up for the Fourth of July festivities tomorrow. "They should have done this weeks ago! Where are the lamppost decorations? The red, white, and blue twinkle lights? This town *needs* its twinkle lights. That Rose Howe has no idea what she's doing. Why did they let *her* take over? You should have had the committee meeting here, Michaela, so I could have had input."

"I'm sure it will be fine, Mammie," I muttered while glancing over our expected guests for the night—all two of them. I hoped they didn't mind the unanticipated construction zone.

"Oh, there's Adelaide. She'll straighten them out." Still, Mammie wrung her hands as she floated back and forth in front of the window.

My aunt, aka Madame Luiza, aka Mammie, had passed four months ago, right after I'd first come back to Havenwood Falls on a weirdly arranged job offer at the inn. She'd returned in this new form, her silver hair in a bun and wearing the purple ball gown I'd dressed her in before she died—but a little less solid than she'd been before. Her death had been the last in a string of deaths in our family, including my parents, leaving Gabe, Aurelia, and myself on our own. Mammie couldn't bear to leave us quite yet, for which I was grateful. Surprised as hell the first time we saw her, but incredibly grateful. I wasn't quite prepared for what it would mean to finish raising two teens while simultaneously trying to save the family business that was over a century and a half old and on the verge of bankruptcy.

Although I knew her worry for us was the real reason Mammie visited our realm, she claimed she came to help the business. She was a marketing ploy.

"Looks like our efforts last night worked," I said to her as I read the comment card left by today's departing guest.

"Only because of you," she said, distracted. "He was a tough nut, wasn't he?"

"Oh, he's experienced. He wrote, 'I've been to several hotels and inns in Colorado that claim to be haunted, but this is the real deal. Watch for the woman in the purple gown. She particularly likes windows. Besides an incident involving my backside, she seems harmless enough, but there is something more sinister that lurks in the shadows. I felt like it might want to eat me.' Ha! We did it! But what does he mean about his backside?"

Mammie looked over at me with a coy smile. "I'm dead. It's time I start living."

I sucked in a breath. "What did you do?"

She patted her hair. "Oh, well, I might have pinched his butt."

"Mammie!" I squeaked as laughter bubbled up.

"The dead don't need to be proper. I've decided I wasted my life being good, and look where that got me. Just as dead as the ones who had all the fun." She shrugged. "Now it's my turn. And it gives the guests more to talk about."

Mammie served as the resident haunter of Whisper Falls Inn, scaring guests (or, apparently, sexually assaulting them) just enough to thrill them into leaving enthusiastic reviews. The memory wards surrounding the town meant tourists never remembered visiting Havenwood Falls once they left, so we had to capture their excitement to paper before their departures. For really tough customers, like this guy, I vamped out in dark corners or reflective surfaces, leaving them to question what they saw, but with a spike of fear flowing in their blood. Nobody could accuse us of false advertising. In fact, we were more authentic than most.

"What is Adelaide doing? She's walking right past them all and not saying a word." Mammie let out a sigh, before turning and giving up her post at the window. The guy was right about her liking windows, particularly one on the top floor in the far back of the inn. She stared out it, but at what, I wasn't quite sure, because it looked upon the back of the row of businesses on Main Street and the alley that ran behind it. "The mail came, dear. Maybe while you're out there—"

"I'm not going to tell those people how to do their jobs, Mammie." I walked around the front desk and headed for the door.

"Somebody needs to!"

Snickering, I hurried out to collect the mail, then sighed as I ruffled through the envelopes on my way back inside. Bills, bills, and more bills.

Tase had paid off the mortgage, and Mammie's hauntings had helped to keep the inn afloat, but we were still in deep. The inn had fallen into some disrepair over the last several years, thus the need for all of the work. Our current services were only the basics—besides our outdated guest rooms, we offered muffins, scones, and coffee provided by Coffee Haven each morning and that was pretty much it. Our kitchen needed to be completely redone, and the dining room needed updates. I could have tended the bar, but without diners in the restaurant or overnight guests, we had no reason—nor funds—to keep it stocked.

Mom and Mammie had been unable to keep up with everything after Dad's death, and Mammie had an especially hard time after Mom passed. But the inn's misfortune had started even before Dad died, when Tase bought the ski resort. He'd been engaging in shenanigans with a witch to draw out-of-town visitors to the resort's new cabins and simultaneously drive our business into the ground. He'd almost succeeded.

He claimed to have seen the evil in his ways and changed. Possibly because he had a death sentence hanging over his head. Maybe because he actually felt real guilt for everything he'd done to our family. I wasn't sure it was possible for Tase Roca to feel anything at all, but it explained why every single bill in today's pile—and every day's pile—was marked "Paid in Full." Along with McCabe's and Weston Design's invoices.

"Looks like that boy's not going to give up." Mammie looked over my shoulder, near enough that her cold breath sent a chill down my spine.

"He's pretty damn persistent."

"Good. Let him be. We need to bring in more guests, Michaela. There's nothing more to it. That boy owes us. He and his father. Let him pay their debts."

I didn't reply as I left the front desk area for the back office to drop the invoices on my desk. She wasn't wrong about needing more guests, but more guests meant we needed all of our rooms not just habitable, but comfortable and nice, and our dining room and bar functional. Which meant I needed the work to be done if I ever wanted to earn enough money to pay for the work that needed to be done. Without Tase's help, we were between a rock and a hard place.

I really hated letting Tase Roca get his way, though. Everything wrong in my life was about him getting his own way, including everything wrong between Xandru and me.

"Isn't it coffee time with Adelaide?" Mammie asked, as I came back to the front desk. "It looked like she headed to Coffee Haven."

I glanced at the clock. Addie had been my best friend since preschool, and we had a standing coffee date—whenever we could both get away, anyway. "Yeah, I guess it is."

"Talk to her, will you, dear? *She'll* tell those men how to do their jobs."

"Yeah, sure. If Xandru comes in, tell him where I am."

The sun was actually, *finally* warm as I crossed the front lawn of the inn that sat on a diagonal facing the corner and Town Square Park across the intersection. Once I crossed Eleventh Street, though, the Main Street buildings threw shade onto the sidewalk, and it was still a little chilly for my thin blood. It'd probably be a year or two before I adjusted from Hotlanta to the mountain climate. At least once I passed Callie's Consignments and crossed the alley, I was back in the sun, where I found Addie sitting at an outside table at Coffee Haven.

She wore a black tank top, displaying the tattoos that covered her arms, cutoff jean shorts, and purple Chuck Taylors. A bandana covered her head, her brown hair snaking out of the bottom in two braids. Round sunglasses had replaced her regular eyeglasses. She hunched over the small book she carried with her everywhere, two cups on the metal table in front of her.

"I didn't know you BuJo'd," I said as I took a seat and a cup.

She looked up at me. "I what?"

"Bullet journaled?" I motioned at her book, the pages filled with writing and drawings in a colorful array. "Or is that a Happy Planner? I'm not quite sure about the difference."

"What the hell is a bullet journal or Happy Planner?" she demanded.

"Um . . . that. Sindi had them, too."

"Sindi? You mean the other Addie?"

I laughed. Sindi was my old roommate in Atlanta, and while I'd been there, she'd been my best friend. It was kind of funny how similar she and Addie were, although it made sense. I supposed they were my "type" for besties.

"Don't worry, nobody could ever replace my Bratty Addie," I cooed as I reached over to tweak her nose. She slapped my hand away. I gestured at her notebook again. "Anyway, Sindi would never admit it, but she was a planner freak, and she loved her BuJo. She planned out her days, used them as a journal, and tracked all her crap, from when to change the water filter to the last time she had sex and with who. She had all these stickers and tapes and a gazillion markers and pencils for her color-coding system. I even caught her using Pinterest to pin all these elaborate, artsy layouts." I laughed at the memory of her flushed face when I teased her about it. "I'll admit, I've been tempted to start one myself to keep track of everything going on. At least give myself the illusion that I have my shit together."

One side of Addie's lip curled up, as if she were appalled by the whole idea. Then she leaned forward and hissed, "This is my Book of Shadows."

I stared at her.

"My grimoire." She huffed out a breath at my ignorance and leaned even closer, whispering, "My spell book, you idiot."

"Ohhh," I drawled out. Then I whispered back, "Your *magic* BuJo."

She threw a piece of scone at me. I caught it and popped it in my mouth. Aster McCabe may not have been around here anymore, but her scone recipe remained. And her scones were not something to be wasted. In fact, doing so felt like an affront to her memory.

"Still no news on your skinwalker, which is really pissing the Court off," Addie said. "Some of them are worried we won't be able to detect it if it's wearing someone's skin who's already registered and known by the wards."

"Is that possible?"

"You gave us," she wrinkled her nose, the stone piercing twinkling in the light, "tissue samples. That should be enough for the coven to track it if it were in town."

"So, you think it left?"

"I don't know. These things are skeevy as hell. But we can hope, right?" She took a sip from her cup, eyeing me over the rim. "So, speaking of the Court . . ."

I made a face and blew out a sigh. As the Court's business manager, Addie had apparently been given the job of persuading me to claim the moroi seat, because it came up nearly every time we saw each other. "After what they did to the McCabes, I don't know that I want to be a part of that."

"Maybe you could have changed the outcome."

I lifted an eyebrow.

"Okay, probably not," she admitted. "We do have laws in this town. If you don't want your seat, though, you'll have to give it up to a Roca. And you know what that means."

"Yeah, yeah, I know."

Saundra, Addie's grandmother and one of the leaders of the Luna Coven as well as the Beaumonts' member of the Court, had already explained it to me.

The Petrans—my father, specifically—had always held the Court seat for the moroi vampires, since the very beginning, because at the time, the Rocas had been my family's servants. When my father passed a couple of years ago, there had been a huge uproar by the Rocas, who hadn't been servants for over a century, because the seat was offered to my mother instead of Mr. Roca. That's how all seats were passed along, from family member to family member. But Mr. Roca was, among other things, a misogynistic and self-righteous ass, and thought he deserved the seat rather than my mother.

Then again, I couldn't entirely blame him. After all, the Rocas had never had any true say in things in our little town. My father had always spoken for all of the moroi, and I doubted he consulted the Rocas before making any decisions with the Court. When Mom passed, Mammie took the seat. Now it was meant to be mine.

If I didn't want to claim my place on the Court, I could offer it to another moroi vampire. And since my siblings were minors, that meant one of the Rocas. I'd honestly considered offering it to Xandru. Since I'd been gone for over five years, he had a much better understanding than I did of the town's secrets and things that went on beneath the surface. But Xandru wasn't the eldest of his family.

Tase could rightfully dispute the offer, and since he was unpredictable these days, we couldn't take the chance. The only way to guarantee he didn't get the seat and Xandru did was to prove to the Court that Tase was incapable of fulfilling the duties of the position. And while that might have been true, we didn't want to go that far yet with Tase, especially with the Court. That would have meant giving up hope on him, and not even I was at that point. Even if I were, I couldn't do that to Xandru.

Or to Addie, who'd never give up on him, even if her love was unrequited.

I gnawed on my bottom lip as Addie drummed her fingers on the table's edge while studying me.

"You're not ready for the commitment, are you?" she asked.

"What?"

"To the town," she clarified, then she cocked her head. "To Xandru?"

I shook my head. "What are you talking about?"

She leaned forward, resting her arms on the table. "Kales, I love you. You're like a sister to me, and I missed you so much while you were gone. We all did. But I get it. You didn't even remember us, so you couldn't possibly have missed us."

"But now that I'm here and I remember—"

"It's not the same, is it?"

I sucked in my lip and chewed even harder on it, as feelings I didn't realize I'd been harboring stirred within.

"You're not the same," she said pointedly.

"What do you mean?"

She smiled, and although I couldn't see her eyes, I could sense the sadness in them. "You've had a big taste of life outside this sleepy little town. Big city life. You're different."

I leaned forward, too. "You really think so?"

"I don't think so. I know so. You're . . . darker. Less confident than you used to be. More hesitant. The old you would have been the one to BoJu or whatever you called it, because you always had so much going on, and you loved organizing and color-coding. The old you was the bubbly and social one, while I was the weird, awkward, and ugly best friend. The old you always dove headfirst into whatever crazy idea we came up with. We were practically fearless together." She dropped her voice to a soft whisper. "And the old you wouldn't have gone this long without jumping into bed with the man she loves."

I frowned. "That's not all me. To be honest, I don't think Xandru likes me anymore. Not in the same way."

Addie spluttered on her coffee. "Oh, trust me. I don't think that's an issue."

"I don't know . . . I mean, sometimes I wonder how he can even look at me." I dropped my voice to a whisper as guilt flooded through me. "I killed his parents."

"He doesn't blame you for that," she said softly.

"Not out loud."

"Kales, I'm sure that's not an issue, either. Not for Xandru."

I exhaled slowly. "Well, there definitely *is* an issue. It's just . . ." I couldn't finish my thought, not sure what words to give it.

"This life is not what the two of you had always planned and daydreamed about before," she finished for me. "It's not the vision you'd created in your sweet and innocent minds."

I slumped back in my chair. "No, it's not," I admitted. "Maybe it is me. Maybe it's everything I've been through."

"It's getting to you both. He's been through a lot, too. He lost his world when you left."

"I know. We both did. I left this town as a young girl who didn't know half of what was going on behind all the pretty lights and small-town charm. I came back after having my life ripped away from me. Twice." Once when my parents sent me away with my memories wiped, and once when my gene was triggered, turning me. "And even now . . ."

I swallowed against the lump in my throat. Addie was my best friend, and I should have been able to say anything to her. But what I was thinking felt almost like a betrayal. One I couldn't bring myself to say aloud.

But she could. "Even now you feel like this life has been forced on you."

"How did you know?"

She shrugged. "I would have felt the same way. After everything you've been through, it's not surprising. You came back to a life you didn't remember, only to have two kids and a failing business dumped in your lap. And while you and Xandru always seemed to be meant for each other, that was before."

"Before I changed."

"Before both of you did. Before shit happened. Before you both let fear get in your way."

"I'm not afraid of anything," I protested automatically. She lifted a brow.

I twisted my hair around my finger. The backs of my eyeballs pricked, but I refused to tear up. Her hand landed on my forearm, and she gave it a squeeze.

"Nobody would blame you if you took off, you know. I'd hate you, but I wouldn't blame you."

"I can't."

"You can. If that's what you really wanted."

"I couldn't do that to Aurelia and Gabe. They need me . . . The inn does, too."

"The town would rally around them and make sure they were

taken care of. Or you could take them with you. Let them see the world before their genes are triggered. *Are* you going to trigger them?"

I blew out a breath. "I haven't even thought that far ahead. It's not like anybody's at risk if I don't."

Normally, if the moroi gene wasn't triggered by age twenty-one, the whole bloodline before them would begin to age and die like a human. But there was nobody left before us, no previous generations at risk. And if my siblings' genes weren't triggered, they'd continue life as humans, having children with dormant genes that didn't have to be triggered. That was the life my parents had tried to make for me, before Tase turned me.

"You could take them far from here and let them lead the normal life you were supposed to have," Addie said. "Get away from all the craziness of this town."

"Are you trying to get rid of me?"

"I'm trying to point out that you have options, Kales. You don't have to feel like this is all forced onto you. You can choose this life. I mean, it's kind of like what you'd always wanted, just a little twisted up. Or you can choose something else. And it's about damn time my girl was allowed to choose for herself. Wouldn't you say?"

I looked up and behind her, at the mountain rising high into the sky, a tiny bit of snow left on the tallest peaks. We were surrounded by magnificent beauty in this little box canyon of ours. But there was a whole world out there beyond.

I'd been happy out there before. Sort of.

I'd been happy here. Once upon a time.

"What about Xandru?" I whispered.

Addie gave my arm another squeeze. "I think you have some hard decisions to make. Just remember—you *do* get to make those decisions. Make them yours and nobody else's."

I considered that for a moment. How glorious it sounded to be able to make my own decisions about my life. I'd tried it before, though. I'd had a life I'd created on my own, once. But she was right about my fears. "What difference does it make if my life just gets ripped out from under me again?"

"Oh, Kales," Addie said with a sigh. "I'll do my damnedest to make sure nothing like what you've been through happens again, but I can't guarantee anything. All I can say is that you can't let that fear hold you back, or you'll never be able to move forward. Take the power you do have and use it."

Tilting my head, I studied her, letting her meaning sink in. "When did you get so wise?"

She smiled. "My destiny is to be a wise old witch, so I may as well start working on it now."

"Good thing you have a lot of years before you get to the old requirement, so you can practice the wise part," I teased.

"Aw, come on. I thought I did good for my first time."

I laughed. "If imparting your wisdom means leaving your subject more confused than ever, you'll make a fine wise old witch, Bratty Addie."

She considered this for a moment and nodded. "I'll take that. So, you don't know what you're going to do?"

I stood and grabbed my nearly untouched cup of coffee. "I'm going to think. That's what I'm going to do. Because you're right. It's time for me to woman up and be the boss of my own life."

CHAPTER 4

XANDRU

*C*alling it quits for the day, I locked up the workshop at Roca Metal Works and strode the sloping gravel driveway toward the house. Dad had built our log cabin-style home at the eastern end of Mills Avenue and built the shop up the hill, closer to the banks of Bels Creek, which twisted and turned along the bottom of Mt. Sousa. He claimed being close to the creek's icy water was more efficient for our work, but manipulating metal was our gift. We rarely used fire or had a need for the cold water to set our designs.

I'd always believed the real reason was to have a better viewpoint to look down at the town—rather than them looking down at us—but as I made the walk by myself in recent months, I began to think that maybe he simply enjoyed the beautiful view. Right now, the trees were all filled out and various shades of green. In barely more than a month, the aspens would be bright gold surrounded by the reds and oranges of maples and oaks. Not long after, I'd be looking down on a winter wonderland. Maybe my dad did have a soft spot in that icy heart of his.

I'd just reached the back deck with a cold shower, a colder beer, and a call to Michaela on my mind, when my phone buzzed with a text.

AB: We need to talk.

Me: Did he go?
AB: Yeah. He's done. Something's not right tho
Me: Give me 15

I rushed through my shower, my mind flipping through a dozen things that could have gone wrong at Tase's check-in with the Court today. After throwing on a T-shirt, jeans, and boots, I hurried out to my truck. If it weren't for human eyes, I could have been downtown in five seconds by foot. Instead, the drive took five minutes because of the 15 mile-per-hour speed limit of the residential streets. I found Addie Beaumont pacing impatiently outside the back of City Hall, and she jumped into my passenger seat when I pulled into the parking lot.

"Didn't go well?" I asked, shifting into park before turning to face her.

She pushed her glasses up, the light of the afternoon sun glinting on the stone in her nose, frustration painted on her face. "What did he do?"

"Hmm . . . you'll have to be more specific. Which time?"

"I don't know, Xan. Any time!" She threw her hands into the air. "It's a good thing they had *me* renew the protection spell, because I swear he was resisting it."

I arched a brow. "Tase is resisting your magic? The magic that's keeping him from going off his rocker?"

"Not completely resisting, but definitely trying. And not him, not on purpose. It's the curse, I think. It's growing stronger. Something's changed in the last eight weeks, since his first check-up." Worry filled her eyes. "I tried to cover it up, but there's a chance my grandmother sensed it. If she did . . . if she thinks she needs to start doing the spells herself, she'll notice. And then if she says anything to the rest of the Court . . . if they think he's getting worse . . . they'll start taking further action. You have to tell me if he's done . . . something."

I shrugged. "He's a grown man. I can't babysit him twenty-four seven."

"*Please.* Anything you can think of. The more I know, the better the spell I can create to protect him." Pausing, she angled toward me more and tilted her head. "Did something happen in Montrose maybe?" she fished.

I played innocent. "Montrose? Why would you think that?"

"Stop being a pain in my ass!" Addie lifted her hand from her lap, holding it in a fist. Not in a threatening way. At least, not in a traditional threat. "I have all sorts of ways I can force an answer out of you," she said through clenched teeth. "Don't make me use them."

"You would use magic on me? You're that serious?"

"I'm. That. Serious."

I stared at her for a moment. "Why?"

The question seemed to catch her off guard. Her fist dropped a few inches. "What do you mean?"

"Why are you so dead set on helping him? After what he did to your best friend and her family? After everything he's done to *you*?"

She looked away, gazing out the windshield for a moment before looking me in the eye. "You know why. I'm a masochistic schmuck. Now, are you going to help me save your brother from an imminent execution, or what?"

"I'm not sure there's anything I can do."

"Tell me everything that happened in Montrose. He told the Court about the girl and being set up, but I don't think we got the full story."

"Really?" I was surprised he'd told them anything.

"By the way, you *will* have to babysit him now, because he's not allowed to leave town without a chaperone. Specifically, you. Not if someone's trying to set him up to kill."

Fucking awesome. As if I had nothing else to do. Of course, I'd been going with him on every trip out of town since then anyway, but being ordered by the Court made me want to do the opposite. Blame the Roca blood.

"So you know he drank some human blood?" I said.

"No! How much?"

Oops. "I don't know. She'd already bled out some, but she was unconscious by the time I pulled him off."

"Damn it. Damn *him*! He said he restrained."

I snorted. "Hardly. But do you really think he'd tell the Court otherwise?"

"He could have at least told me." She sighed, then nodded. "Okay, that explains a little more. I guess the curse could have gained some strength from a certain amount of blood."

"He didn't even come close to draining her, and that was over a month ago."

"Yeah, I know," she said with another heavy sigh. She watched her hands in her lap, her finger tracing over the stones in one of her many bracelets, her teeth working on her bottom lip.

"What are you thinking?"

She looked back up at me, then out the window again, then back at me. "Did he . . . did he kill anyone then? Human, specifically?"

I exhaled sharply at the blunt question.

"You'd tell me if he did, right?" she continued. "You have to be honest with me, Xandru. It's the only way I'll know how to formulate the best potion or spell."

A lie danced on the tip of my tongue, but Addie was right. The more knowledge she had about what she was working with, the more accurate her magic would be. If she and the rest of the Luna Coven, all powerful mages, knew what had gone into the curse itself, they could have developed a counter to it. But they didn't know. Putting in temporary blocks was the only remedy they had for now, but those wouldn't work if not done properly.

"I don't know," I finally admitted. Her face fell, so I quickly added, "But I don't think so. I wasn't with him the whole time while he looked for whoever had left the girl. He said he didn't find anyone, and I never smelled or sensed anything that made me think he was lying. Besides, they were supernatural, so it wouldn't have affected him, even if he did. That's the best I can tell you."

She blew out a long breath, as though she'd been holding it since asking the question. "Okay, I guess that will have to do." She glanced at the City Hall building. "I need to get back inside. Court's about to reconvene. Busy night. Oh, hey, there's Michaela."

I followed her gaze out the windshield to see my girl round the corner to the back of City Hall. She looked sexy as hell dressed in a skirt and jacket, her dark hair pulled up in a twist, and her long legs seemingly endless in those heels. I suppressed a great urge to jump out of the truck, run to her, and sweep her into my arms, every bit of me wanting to go all Neanderthal and claim her as *mine*. But I knew that was the last thing she'd want. I'd been doing my best to hold back and give her as much space as I could possibly stand. If it were up to me, we'd have sworn vows by now and be spending every waking moment in bed. But I'd promised myself I wouldn't pressure her.

Addie did what I couldn't—jumped out of the truck and rushed over to Michaela. The two talked for a moment, then looked over at me. Michaela waved and started walking toward me. I slowly edged my way out of the truck seat and sauntered over to meet her.

"Hey," she said.

"Hey, yourself. I was going to call you as soon as I was done with Addie. See if you wanted to grab a pizza at Napoli's."

She looked over to where Addie was slipping through the metal door at the back of City Hall, plain as could be except for the moon emblem embossed into it. Dad's work. "Oh, well, I'm glad I caught you here then. I won't be around tonight."

"No?"

Her gray-green gaze came back to me. "No, sorry." She motioned toward the metal door. "I'm meeting with the Court."

Something flickered in her eyes that made my stomach drop and a lump form in my throat at the same time, but I couldn't say what. I cleared my throat, but my voice still came out hoarse. "About what?"

She gnawed on her bottom lip. How I wanted to be the one gnawing on it. "Um . . . well . . . about my future. And Aurelia's and Gabe's, too. You know, what's next for us. Where we go from here."

It took everything I had to keep my expression neutral. But . . . what the fuck did that mean? Where was she planning to go? Away again?

"What our options are," she added, and that just about undid me.

Options? What kind of options? My chest ached with the desire to tell her there was only one option: me. Nothing else mattered. But she'd had enough forced on her in her life. I wanted to be her *choice*. And if I wasn't . . . well, I'd survived the first time she left. Not well, but I had. I could only hope I could handle it again.

"I see." I smiled for her as I pushed a lock that had popped out of her twist behind her ear. "You have every option you want, Kales. Don't let them choose for you."

Her eyes darkened for a moment, but then she returned my smile with an appreciative one. "Thank you, Xandru."

She tilted her face up and lifted on her toes at the same time—even in heels she was nearly a foot shorter than me. She pressed her lips against mine and lingered for a long moment before she turned away and hurried for the metal door that led to the meeting room of the Court of the Sun and the Moon.

My very favorite people, said no Roca ever.

Once in my truck, I considered going home for that cold beer, but decided to head to the Dirty Knuckle instead. I drove down Fourth Street almost to the entrance to the ski resort. The lifts ran on the weekends during the summer for those who wanted to go up the mountain to enjoy the view and a bite to eat at the snack shack Tase had built up there, but they were closed today. That meant the Knuckle wouldn't be as busy as the Haven Saloon on the square, where both locals and any tourists would gather. I had enough noise in my head. I didn't need it all around me, too.

The lighting was dim, and the air cool and welcoming. I grabbed my usual stool at the bar and shot the shit with Rhys Graywalk, the fae owner, whom I didn't usually see behind the bar. Everett Weston came in and straddled his own favorite stool two down from mine. We had a few beers and shot a couple games of pool. Everett was easy to hang out with. He didn't feel the need to fill every moment with conversation, unlike the girls when they were here, and was a no-drama, no-bullshit kind of guy. Unlike my brothers.

When I left a few hours later, I admittedly didn't take the most direct route home. I meandered my way through the streets with the windows down, turning down Main Street and slowing to a crawl as I neared the inn.

"Are you stalking me?" a familiar voice called out from the sidewalk.

Shit. Hadn't meant to get caught.

I pulled over to the side of the road in front of Madame Tahini's and the pawn shop, where Michaela stood. She opened the door and slid into the passenger seat.

"Court just got out, and I was on my way home. Give me a lift?"

I smiled as I looked through the window at the inn across the street. "Any time, my lady."

When I pulled into the driveway and parked in front of her cottage thirty seconds later, she didn't immediately move to get out.

"So . . . did you find out your options?" I asked, turning toward her.

She twisted in her seat and smiled. "Yeah. I did." Her gaze drifted, and her smile faded. "I've been thinking a lot lately."

Shit. Not good. I mean, not the thinking part. Just the thinking part combined with the talk about options and the future and meeting with the Court and . . . shit. Just not good.

But I'd known something had been up. She'd been even more distant than usual the last few weeks. The little bit of time we'd been able to spend together, grabbing a coffee or when we had drinks with the gang at the Knuckle, she'd get this look on her face when she thought I wasn't watching. More than simple thoughtfulness. More like she was trying to figure out a complicated equation or solve the meaning of life. But every time we had a moment for me to ask her what had her preoccupied, we'd been interrupted.

"Good thoughts, I hope?" I asked.

Her gaze came back to me as she exhaled a breath. "We need to talk, Xandru."

Aw, fuck. No. Not yet.

My whole body stiffened, every muscle tensing and locking, as though paralyzed. This couldn't be happening. I needed more time. More time to get my shit together. To get Tase's shit together. That motherfucker. I knew he'd ruin everything. I turned back toward the steering wheel and gripped it tightly until the metal began to soften and I had to let go.

"Xandru." Michaela took my hand between hers and brought it to her lap. "Look at me."

I inhaled deeply before turning to face her again. The only person I could say without a doubt I'd ever loved completely.

Wholeheartedly.

The only person who'd broken my heart before and could do so again.

"I owe you a date, right?" she asked.

"What?" I asked with bewilderment.

"We never went on our date. I owe you."

"Oh. Uh . . . I'm pretty sure I owe you. A lot of them. Like a lifetime of them." Shouldn't have said that. *Don't pressure her, Xandru. Take it easy, dumbass! She wants to fucking* talk.

"I think the last one didn't happen because of me . . . or because of my life, anyway," she insisted. "The Day of the Goo? I can't believe that was like two months ago . . ."

She trailed off, blushing.

I gave her a small smile, all I could muster, because my mind raced and my heart pounded. She could surely hear it. She was all over the place tonight, talking about options and the future like she was leaving and then bringing up dates? Did she want one? With me? Damn it, I hated games. Why couldn't we just say what was on our minds without fearing that we'd freak each other out?

I blew out a harsh breath.

"Michaela, will you go out on a date with me?" There. I did it. I sounded like a fourteen-year-old idiot, but I did it. Said what was on my mind. Sort of. It was a start. Because *I* didn't want to fucking talk.

She grinned. "I would love to. But—" She paused, drawing out that *but*, probably trying to kill me. I wouldn't have to worry about a broken heart. She'd kill me first. "But, we have to promise each other —both of us—that we *will* make this date happen. No matter what. We need to—"

I cut her off, not wanting to hear the stupid t-word again. "I promise. Saturday, you and me. Nobody else. A real date. I'll pick you up at seven. Wear that sexy black dress again."

She laughed. "I can't. I wore that on our first date." She paused again before correcting herself. "Well, our new first date."

I chuckled. "It's been over four months. I think this is a new-new first date. Wear it."

Her smile fell away again. "That's depressing, isn't it? Well, no promises on the dress, but I do promise back to you that I will go on a date with you this Saturday. No matter what, Xandru."

"No matter what, Kales."

CHAPTER 5

MICHAELA

*S*tanding behind the front desk, I scrolled through the email, skimming over everything to ensure I didn't miss something important, then checked the inn's reservations one more time.

"Okay, Mammie," I said, "we're all set. The last guest leaves on that Thursday, so no worries there. Our own arrangements are made, and we leave for Denver on the eighteenth. I can't wait to see Sindi!"

Madame Luiza wrung her hands, and a frown creased her forehead. "I don't know what I'm going to do without you, Michaela. It'll be so quiet here. *Dead* quiet."

I snickered at the pun. "Oh, Mammie, you'll be fine. Surely you have better things to do than watch over our mundane lives. Maybe things to do in the other realm? People you know?"

Her gray eyes brightened—if that was possible. "Yes, yes. Maybe I can find Maxwell in the other realm."

"There you go," I encouraged, although the name was only vaguely familiar and I had no real idea of whom she spoke.

I knew she'd tried to find my parents at one time, but, sadly, hadn't been able to. Eloise Sinclair hadn't been able to reach them, either. I'd gone to see the psychic scribe in her little shop on the square back in my "dark days" of March and April, when I'd first returned, hoping to be able to make some kind of connection with my parents. Eloise could communicate with the dead, channeling their spirits. Addie said there was nobody better.

Eloise had frowned when she'd tried, though, her brow furrowing with concern.

"I'm coming up against a wall of darkness." She'd shuddered and shook her head. "It's terrible. *Frightening.*"

The fear in her voice had sent a chill down my spine, so I made her stop.

"Why would that happen?" I'd asked her before I'd left, once both of our hearts had slowed.

"I'm not sure. I knew your parents. I don't know why they'd be surrounded by such darkness. I'm so sorry I can't help you."

Part of me had wanted to ask her if we could try again another time, but I knew I couldn't put her through that again. I didn't really want to go through it myself. So I'd decided then it was best to leave the dead alone.

I shuddered, bringing me back to the inn's lobby and Mammie's ghostly face staring at me, making me jump.

"Sheesh, Mammie," I muttered as I glanced down at the desk in front of me, reorienting myself.

Oh, yeah. Denver.

"Hey, Gabe," I called to the parlor where my little brother sat hunched over the coffee table, "did you hear that? We're leaving for Denver bright and early a week from Friday. Don't save your packing for the last minute."

"Bright and early for you or for normal people?" he muttered.

"Probably for me, funny guy, since I'll be driving."

"Yeah, don't let Aurelia. She'll get us all killed." He looked over at me with goggles pushed up on his head—the old-fashioned round kind like what motorcyclists used to wear, except these had several lenses that could be switched up and down, along with gears and levers—we couldn't decide whether they were decoration or were somehow functional. "Kae, did you see this?"

I crossed the lobby and joined him in the front parlor, sitting on the sofa that had been at its height of comfort and fashion at least ten years ago. I couldn't wait until we started work on this unusual room, with its peculiar octagon shape that jutted out of the west corner of the inn. Graysin Ravenal, an interior designer and a friend, had sent me some design ideas that would brighten it up, which it seriously needed, with all of its dark wood paneling and trim.

Gabe had spread out an array of items on the wooden coffee table, all things he'd found in the walls and under the floorboards during the renovations. Most was junk—a plastic army man, a cubic zirconia earring, a single tarnished cufflink, a mitten, and other long-forgotten items. He'd already found three small leather pouches that Mammie immediately had me confiscate and give to Addie, because they'd been hex bags once upon a time. Since we'd discovered the first one, Addie and Eloise took turns coming in and cleansing the inn on a regular basis with white sage smudge sticks. Out of all the junk, there were a few worthy, or at least interesting, items, such as the goggles.

"Oh, this is cool," I said, picking up a leather cuff that was too wide to be a bracelet, but looked almost like a protective brace. It was decorated with metal eyelets, buckles, and several gears that looked like they came out of an old-fashioned clock. A brushed nickel piece with scrolled edges lay across the top of the wrist, its center concave and quite plain compared to the rest of the piece. "It looks like something's missing here."

"Yeah, Mammie says a timepiece probably went there. They used to wear stuff like that back in the olden days, when she and Mom and Dad first came here and built the inn. I found it under the floor in the conservatory. This, too." He held up what he'd been inspecting earlier—a small dragon figurine made of metal hardware, wire, and more clock gears. "Mammie said the kids played with toys like this back then."

He lifted its tail, and we both gasped as a puff of green fog spewed from its metal mouth and right into my face.

"Oh god, that is gross!" My hand flew to cover my nose and mouth. I tried not to gag as the substance floated and settled, smelling like a rotten egg had exploded. "Gah! It's a good thing I hadn't taken a shower yet!"

"Xandru should know by now that you're a stinky girl." Gabe laughed hysterically at the look I gave him. He fingered the dragon's tail again, and I snatched it away.

"You be careful with that," Mammie said as she floated in. "We had better hope that wasn't old stored-up aether."

"Aether?" I asked.

"An old form of magic," she said, as though that was enough explanation.

"Sheesh. Is anything normal or safe around here?" I muttered as I headed for the back of the inn, unable to stand myself one minute longer. "I'm off to shower and get ready for my very important date."

I couldn't believe how smelly I was on date night. Again. No amount of scrubbing or standing under the scalding shower seemed to be enough to wash away the stink. By the time I shut the water off, I hoped the odor was all in my head, my olfactory nerves still recuperating, because I was running late. I glanced at my phone. *Yep.* Xandru was supposed to pick me up in fifteen minutes.

I didn't want to make him wait, even when part of me felt like he deserved it, considering all the times he'd been so badly delayed, he just hadn't showed. Tonight was supposed to be different, though. He'd told me on the phone earlier that he'd planned for tonight to make up for every date we'd attempted since I'd been back, but had never been able to make happen. He wanted it to be perfect. I told him I'd hold him to it.

Still, I couldn't deny my shock when there was a knock on the door at seven o'clock sharp.

I finished applying the last coat of mascara, framing my eyes with thick, dark lashes that still wouldn't compare with Xandru's natural ones. After a quick check of my updo, I smoothed my hands down my slinky red dress. The dress I'd put on for the third time in as many months, yet nobody had seen me in it. Not even Xandru. I looked damn fine, if I said so myself.

Satisfied, I headed for the door. When I opened it, Xandru stood on the porch with a bunch of wildflowers and a bottle of Stone Falls Winery's Blood Like Velvet "wine" in his hands. He really was going all out.

His gray-green eyes were unusually bright tonight, making him even sexier than usual. His gaze traveled down my body, lingering on my legs before coming back up as a slow smile lit his face by the time his eyes locked with mine.

He gave me my favorite look, the one that made me feel as though nobody and nothing else mattered. This was why I stood in this doorway, even after everything. This was why I was ready on time for a date that I couldn't have been positive would happen, when all the others hadn't. This expression in his eyes, in his face, that was much more than adoration, but as though I was his entire world . . . his universe . . . his life.

This look that was full of love. And lust.

His eyes smoldered as he rubbed his thumb across his full lower lip.

A whole hell of a lot of lust. On both sides.

My tongue slipped out, wetting my own lip, wishing it was his.

"And I thought I liked the black dress . . ." His voice came out husky as he gave me another visual appraisal that sent warm tingles over my skin.

"We're going on this date," I said preemptively, before he persuaded me to spend the evening home . . . in bed . . . my sexy red dress on the floor, never to be seen in public.

Nothing like that had happened yet. It wasn't about to tonight. I'd rehearsed everything over and over, and I needed this night to happen. *We* needed it to happen.

"Of course. A promise is a promise." He held his hand out for me. "My lady?"

"Should I put that inside first?" I motioned toward the flowers and black bottle.

Xandru handed them to me, and I took them inside. I moved quickly to put the flowers in water before grabbing a shawl and a little evening bag. As soon as I joined him outside, he took my hand

and pulled me close to him so my chest pressed against his. Electric butterflies danced in my core. Although I remembered most of our past together, there was still so much new about what we had. Or what we were *trying* to have, anyway. So much mystery and anticipation. So much exploring still to do.

So much history to overcome.

I had to crane my neck back to look at him as his arm slipped across my lower back, holding me even closer. He smelled divine— manly but godlike. He leaned down, our noses nearly touching, pausing before coming in for the kill. His mouth actually might kill me. It was perfect. Always perfect.

But gone entirely too quickly.

"What's that smell?" he asked, pulling away. His lip curled.

I sucked in a sharp breath. "Holy hell! You've got to be kidding me!"

I spun out of his embrace and headed back for the door.

"Hey, where are you going? What are you doing?"

"I cannot go out smelling like this! Just go. The night is ruined. Again."

"Kales." His large, warm hand landed on my shoulder. "We made a promise to each other."

"I smell like rotten eggs! Gabe found this old toy that might have aether in it, and something gross blew out all over my hair and face, and I scrubbed and scrubbed, but hell, if the stink's still here, there's no way I'm going to get rid of it with another shower. We'll just have to do this date another time. Once it wears off . . . or whenever." I threw my arms in the air before grabbing for the door knob, willing away the pricking in my eyes and at the back of my throat. This was not how tonight was supposed to go, damn it!

"Michaela." Xandru's voice came out firm. His hand on my shoulder squeezed and pulled, turning me back toward him. "You are not getting out of this."

"I don't *want* to get out of this," I protested. "But I stink."

"I don't care."

"I do! It's embarrassing. Not sexy at all."

The corner of his mouth twitched, as though he fought a smile. "Woman, I don't care if you just crawled out of the pits of hell smelling like brimstone and sulfur, you're still the sexiest damn thing I've ever seen. You always will be. Now come on this date with me and let the world see you in that dress before I bring you back here and turn it into rags."

Gasping, I pressed a hand down my little red dress. "You would not!"

His mouth curled into a small, sexy grin. "Oh, I will. I've already pictured it five times since you opened the door. Just not sure yet if it'll be my hands or my teeth shredding it off of you."

I laughed. "You're terrible."

"You will soon find out just how good my terrible feels." *Holy sex bomb.* My panties might have wetted with that little promise. He held his hand out once again. "Are you coming with me or not?" I hesitated. "If it makes you feel better, I could only smell it on you when I was close. And I have vampire senses, you know."

"And half the town has a heightened sense of smell."

"Not quite half. And anyone who comes close enough to smell your hair will be worrying about other things than what you smell like. Such as their lives."

"Ah, such the chivalrous gentleman you are."

"No, love. Not a gentleman. Just someone who refuses to share."

I took his hand and let him lead me to his truck, where he was most definitely the gentleman, opening the door and helping me inside. While he rounded the front of the vehicle, I couldn't help but think about how much sharing we both had to do. I'd been thinking about it a lot lately, ever since my conversation a month ago with Addie outside Coffee Haven. Family always came first, and work also found a way to steal our time from each other, because family and work were so intertwined for the both of us. Only, I'd been able to steal some time back much more often than he had.

Of course, my brother wasn't knocking on death's door, so there was that. Even if I couldn't stand Tase and he wasn't exactly Xandru's favorite person, either, he was family. So I did my best to understand. I practiced a lot of patience.

My patience had worn quite thin.

Xandru drove up Mt. Alexa on Alverson Road to Fallview Tavern & Grille. The large lodge had a log cabin look to it, which wasn't exactly white-linen fancy, but it had one of the best views in town. Sitting on the edge of a cliff, it overlooked the great falls with the lights of town sprinkled down below. Simon, the cook and a dragon shifter, also made the best steaks in town. I'd asked him once if he secretly flame-broiled them with dragon fire. He never gave me a straight answer.

We sat outside in the mist and roar of the falls, at a round wooden table near the edge of the deck to take advantage of the view. A candle in a square glass holder flickered, the flame causing shadows to dance over the table and across Xandru's face.

"To my life." Xandru held his wine glass up, his head cocked in a way to indicate he meant me.

"To *our* lives," I said as I clinked my glass against his.

"I know it's not what we'd always hoped for, but it'll get better. I promise you."

There was so much to say to that. Everything I'd rehearsed, actually. But not yet. I wanted to save it for later and enjoy our dinner now. So I gave him a smile as Serena Alverson, our waitress for the evening, approached with our steaks. The teen placed our plates in front of us without a word, although the look on her face showed she had much to say.

"Are you okay?" I asked her.

Her blue eyes widened. She glanced down at my steak, then spun on her heel and hurried away.

I groaned. "She could smell me."

Xandru laughed. "She's a vegan, according to Simon."

I looked down at my extremely rare steak, oozing the blood I craved even more than the actual meat. "Oh! And it all makes sense now. Poor thing shouldn't have to serve us flesh-eaters, then."

"To each their own," Xandru said, lifting a bite of bright red meat to his mouth.

I began to cut into my own steak when Xandru's phone went off.

"Ignore it," he muttered, hitting the decline button before slipping the phone into his pocket.

Three more times in the next ten minutes made it impossible to ignore, even in vibration mode and hidden away. He finally answered with a growl as he stood and walked away to take the call. I tried to enjoy as much of my meal as I could, expecting it to be coming to a premature end.

Before I'd had a chance to say what I needed to say.

Xandru returned to his seat with a tight smile.

"Do we need to go?" I asked.

He nodded at my plate. "Finish your meal, love. This is *our* night."

But I could sense his tension and worry. Something was wrong. He tried to pretend that it wasn't for the rest of our meal and as we finished our bottle of wine, but I knew better.

"It's Tase," Xandru finally admitted. Of course it was. While he paid the check, his phone rang again. "Let me just take this, and then I'll shut my phone completely off, okay? Then it'll just be you and me."

I nodded and managed a smile, feeling guilty that my first thought was that he should have turned the phone off before he even picked me up. But considering the whole situation with Tase, I knew that could be dangerous, and I wouldn't hold him to it when he returned.

I leaned my elbow on the table and dropped my chin in my hand as I gazed out over the falls and the town below, going over my prepared speech in my mind.

It had taken several weeks to come to the conclusion that I had. To figure out what I really wanted in life and to gather the courage to go after it. It had been a TV show that finally made me see the so-called light.

Gilmore Girls had been my favorite show when I was in Atlanta.

While I made fun of Sindi with her BuJos and Happy Planners, she made fun of me for my obsession with *Gilmore Girls*. And it was a true obsession. Utter embarrassment kept me from admitting how many times I'd binge-watched all seven seasons. We really couldn't figure out why I liked it so much, considering I'd thought I'd come from a shitty small town and a life I'd never want to return to. Now it made sense. Something deep inside my brain must have noticed the similarities between Stars Hollow and Havenwood Falls. Something had connected it to home.

I'd been watching it the other night while working in bed when my favorite scene of the entire show came on.

Leaving me curled up in a snotty, blubbery mess of a ball.

Then I tried to call Sindi in Atlanta, at about four in the morning her time. She'd been my best friend while I was gone, my savior in more ways than one. While I loved Addie as a sister, no matter how much she encouraged me to take the reins of my own life, I knew deep down that she couldn't be entirely objective. Sindi would lay it out straight, tell me what I needed to hear. We'd barely talked since I'd left Atlanta, thanks to our crazy schedules and the crappy phone service here. By chance—or not—she picked up my call that night, and we talked for hours.

As expected, she helped me make sense of my life, and the answers clicked into place. We made plans.

I knew what I needed to do, what I needed to say to Xandru.

A large warm hand landed on my shoulder when he returned from his call. "Are you ready?"

"Um . . ." I motioned toward his seat. "First . . . can we talk? Before I lose—"

He winced. "I'm sorry, Kales. Something's come up that I need to take care of."

He held his hand out to me, and I hesitated before taking it and standing. We walked out to the truck in a thick, heavy silence.

"Do you mind if we make a stop before we continue the night?" he asked as he helped me into the truck. Surprised, I looked up at him. He gave me a devastating grin. "Ah no, it's not over. *Our* night, remember?"

He leaned down and delivered a kiss to match that grin, leaving me breathless as he closed the door. When I realized I still had a chance to do what I needed to do tonight, butterflies began to dance in my full belly. Not the giddy ones from earlier. Anxious ones.

He knew I wanted to talk, but every time I mentioned it, he freaked out. I'd seen it all over his face. He'd been avoiding me all week, and I couldn't help but wonder if he still was. At least, avoiding the talking part. Because I knew that was the last thing he wanted to do.

But I couldn't avoid it. Not anymore.

Even if what I had to say could possibly ruin everything.

The stop he needed to make was at the Rocas' family home on the opposite end of town, at the base of Mt. Sousa. When we were teens, it was nearly a second home for me. My last time inside, though, had turned it into a place of nightmares. I waited in the truck.

"I'll be right back," Xandru promised, before opening his door. "Then we can do whatever you want to do." He leaned in to give me a quick kiss. "Even if all you want to do is talk."

I blinked against the sting in my eyes as I watched him jog up to the large log cabin.

Apparently, whatever was going on with Tase now was worse than Xandru had expected. After fifteen minutes, he finally texted me.

Xan: I'm sorry. It's going to be a while
Me: Should I come in?
Xan: Not a good idea
Me: Go home?

Several more minutes passed. Loud shouting came from inside the house, followed by a long moment of silence. Then my phone dinged.

Xan: I hate for you to sit in the truck all night long

I waited, but the conversation ended with that. I bit my lip, refusing to cry—or shout obscenities—before climbing out of the truck.

"It's about damn time," a female voice called from the dark front porch. Alina, the older of Xandru's two sisters, a year or two out of high school, leaned against the log post. There was just enough age difference between us that we'd never been remotely close to friends. Of course, her typical Roca attitude toward the Petrans—and the world—had a lot to do with that, too.

"About time for what?" I asked.

"About time you went home. My brother has more important things to worry about. You need to leave him alone. He needs to focus on what's important, and that's not you."

My jaw clenched and my hands fisted, but I forced myself to bite back several comebacks popping through my head.

"Tell him he knows where to find me."

"I won't. He doesn't need to go looking. He needs to stay here and take care of his family, not be fucking around with the whole reason we're in this mess."

Nostrils flaring, I turned my back and started down the street without another word. Starting drama with Xandru's little sister wouldn't help anything.

"And you smell like shit," Alina called from behind me. "Take a shower once in a while, pig."

A low growl caught in my throat. *She's still human*, I had to remind myself. It'd be a crime to kill her. The Court would lock me up, and since I hadn't officially been sworn into the Petran family seat yet, they'd likely throw away the key. Or banish me, sending me out of town, never to return this time.

Perhaps that was what I needed.

No. Leaving town will be my choice this time. Nobody else's.

As I opened the door to the cottage, my phone buzzed several times with new text messages. Xandru had apparently lost signal, because he'd sent the same text eight times.

Xan: Please forgive me

CHAPTER 6

XANDRU

*W*ith my arms crossed and jaw muscles twitching, I glared at Tase. Dressed in jeans and a button-down, he stood at the liquor cart in front of the sliding glass doors that opened to the deck, Mt. Sousa looming in the darkness beyond. He reminded me entirely too much of our father as he poured a glass of bourbon and held it out to me. I didn't budge.

He held out his other hand, fingers pinching a fat blunt, its end orange and hot. The definitive odor of pot was admittedly enticing, but I still didn't move.

"You sure?" He downed the amber liquid, then poured another glass as he toked, holding the smoke in when he spoke. "You look like you could use both about as much as me."

"It's not a drink or a hit that I could use," I muttered.

Exhaling the smoke, his dark brows lifted, his forehead wrinkling in the same way our father's used to. The same way all of ours do. It's a Roca family trait.

"Oh yeah?" His arms flew out to the side. "Come at me, bro. Is that what you want? A fight? Need to take out your anger?"

Tempting. But I remained a statue. "What I need is for you to stop acting like a fucking idiot. You held a human hostage tonight, Tase. What the hell is that shit?"

He shrugged, blowing it off like it was nothing. Thirty minutes ago, he was about to kill some guy who was probably barely old enough to drink. I'd walked in just in time. Our other siblings couldn't control him like I could, not even Adrian, who was also turned. Hell, I struggled tonight. Addie was right—something had changed. He'd gained strength since the last time I had to take him down. His temper had grown nastier in the last few weeks, too.

I'd been trying to watch him more closely since my conversation with Addie, but nothing specific caused the change. Just the curse itself strengthening. Or, perhaps, he'd simply given up and stopped fighting it, letting it take over. Leave it to my brother to take the easy way out, even if it would kill him.

"He was trying to steal from me," Tase answered. "Rocas don't put up with that bullshit."

He quoted one of Dad's favorite lines.

"Run a con business, and you're gonna get conned. What'd you expect?"

"I expect some damn respect!" Another of Dad's lines.

"Then why don't you try doing the right thing for once?"

"Hey!" He gulped down another glass full of bourbon, then held his finger out from the rim, jabbing his whole hand, glass and all, at me. "I'm trying, man. I'm doing this all for us. For our family. And for that woman of yours." He took another hit off the blunt, then burst into a coughing fit. When he spoke again, his tone dropped. "I owe her. I know that. I owe all of you. I'm trying to get everything set up right, before—"

I wouldn't let him finish that sentence. I refused to believe there was an after. *I* wasn't ready to give up yet, even if he was.

"If you want to do right by Michaela, then stop making me disappoint her. Do you realize you've fucked up every single date we've tried to have?"

He smirked. "Maybe that *is* how I'm helping her. She deserves better than you."

Well, I couldn't argue with him there. "And Addie deserves better than you."

"Touché. Which is why we're not together and never will be."

After watching him for a moment, I crossed the living room to the bar cart, deciding I did, indeed, need that drink. "She deserves a better *friend* than you. She's busting her ass trying to save you, and what do you do in return? Offer to be a fuck buddy every once in a while?"

His smirk grew into a cocky grin. "But I'm an awesome fuck buddy. At least there's that."

"You're an asshole."

"Not news, brother." He sighed. "We all know I can't be what she wants."

I threw back the bourbon, the liquid burning its way down to the pit of my stomach. "And for some reason, she's still always there for you."

"I know."

"Then keep your shit together, so when she succeeds, she doesn't regret it. And be honest with us." I turned toward him to look him dead in the eye. "Did you kill anyone when we were in Montrose?"

He flinched. "What the fuck, man? No! Like I said, I'm *trying*."

I wasn't sure if I believed him. Vampire senses made it easier to detect a lie—we could almost smell it coming off the skin, see it in the subtle changes to pupils and expressions not visible to the human eye, hear it in the liar's fluctuating heartrate. I detected nothing now, but I had no doubt the curse's effects were escalating.

"Try harder." I poured another drink. "To start with, stop with the illegal shit. You do know pot's legal now, right? I mean, our brother owns the damn dispensary in town. Isn't that enough? You gotta sell the hard stuff?"

"Eh. Legal's no fun, bro."

"Tase."

"Xandru." He mocked, taunting me, but I refused to bite. He was pulling me in. Again. "This isn't about drugs. Not even close. I promise you. This is a mess I'm trying to clean up. I swear."

"By holding a human against his will? By killing him? If the Court gets any wind of this—"

"But they won't, right? The only way they would is if someone here told them. I know the rest of the family wouldn't say anything. That only leaves you."

"And the human?"

"He's compelled."

"And if it doesn't stick?"

His smirk grew, something flickering in his eyes. "Like everything else, that power is growing."

Awesome. He was even admitting to it. This wasn't good. I needed to talk to Addie.

I rubbed a hand over my face. "You're gonna fucking kill me, bro."

"Nah. You have too much to live for."

"You could, too."

He shrugged. "Maybe if I cared enough. Look, I got one more job and some loose ends to tie up—"

"Damn it. You've said that before."

"One more. I swear, just one more, and I'm out."

I looked up at him, studying him. He held his palms up to me.

"One more," he repeated. "I promise."

I rubbed the back of my neck, but didn't answer. If he wanted permission, he was asking the wrong person. Of course, Atanase Roca never asked for permission for anything. He was more an ask-for-forgiveness type. I supposed we all were. Our parents had taught us well.

When he realized I wasn't going to respond one way or the other, he poured himself more bourbon, then dropped onto the leather sofa. "Is everything progressing at the inn?"

I sank down on the opposite sofa. "Yeah, it's moving along. Weston and McCabe say it should be open before the first snowfall."

He offered me what remained of the blunt, and this time I took it. "Have they started on the conservatory?"

I tilted my head, wondering why he cared. "This next week, I think."

He nodded. "Good. Maybe I'll give McCabe a hand, since it's a metal framework. Is she still bitching about me paying for it all?"

"You know . . ." I thought about it. "She really hasn't lately. I guess she's come to accept it."

"She doesn't really have a choice."

"I don't know why you're wasting your time and money," interjected a female voice. Alina leaned against the rail that set off the sunken living room, apparently sensing that the tension had eased and Tase wasn't going to bite off anyone's head tonight. Literally. He'd spilt bourbon all over her earlier during the scuffle, so she'd showered and changed into fresh clothes. Her wet, brown hair hung to her shoulders, dampening her shirt. "She doesn't deserve shit."

"Shut up," Tase and I both growled simultaneously.

She snarled in response. "The bitch killed our parents! And you both think *we* owe *her*?"

"Don't twist the story," I warned. "You know the truth."

She snorted. "Yeah, I do. Their family treated ours like shit since forever. She and the rest of them had what was coming to them. *You're* the one who's twisted the story, Xandru, acting like the Petrans are the victims in all this. You even have Tase believing it half the time. But if not for them and their stupidity, none of this would be happening in the first place. Our parents would still be alive—right when things were finally getting good around here."

"The only reason they were getting good is because Dad was screwing over everyone in town," I reminded her. "Including the Petrans."

"Hey, I helped," Tase jumped in, his words beginning to slur.

"Bro. Not something to brag about. Between the two of you lying and cheating on every business deal you ever made, the Court was going to come around looking for your heads anyway." I snuffed out the blunt in an ashtray on the end table and turned back to Alina. "We have a chance to make things right."

She rolled her eyes and turned on her heel. "Are you really going to let the Court be your alpha and bare your neck to them?" she called over her shoulder.

I growled at the shifter insinuation. A *wolf* shifter, no less.

"She has a point," Tase slurred. "Rocas deserve some damn respect."

"Respect and fear aren't the same thing," I reminded him. "Especially in this town. Provoking fear gets you killed."

Tase snorted. "She's been back for what? Four months? And you've already gone soft on me."

"Almost five." I shrugged. "I have something to care about again. And I'm not letting you ruin it." I leaned back in my seat. "So what the hell was that tonight?"

Now that we'd both cooled down, maybe I could get some answers. My brother's eyes glassed over for a moment, and I thought I'd lost him. Sometimes, liquor mollified the violent mood swings; other times, it seemed to feed them. The pot helped, but Addie's magic was the only sure thing that worked. I wasn't about to invite her over tonight, though, with the way Tase had been when I'd walked in.

"I don't know," he finally said, his voice soft. "That kid just . . . he got to me, Xan. I lost it."

"No shit. You really were going to kill him."

He leaned back, his eyes drifting closed. "Not at first. Just needed to scare him. He can't be pulling shit on me, stealing product." His lids lifted a little. "I didn't mean to lose my temper like I did, but I have to finish this out. I have to follow through and can't have some little snot messing it all up."

"What are you into? Who are you tied up with? If it's not that witch anymore, then who?"

"You don't want to know, bruh. You don't want to know." His eyelids drifted down again. "Hey, you wanna go to Vegas tomorrow?" he asked sleepily.

Where did that come from? "What the fuck are you talking about?"

His head rolled to the side, his mouth open. He drew in a loud snore, out cold.

I scrubbed my hand over my face and through my hair before pulling out my phone and glancing at the time. Just past one in the morning.

Me: You up?

Long pause. Not good. I knew she'd be up for several more hours.

Kales: Working. Everything ok?

Me: Same as always. Want to finish our date?

Another long pause. *Way* too long.

Me: Guess that's a no?

Kales: No

I threw my snoring brother a hateful look. My phone vibrated again.

Kales: I mean no, it's not a no. Come on over

Standing, I debated for a moment whether to haul Tase to bed, but decided to leave his ass on the couch. I stopped briefly in the downstairs half-bath to make sure I didn't have any blood or anything else splattered on me. As I opened the front door, my mind scrolled through ideas for how I'd make this up to Michaela. I walked out onto the front step to find Sheriff Ric Kasun and Deputy Conall Kasun walking up, Ric in his usual flannel and jeans, and Conall in his tan uniform.

Had they heard Alina's wolf comment and come sniffin'? I laughed inwardly at my stupid joke. The THC was kicking in.

"Tase around?" Ric asked, somewhat cordially, which I had to give him credit for. Our kinds weren't exactly besties. Our family wasn't exactly the Kasun pack's favorite.

"He's out cold."

"Then you got a problem. The ski resort's alarms are going off."

Muttering a string of profanity, I pulled my phone out and texted Michaela.

~

THE METAL BAR was like clay in my hands. Gripping it in both fists, I squeezed, varying the pressure of my fingers while moving them up and down, molding and shaping what had once been a rod into an elaborate sigil. Many people in town looked down at our ability to control metal as evidence of the Rocas' blue-collar status. They were idiots. Our creations were art. They were functional. Oftentimes, they were both.

Stepping back, I examined the iron gate commissioned by Emilian Xavier, alpha of the black bears. It wasn't my most creative design, but it was what he wanted, and traditional methods would have never achieved the lines and curves my hands did. I'd worked on it all last night and today, after Tase and I had returned from a quick trip to Vegas for his "one last job."

The bears' alpha and my dad had been friends, in their own way, and when I visited the bears' property to take measurements for the piece, Emilian had seemed like he wanted to be my friend, too. He'd invited me in, showing me around the bears' magically cloaked estate, which he called a palace. It was impressive, but so were many of the elaborate manors that dotted the town and the mountain sides, homes referred to as palaces only in jest. The bear alpha wasn't joking.

Emilian treated his staff like slaves, which I didn't appreciate at all. My family had once been servants, and not even my dad would have said they'd been treated with such arrogance. From what I could tell, the only reason this Xavier guy and my dad had been friends was that they both hated the Court and the Old Families.

I'd met Emilian's son, Harrison, a couple of times at the Dirty Knuckle. He seemed all right, but his father was a dick. This was the last project I'd be doing for him, even if he did pay well.

A glance at the time revealed I had a few minutes free to work on my pet project, a small but intricate piece of various metals I was creating for Michaela. I'd started and stopped it several times, scrapping it over and over in my determination to get it just right.

"Why don't you just make her a ring and get it over with?" Tase's voice emerged from the workshop's doorway as I tilted the piece in the light, catching all the imperfections.

"Why don't you just shut the fuck up?" I tossed it in the scrap pile.

Tase threw his hands up in mock innocence. "Why you so mean, bro?"

"What do you want?"

"Who says I want anything?"

"Tase, my brother, you always want something." Gripping the edge of the worktable, I glared at him.

"Seriously, man, why the hate?"

I lifted an eyebrow. Did he really have to ask?

"You need to get laid," he concluded.

Well, he wasn't wrong about that. "As long as you're in my life, that's not likely to happen."

"What the hell do I have to do with it?"

It took every bit of self-control I had not to jump him and throw him to the ground. "What do you want?"

Sauntering up to the work bench, he lifted his hands again. "Maybe I just want to help you."

Yeah, right. "You have your own work to do."

"I mean, help you make Michaela happy. Happy wife, happy life. Isn't that what they say?"

"She's not my wife," I ground out. "Far from it, and the way things are going, she never will be." Scrubbing a hand through my hair, I grimaced. "I think she's on the verge of breaking up with me."

Not that we had much to break up.

"What makes you say that?"

"I don't know. Maybe because we can't even have one night to ourselves. Since our last attempt, I've been in town for a whole forty-eight hours and worked the entire time. Or maybe because she keeps saying she wants to talk."

Tase made an awful face. "Ah, shit."

"Yeah. No kidding. She's gonna call it."

He walked around the table and clamped a hand on my shoulder. "Not gonna happen. What do we need to do to ensure that? How can I help?"

Shrugging him off, I moved away from him and slanted my head toward him. "You can start by keeping your promise."

"Which one?"

I snorted. Should have known he'd broken more than one. "About one more job. Remember that one not too long ago? You said one more job to finish out, then you'd stay on the straight and narrow, take care of your own shit, and let me take care of mine."

He leaned against the workbench, stretching out his jeans-clad legs and crossing one motorcycle boot over the other. "Ah. But I haven't broken that promise. It's a multi-part job. A long-term project, so to speak. It'll take a bit longer to wrap it up."

My jaw clenched. He'd failed to mention that before.

"Is it for Ronan Bishop?" I asked. "Is it the Bishops you're all tangled up with?"

He looked at me askance. "No."

"I saw Ronan in Vegas. In the same hotel as us. Don't tell me that was coincidence."

He shrugged. "Must have been. I didn't see him." Lie.

"You're an asshole."

"You've said that before." He shrugged again. "And I've been called a lot worse."

"Leave me alone, Tase. I have work to do. Work I haven't been able to get done because I'm always having to do *your* work or make stupid trips to Vegas with you. Did you get that shit with the resort's alarms taken care of? I don't exactly like opening the door to find the dogs on our front steps."

"The cops won't be back around. It's taken care of." He turned and leaned his elbows on the bench. "So, what do we need to do about Michaela?"

"*We* don't need to do anything."

He picked up a hand broom and half-heartedly dusted shavings into a pile on the table. Why was he so restless? "Surely there's something I can do."

"Stay out of our lives. That's a start."

"God damn it, Xandru!" he suddenly roared, slamming his fist on the bench. The force sent several items rattling to the floor. Red, veiny streaks filled his face, the green in his eyes brightening as he leaned toward me. I didn't budge, refusing to show any kind of reaction. "We have to take care of her! I need her to be happy!"

What the hell? "Why do you care about her happiness?"

He growled, the sound much more animalistic than vampire, and bared his fangs at me. "Why don't *you?*"

I didn't justify his question with an answer. Antagonizing the beast would accomplish nothing, so I maintained an outward calm, while inwardly preparing to act if needed. His mood swings had signs, and I was learning them, as well as how the curse affected him. This outburst was caused by real anger, not the curse. The strigoi monster fed off anger, so it could turn bad quickly, but I didn't think it would. As expected, he backed off, and his breathing slowed.

"I just want her to be happy," he finally said, his voice back to normal. "I owe her that."

Without another word, he turned and strode out of the workshop.

"Nope, not buying it," I muttered as I watched him go. He had way too much interest in Michaela, her business, and her happiness. As much as I wished he had true altruistic feelings, I knew my brother better than that.

Strangely, he made himself scarce over the next few days, except when something needed to be done with one of the family's businesses. Then he jumped right in, taking care of it so I didn't have to. I didn't trust him or this shift in behavior, but his help freed up some time for me to spend an evening with Michaela, and I wasn't about to pass that up. If I didn't show my face at her place soon, she'd think I was purposely avoiding her.

When I arrived at the inn, however, it was all locked up, and none of the Petrans were around. Walking around the side of the building, I checked various doors along the way, until I eventually noticed the silence—there were no workers, either. Where was everyone?

After trying the back doors, I went to the cottage, but nobody was there, either. I stood on the porch and dropped my hands to my hips, a growing feeling in my gut telling me something was wrong. Then a sudden noise and movement came from the conservatory.

The only person on the whole property was the last person I ever expected to find here.

"Tase?"

He dropped a shovel as he looked up at me.

"What are you doing?" I asked.

He glanced around, gesturing at the pipes and metal work. "I told you already—thought I'd help McCabe."

"Does Michaela know?"

"I don't think Michaela cares," he said slowly. "She's gone."

My chest tightened. "*What?*"

He fished for something in his back pocket, then offered me an envelope. "I guess she and the kids took off early this afternoon. She left this on her door. Thought I'd bring it to you, but hey, here you are."

My name was written across the front in Michaela's loopy handwriting.

I stared at it for several heartbeats, then shook my head, jabbing my finger at him. "No."

I refused to take what could only be a Dear John letter.

He arched a brow. "Seriously, dude?"

With a growl, I snatched the envelope from him and stomped out, toward my truck. No way was I reading it in front of him. I didn't want to read it at all. I needed a beer or six first.

An hour later, I still sat on my favorite stool at the Dirty Knuckle, nursing my fourth beer and trying to ignore the damn envelope that lay on the bar, mocking me, when my phone buzzed.

AB: Need you, Xan. There's been an accident.

Me: Tase

I didn't even make it a question.

AB: No

A lump filled my throat. My shaking thumbs couldn't manage to type out my question, and Addie's response came first.

AB: M and the kids

CHAPTER 7

MICHAELA

*G*abe kept a death-grip on my hand as he lay in the hospital bed, his brown eyes wide and full of fear. His whole body trembled, shaking my arm that he refused to release.

"I'm so sorry," he whispered repeatedly, the only words he seemed capable of saying.

Bruises had already started to bloom over his face and arms, and his skin was swollen around the numerous cuts covering his body. He was lucky, especially since he hadn't been wearing a seatbelt at the time of the crash. My own injuries had healed almost immediately. Aurelia, on the other hand, had been rushed to emergency surgery within the first ten minutes of our arrival at the hospital in Vail.

"I'm so sorry," Gabe muttered again.

"I know, buddy. I know." I didn't know what else to say. I just wanted them both to be better, so I soothed him as best as I could.

I'd been so close to giving them my blood at the scene of the accident, my wrist held to my fangs, but thankfully the ambulance arrived, stopping me. I hated to see them in so much pain, but it was temporary. Triggering their moroi gene was not. The damage it could cause at their ages was unknown and would last forever. If only Sindi had been with us at the time. She was a different kind of vampire, and her blood could heal them without triggering their genes.

But we'd still been hours from Denver, never making it to the hotel where my friend and former—soon to be current—roommate from Atlanta had been waiting for us. As a vampire, she couldn't have left her hotel until after sunset anyway, or she'd have burst into flames.

"Aurelia," Gabe whispered.

Well, at least he'd found a new word. "She's still in surgery."

"My fault." Intense guilt filled his tone.

I sat on the side of his bed and pushed his sweaty hair off his forehead. "What happened, Gabe?"

"I . . ." He rocked his head back and forth on the pillow, tears seeping out of the corners of his eyes and down his temples. "I don't know."

Neither did I. After packing up Mom's SUV, we'd left home around two this afternoon and four hours later, we'd just passed Vail on I-70, headed for Denver. One minute we were cruising through the mountains, music blaring, Aurelia singing along in the front passenger seat while Gabe sat in the back, keeping himself occupied. The next minute, Gabe launched himself between the front seats, arms flailing and teeth gnashing. He behaved like a rabid animal, and if he were any other kid from Havenwood Falls, I would have suspected he was shifting for the first time.

Whether he meant to or because his hand latched on to whatever it touched first, he grabbed the steering wheel and whipped it out of my grip. We careened across the highway, narrowly missing several cars, before plowing through the guardrail and slamming into a tree . . . only feet from plunging down a ravine. If we'd gone the other way, we would have smashed head-on into the rock wall of the mountainside.

"I wasn't . . . me," Gabe added, a tear rolling down his cheek.

"Michaela." The deep voice came from the door behind me, and my whole body froze.

Then I jumped off the bed and turned to face Xandru, his large body filling the doorway. "What are you doing here? How—"

Addie's head bobbed over his shoulder. "You didn't really think I wouldn't tell him?"

Xandru crossed the room in three strides, and as soon as his arms opened, I fell into them. His warm, muscular body wrapped around me, his scent cocooning me in familiar comfort. I leaned my head against his chest, and my breathing became hitched as I held back the first tears that had threatened since the accident.

I peeked over his arm to see Addie standing by Gabe's bed, her hand caressing the side of his face. She soothed him, I assumed with a touch of magic, because for the first time, his body stopped trembling, and he finally relaxed. Addie nodded toward the door.

The three of us exited the room and found a small waiting area with coffee and vending machines—and too many people. Addie led us through double swinging doors that exited to the ambulance bay, which was currently empty. Beyond the portico, the western sky showed the tiniest hint of light, a glow behind the mountains left from the sunset barely more than an hour ago. My brain felt like it should be midnight. How was this day not over yet?

"Has Gabe or Aurelia been exposed to anything recently?" Addie asked me as soon as the door closed.

"What do you mean? It's summertime. I don't think any of their friends have been ill."

"I sense . . . something," she said. "It's kind of like dark magic, but not really. It's such a minute trace . . ." She shrugged. "Maybe it's nothing."

"Could it have made him lose his mind?" I explained to them what had caused the accident.

When I was done, Addie shook her head. "I don't know. There's not enough there for me to even know what it is. So I doubt it."

"You don't think he could have been bitten by a shifter at home, do you?" I asked.

Both she and Xandru reacted with surprise. If they'd seen Gabe at the time, they would have understood.

"We can test his blood, if you think we need to," Addie said, realizing I was serious. "We'll talk about it later, after we get out of here."

I nodded. "Hey, how did you two get here so fast?"

She tilted her head toward Xandru. "He refused to take the time to make the drive, so I made a portal. I told him we'd need a vehicle to get home."

"We'll rent one," Xandru said curtly.

"How's Aurelia?"

I sighed. "Still in surgery, as far as I know."

"Actually, she's out. They came looking for you." The familiar female voice called from the double doors. Standing in the spotlight over the doors, a tall, thin, twenty-something woman with dark red hair and porcelain white skin lifted her hand in a brief wave.

"Sindi!" I rushed over to her and wrapped her in a hug. She hated hugs, but I didn't care. I'd had a bad day. "You made it. And so soon."

"You know I have mad driving skills." Before pushing me away, she whispered in my ear, "I took care of Gabe for you."

I pulled back to look into her face. Her plump red lips tilted in a small smile. "Thank you."

Her voice rose as we stepped away from each other. "I went to the room number you told me, but you weren't there. Then a nurse came looking for you."

We hurried inside to the nurse's station.

"She's in recovery. Only you can go in, dear," the middle-aged woman said to me.

"I'll meet you back in Gabe's room," I told the others before turning toward a bank of elevators.

"I'll go with you," Xandru insisted, still not releasing my hand, both his voice and his grip tight. He was mad, likely at me. Once we were on the elevator, we stood facing the doors, not even slightly angled toward each other, tension growing thick. "You didn't want Addie to tell me?"

"I didn't want you to worry."

"You didn't want me to come."

I didn't reply to that. I didn't know how. Was his being here his answer to my note? Did he feel coming was an obligation?

He sighed heavily when I remained silent. "You were in a bad accident, Kales."

"And I'm fine. You should have known I would be."

"Physically, yes, but emotionally? And your brother and sister are not fine. They're like my family, too."

I snorted. "You have your own brothers and sisters to worry about."

"Kales—"

"Not now, Xandru. Please."

We had so much to talk about, but I just didn't have the brain or heart capacity at the moment.

The elevator dinged before the doors slid open.

"I understand," he said, following me out. "But we do need to talk."

No. Shit. I'd been telling him that for weeks, and he'd been avoiding the issue. *Now* he wanted to talk? Figured. *Men.*

"Just tell me what I can do for you now," he said as we stopped in front of the doors to the ICU recovery room, giving my hand a squeeze.

I glared at the doors as though I could see through them to check on my sister, but since that wasn't possible, I looked up at Xandru. "Honestly, we need our things. Whatever's left, anyway. Mom's car is surely totaled, but our stuff is in it. We have no clothes, nothing. Wherever they took it is probably closed by now, but . . ."

I let my voice trail off. Nodding his understanding, he brushed a finger over my cheek. The touch was gentle, but his jaw muscle ticked. He was still mad. "I'll take care of it. You go take care of your sister."

I gave him an appreciative nod, then pushed through the doors to find Aurelia on a hospital bed in a large room with several other beds, all of them surrounded by beeping machines. She looked so tiny, her thin body barely noticeable under the layers of covers draped over her. Tubes and wires were attached to her head and face and snaked under her hospital gown. Approaching her bed, I realized she was still asleep. I took her hand and stood by her side for an unknown amount of time, willing her awake.

"She should recover nicely," said a warm voice at the foot of the bed. The short, stout man in a white coat held out a hand. "I'm Dr. Pepper, Aurelia's surgeon."

In any other situation, I would have been suppressing a chuckle. Good thing Addie wasn't here, or we both would have been joking and laughing inappropriately.

Dr. Pepper went over everything with me, although I tuned out most of it. As soon as Sindi could see Aurelia, none of it would matter anyway. I was just sorry my poor sister had to go through as much as she already had.

"Thank you, doctor," I said when he finished, unable to say his name with a straight face. "When will she get her own room?"

"We'll have to see how she is when she wakes," he said. "She may need to stay in the ICU for a night or two."

That wasn't happening. "How long until she wakes?"

He walked up to the side of her bed and checked on the machines and her vitals. "It could be a while. She's heavily sedated. If you want to go back to your brother, I'll have the nurses let you know when she starts to wake." He glanced at his phone. "I have another patient to see."

I nodded. "Of course. Thank you. Again."

Once he left, I leaned over Aurelia and planted a kiss on her forehead. "Don't worry, baby girl, there's no way I'm making you suffer that long. I just need you to wake up, so we can get you out from under their eyes."

It took longer than I expected, and I was about to go check on Gabe when Aurelia's lids began to flutter.

"Oh, thank god," I muttered, giving her hand a squeeze.

Her eyes opened, looking foggy and distant. It took a few moments for them to clear, then the brown orbs found me. She tried to talk, but she had too many tubes coming out of her.

"Shh," I soothed. "You're okay. You're in the hospital."

Her eyes popped wide open.

"You don't remember what happened?"

She gave her head a small shake, cringing at the movement.

"Don't move. Just blink. Twice for yes, once for no."

She blinked once.

I nodded, figuring as much. "We were in an accident. They rushed you off to surgery before I could do anything, but we're all going to be okay. My friend Sindi is here, and she'll get you all fixed up."

She blinked twice, indicating she understood. I'd already told Aurelia and Gabe all about Sindi, considering we'd be spending a lot more time with her now. They were quite intrigued about how her vampirism differed from the moroi's.

"I'm going to let them know you're awake now. Cooperate and do whatever you can to convince them to move you to a private room. Can you do that?"

She blinked twice again.

I caught the first nurse I found, grabbed his shoulders, and locked our gazes. When I felt our energies connect, I compelled him. "Aurelia Petran is awake. Her vitals are clear. She needs to be moved to her own room."

He nodded and walked off. I heard him repeat my orders to the other nurses.

It took another thirty minutes before they finally cleared her to leave the ICU, although it would still be a while before they transferred her. "I'm going to check on Gabe, and then Sindi and I will meet you in your room."

She blinked twice, then closed her eyes to rest.

Back in the emergency area, I found Addie and Sindi leaning against the wall outside Gabe's room, chatting it up.

"Hey, Kales," Addie said, pushing herself off the wall. "Gabe's sleeping."

"Aurelia's awake. She should be in her own room soon. Then we can get out of here." I opened Gabe's door, surprised to find him looking only a little better than when I'd left him.

Addie pushed me inside, Sindi following and closing the door behind us.

"I had to glamour him," Addie explained. "He was healing too quickly, and it'd be suspicious. I was hoping we'd be out of here by now."

"We'll have to sneak them both out tonight," I said. "They're watching Aurelia too closely, and we can't possibly compel them all, the way they come and go. Someone will slip through. I'm sure they'll want to take more blood samples and do all kinds of tests in the morning, so we'll need to be on our way long before then."

"Sindi and I were making a plan," Addie said. "We're waiting on Xandru and a car."

"Sorry," Sindi said. "I only rented a little economy. I thought we'd be making the trip in yours."

"Yeah, you and me both." Exhaling, I rubbed my forehead. "I guess we'll be going back to Havenwood Falls sooner than we expected."

"They should be good as new tonight," Addie said. "You can still go on with your plans."

Sindi and I looked at each other, and she shrugged. "It's up to you, Kaekae. I'm all yours now."

"Ugh. Don't call me that." I bumped her shoulder with mine, then glanced over at my little brother. "I'm not sure what to do. How do I know that what happened won't happen again? It was so weird."

Addie returned to his bedside and appeared to be doing another reading. Shaking her head, she walked back over to us, not wanting to wake him. "Whatever I sensed before . . . it's completely gone now."

"So you think it was a fluke?"

"I don't know. Maybe it's like moroi puberty or something?"

"I don't remember losing my mind like that," I hissed.

"But you don't remember everything," she reminded me. Then

she added, "But I don't remember you doing anything like that, either. Maybe it's a boy thing. We can ask Xandru."

"Ask me what?" Xandru slipped through the door right at that perfect moment. Addie shared her theory. He shrugged. "Adelaide Beaumont and Michaela Petran, I grew up as a Roca. A *Roca*. We lose our shit all the time. How would I know if it was a puberty thing?"

Addie wagged a finger at him. "Good point."

With no clear answers, I didn't know what to do. Our first mission was to extract my sister and brother from the watchful eyes of human medical personnel. Maybe once I knew they were both completely healed, I could better focus on making a decision about what to do next—continue our plans with Sindi or return to Havenwood Falls.

"You want me to go check on Aurelia?" Addie asked.

"You can try, but I don't know if they'll tell you anything."

"Why wouldn't they? I'm her aunt, as far as they need to know." She left the room with a mischievous grin.

"I didn't know how long we'd have to wait, so I brought Gabe's backpack in," Xandru said, slinging it off his shoulder. "In case he got bored."

"Thank you!" Gabe's voice came loud and clear, not a trace of pain or even sleep in it. He smiled at me sheepishly. "Yeah, I might have been faking it. You women are so *boring* to listen to. *Kaekae*."

I gave him the evil eye, and then Sindi, since he'd apparently heard her use the nickname. She gave me a wicked smile in return.

Xandru tossed the backpack on the bed, and Gabe immediately grabbed for it. "I hope it's all here."

Apparently pleased with what he found inside, he let out a grunt that was more of a squeak in his ever-fluctuating voice.

Relief that he'd be okay washed through me, followed by a wave of sudden thirst shuddering through my body. And not thirst for water or coffee.

I was in the last place a vampire losing control should ever be in.

"Let's go outside." Xandru grabbed my hand and briskly led me out into the night before I could even respond. The need for blood must have been written all over my face, and looking at his, I swore he felt the same need. "I don't suppose you brought any blood on this trip of yours?"

"No, and it's probably a good thing, since the cops cleaned up the mess. That would have raised a lot of questions."

He took me to a rented black SUV, not unlike the one we'd wrecked. Peeking through the glare of the parking lot lights on the darkly tinted windows, I saw the back was filled with our belongings retrieved from Mom's car. He opened the door to the backseat. I gave him a questioning look.

"Trust me."

I climbed in and scooted over when I realized he was coming in after me. As soon as the door shut, he let his fangs out and bit into his wrist before holding it up to my mouth. I hesitated, not sure if this was the best thing to do, all things considered. Drinking blood from another moroi was . . . well, intimate.

"After what you've been through, you need to drink, Kales. Hell, I need it, too, and I haven't had nearly the day you have."

The wave of thirst had already passed, leaving only a slight ache in the back of my throat, but he was probably right. No human food or drink would provide what blood could. I latched onto his wrist.

We both moaned in pleasure—me because his blood was a salve to my burning throat, and him for the sensuality another moroi's mouth brought.

"I need some, too," Xandru said huskily.

I lifted my wrist to his mouth. His fangs sunk into my skin, and my pelvis thrusted in response. The next thing I knew, I was straddling him, my fangs at his throat and his on my shoulder. My hips rocked against his as I slid my core along the erection held hostage in his jeans. We moaned and sighed as we drank, me riding him, his hips rising up in rhythm to mine. Our shirts came off at some point I didn't even remember, and I was just reaching back to unclasp my bra, already on the verge of an orgasm, when Xandru suddenly pulled away.

"Not here. Not now," he growled, pushing me off his lap.

I collapsed into the leather seat. He opened the door and jumped out, grabbing his shirt as he did. *Crap*. He must have still been really mad at me, to be able to stop like that.

After catching my breath, I pulled my T-shirt back on and climbed out. Xandru paced behind the car, his hands on his hips, swearing up a storm.

"Can you at least tell me what I did wrong?" I asked, rubbing my arms against the chill of the night and wishing I could change out of my T-shirt and shorts. Or at least grab a hoodie from my suitcase.

Before I could move, Xandru spun, his face livid. He jerked something out of his back pocket and then waved a familiar envelope at me.

"You fucking took off, leaving me a god damn *letter*, Michaela. A god. Damn. Motherfucking. Letter!" He shouted the last word.

I flinched and stepped back, folding my arms over my chest. "Maybe if you weren't so hard-headed and would have talked when I said we needed to, I wouldn't have had to leave a god damn motherfucking letter!"

"Something like this—" He shook the envelope again. "This isn't us, Kales. We don't do this!"

"Oh, really? I wasn't sure, because I don't know what *us* is anymore." I inhaled slowly, counting cars across the way, trying to calm down. How did we get into a yelling match in the middle of the night in a hospital parking lot? "You've avoided me for nearly two weeks. I had no choice."

"I didn't know you were *leaving*! I just needed more time. Another chance—"

"Are you kidding me? How many chances do I need to give you, Xandru?" I had to catch myself, before my emotions blew up again and I said something I'd regret. I lifted my hands in the air and dropped my voice. "I can't do this right now."

The anger slid off his face, and his eyes filled with desperation.

"One more. Just one more chance. That's all I'm asking. I'm here, aren't I?"

"Yeah, here. In a parking lot of a hospital where my brother and sister are inside. I need to go in." I turned away.

"Will you talk to me?"

"I said not now." I strode toward the door.

He followed. "But later?"

I spun, and he almost crashed into me, catching himself only inches away. I flicked my finger against the envelope in his hand, the thick paper making a popping sound. "Did you even read that?"

"No. I won't do it that way. Talk to me, Kales. Not now, but promise me you will later."

"Read the damn note, Xandru."

My phone buzzed in my pocket. Pulling it out, I turned back for the entrance, reading Sindi's text as I walked. "Something's wrong. We gotta go."

I rushed inside and down the hall into Gabe's room, Xandru on my heels. I found Sindi at the foot of Gabe's bed with her hands in the air, as though in surrender. Gabe crouched on his bed, hands out, his fingers crooked like claws, like a bear about to attack.

"What the hell?"

Gabe's head snapped toward the sound of my voice so quickly, I was shocked his neck didn't break. Growling, he sprang off his bed and flew at me. I caught him easily, his tween boy body no match for my vampire one—so easily that I didn't notice his aim at first. His human teeth dug into my shoulder, in the same spot Xandru had bitten me five minutes ago. As soon as the skin re-broke, Gabe started sucking. I pushed at him while Xandru grabbed his shoulders, but Gabe was latched on harder than we realized. Xandru tugged, and I screamed as Gabe's mouth finally broke free, taking some of my flesh with him.

He passed out in Xandru's arms just before a nurse ran into the room.

"What's going on in here?" Her eyes grew wide, her gaze locked on Gabe's unconscious frame in Xandru's arms, blood covering his mouth and dripping down his chin. Her gaze flew to me, and I quickly clamped my hand over my shoulder, covering the healing wound. "What happened to you? Where'd all the blood come from?"

"I got this," Sindi said, grabbing the woman and clamping a hand over her mouth. "Get Gabe out of here."

"Aurelia—" I started.

"Addie's with her. I'll find them when I'm done with this one. We'll take care of Aurelia." She held the woman firmly as she tried to squirm free.

Nodding, I grabbed Gabe's backpack. "Okay. We'll meet you out at the car."

Xandru scooped his arm under Gabe's legs and lifted him like he was a feather.

"I don't think so," Sindi said. "Aurelia's human. Addie's human enough. When I found you after your gene was triggered, you nearly killed the first human you saw."

"Gene . . . triggered?" I echoed softly. "Oh my god!"

I spun toward Gabe, his body looking so small in Xandru's big arms, the hospital gown five sizes too large for his body and his face so young and innocent.

Well, except for the blood smeared on his lips and chin.

Fuck. My baby brother was now a vampire.

CHAPTER 8

XANDRU

"He's going to be parched when he wakes up." I laid Gabe in the backseat of the SUV, and Michaela climbed into the front. "Good thing hospitals are like the market for us."

Michaela didn't say a word. She only stared out the window at the silhouette of the inky mountains against the dark sky. I had no idea what was going through her head.

"Don't worry. I won't be caught," I said when she didn't reply.

I went back inside and followed my senses to where they stored the blood bags. Putting my gifts to use, I slipped in and out fast enough that not even a security camera could catch me. Neither Gabe nor Michaela had moved when I returned to the rental. Sliding slid into the driver's seat, I placed two bags of blood on the console.

"Now what?" I asked. I wanted to take her home. All of them. To where they belonged. But that was my wishful thinking, and not her desire. I couldn't push, no matter how badly I wanted to.

Shivering in her seat, she remained silent, and I began to wonder if she'd gone into shock. I jumped out again to retrieve a couple of blankets they'd brought on their trip from the back. I laid one on Gabe and wrapped the other around Michaela. Still not a peep from her.

When she finally spoke, her voice was small and soft. "I don't know what happened when I was triggered."

I scratched at the stubble on my cheek. "Yeah, I know. Tase was at the bar and saw that douchebag propose to you, so he slipped some of his blood in your wine. He'd followed you there . . ."

She tilted her head to look at me. "You knew that?"

"He told me after you came back."

"Oh." She faced forward again, staring out the windshield and pulling the blanket tighter around her. "I meant, I don't know when it happened. How long until it affected me . . . before I attacked . . ." She paused. "I don't know what to expect. With Gabe." She hiccupped on her brother's name.

I laid my hand on her knee. "You were alone. You had no idea what happened. As if what Tase did to you wasn't shitty enough, he left you to fend on your own. No newborn, no matter what kind of vamp, should be left to figure it out on their own."

"Thank god I had Sindi. It could have been so much worse . . ."

"And Gabe has us. We'll be here the moment he wakes, and we'll help him."

She flipped her hand toward the backseat. "So this is normal so far?"

I looked back at Gabe, out cold, blood all over his face. "Not really. None of us passed out during our turning ceremony. We drank Dad's blood from the chalice, there was a celebration, and about an hour or so later, the thirst kicked in. We were given human blood, and after that, we passed out. For three days. That's when the true transformation takes place, at the cellular level."

"Oh. I thought Sindi knocked me out that long."

"Whatever knocked Gabe out must have been whatever caused him to attack in the first place. Maybe something weird going on with his gene."

Michaela nodded. "Maybe that's what Addie sensed. Maybe he won't wake a moroi?"

She held so much hope in her voice, I couldn't bring myself to reject the idea. But it wasn't likely. It took one swallow of a mature moroi's blood to activate the gene. Unless his gene was completely dormant, which it obviously wasn't, he was going to turn. I was more worried that whatever was different for him, whatever had caused this, would skip him past the moroi stage and straight into strigoi.

"If he wakes with a thirst, we'll know," I said.

"Okay, then we'll wait for that, and go from there."

At that moment, Addie and the tall redhead rushed out of the hospital, Aurelia, still in a hospital gown, braced between them. They hurried toward a small white Toyota and immediately took off as a couple of security personnel ran outside, scanning the parking lot.

"Looks like that didn't go well," Michaela mused aloud. Her phone buzzed, and she read the text. "They're getting a hotel room here in Vail, until we figure out what we're all going to do."

"Find out where."

"I'm not taking Gabe to them! We're not taking him near any humans."

"Aurelia needs clothes," I pointed out.

"Oh. Shit." She tapped into her phone at the same time Gabe began to stir behind us.

I turned in my seat to find him sitting up, his eyes wild and disoriented. He clawed at his throat, his mouth falling open in a silent scream. I grabbed a bag of blood, bit off the cap, and held it to his mouth. He gulped the crimson liquid, draining it all in seconds. I handed him the second bag.

"I guess that answers that," Michaela said, sighing sadly. "Well, at least it doesn't matter if he was bitten by a shifter."

As soon as Gabe finished, he belched, smiled like a drunk, and then passed out again.

"So he's out for three days now?" she asked.

"Sleeping like the dead. So now what? Where do you want to go? I'm all yours."

I cranked the engine over as she rattled off a hotel's name and address. "We'll give them Aurelia's suitcase, then I guess we head home. You probably need to get back."

I plugged the address into the GPS. "Like I said, I'm all yours."

"Yeah, right."

"Kales."

"What about Tase and Alina?"

"Tase can fuck off, and for that matter, so can Alina. She needs to get over herself. I'm all yours."

Sighing, she shook her head. "You're like the king of mixed signals."

I laughed. "*Me?* I've only had one signal, Kales. But if that makes you my queen . . ."

"My signals are loud and clear in that note."

I retrieved it from my back pocket. "Do you want me to read it now?"

Her eyes widened, and she snatched it out of my hand. "No. Not when I'm about to be cooped up in a car with you for several hours."

"It'll force us to talk."

"And when we're done? After we have no more to say?"

She had a point.

"So the hotel, then Havenwood Falls?" I asked while backing out of the parking spot.

"Gabe should probably wake up in familiar surroundings. Mammie should know what to do, too." She sighed. "I can't believe I've blown it already."

"This wasn't your fault."

"It still happened on my watch. If I only knew *why*. First the attack in the car . . . oh! He'd been trying to bite me then, too."

"You? But not Aurelia?"

She seemed to ponder this as we pulled out of the hospital parking lot and headed toward the hotel, only a few blocks away.

"I can't be sure," she finally said. "It happened so fast."

"Hopefully you're right, and Mammie will be able to explain." I pulled in front of the hotel's entry. "I'll wait out here with Gabe."

Michaela hopped out and retrieved Aurelia's suitcase from the back, then headed inside, returning fifteen minutes later.

"Sorry it took so long. Aurelia was a bit of a mess. She'd been driving Mom's car before this trip, and I had to tell her it was totaled. And she was really looking forward to school shopping in the city, so I hated disappointing her, after everything."

"So do you want to stay?"

"No, I don't want to take any chances with Gabe. Addie and Sindi offered to take her shopping tomorrow, so she's better now. Addie will be able to bring Sindi into town."

I shifted the SUV into drive and headed out of the parking lot and toward the highway. "So, that's Sindi, huh?"

"Yeah." She smiled. "That's Sindi. She's pretty awesome, especially taking care of all this."

"She's a good friend."

"Yeah, she is. Not like Addie. Nobody can compare to Addie. Or you. But she is a good friend. It'll be interesting to have her in Havenwood Falls. She's a total city girl."

"How long will she be staying? Did she say?" If my gut was right, that would tell me how long I had left with Michaela, then I could figure out what to do to change that.

She shrugged. "For now, she's committed to go where—and when—I go. I don't know how long that'll hold, though. I guess we'll see."

That wasn't helpful.

We rode for hours in silence. I was lost in my own head, making plans for what I was going to do about Michaela. She'd fallen asleep. *Good.* The day had taken a huge emotional toll on her, and when she was awake, she tensed up every time we passed a car, grabbing at the handholds and bracing herself for another crash. She needed to rest. As we crested the ridge on Burdorf Pass, about to descend into town, she jolted awake from a nightmare.

The sky above Mt. Sousa on the far side of town was just beginning to lighten.

"Home sweet home," Michaela sighed as I pulled up in front of the cottage.

"I guess you weren't planning on being back here, were you?"

"Not already." She stared at the cottage. "I can't believe we left just this afternoon. It feels like days."

My hand covered hers. "I'm sorry your plans were ruined."

I meant it with full sincerity.

"Yeah, me, too. I can deal with missing a couple days in the city, but this . . ." She glanced over the seat at Gabe's still form. "This is a total game-changer."

"It doesn't—wait. What do you mean, a couple days in the city?"

She hopped out of the car without answering.

"Kales?" I asked as soon as she opened the back door. I slid out and ran around the front of the car to help her. "Will you explain?"

She lifted Gabe and slung him over her shoulder in a fireman's carry. She obviously didn't need my help. "I'm taking him inside. Read the note, Xandru."

She strode up the stairs of the cottage. When I glanced in the car window, I noticed she'd left her note in the front passenger seat. Damn it. Couldn't she explain in person? It wasn't like Gabe would have noticed if he spent another five minutes in the back seat. I opened the door, snatched the envelope off the seat, and slammed the door shut. I leaned against it and ripped the stupid paper open.

I read through the letter once, my heart pounding the entire time. Then just to be sure I understood, I read it again, slower now, taking in every word.

Dear Xandru,

I'm sorry I have to say this in a note, but it's been impossible to talk to you. I have too much to say for a text, but I can't carry this around any longer. I can't even wait three more days until I (hopefully) will see you again.

I'm taking Aurelia and Gabe to Denver for a couple of days to go school shopping. They're all enrolled and ready to start next week, but they need clothes. We also wanted a few days just to get away.

My friend Sindi from Atlanta is meeting us in Denver so I can bring her back to Havenwood Falls. I've already cleared it with the Court. She'll be able to help me run the inn, since she can actually touch and do things, and Mammie can't.

I've also claimed my seat on the Court. I still have to do the swearing in or whatever it is they do to make it official, but that's one of the reasons why I met with them last month. They've also helped me put other matters in order so we can actually get on with living life.

This is all to say that I've made my choice—and it's <u>my</u> choice. Not anybody else's. I'm choosing to live this life we have in Havenwood Falls. This is my home. This is where my family and friends are. It may not look exactly like we'd always envisioned it, but this is the life you and I always wanted. And that's how life is—we can plan and dream all we want, we can even make our own choices and decisions, but life has a way of taking things in a whole different direction. That would happen whether we stayed here in Havenwood Falls or not. So I'm choosing to take whatever life hands me right here, where I belong.

All that's left is you, Xandru. I'm choosing you, too, but only if you'll have me. I know things are different. I know I'm different. I don't know if you can accept me and love me the same way you did before— sometimes, it doesn't seem that way. I don't want to force myself on you, if I'm no longer what you want. But I need you to at least know that I love you. That I choose you.

I'm all in, Xandru. This life we have—I'm <u>all</u> in.

Michaela's soft voice floated down to me from the porch, saying the final words as I read them. "I'm all in."

CHAPTER 9

MICHAELA

*X*andru leaned against the black SUV, his long legs kicked out in front of him, one crossed over the other. He gripped the letter, his free hand rubbing his scruffy jaw, something he'd done while reading since we were kids. So I knew the exact moment when he reached the end.

"I'm all in, Xandru," I said, barely able to manage more than a whisper over the lump in my throat. "Are you?"

Slowly . . . so painfully slowly, he lifted only his gaze, looking at me through his lashes as his thumb skimmed back and forth over his bottom lip. He didn't say anything, didn't move in any other way. Just stood there, stroking his lip and staring.

It was pure torture.

I'd wanted to tell him this for what felt like forever now, but in truth, had only been weeks. Weeks of agonizing over his response. Weeks of wondering, and, admittedly, vacillating, if this was the right decision. The right move. But I had to at least try. I had to tell him how I felt once and for all. I'd already moved forward with everything else in this life I'd chosen, except for Xandru. I couldn't let this hang between us any longer. Thus the letter.

Heart pounding loud enough to be heard on the other side of town, I shifted from foot to foot as he continued to scrutinize me.

As always, his gaze was electric, lightning traveling across my skin, through my veins.

Torture. Pure torture.

After what felt like hours, I couldn't bear another moment.

"I guess if it takes you that long to think about it—" I started, but was cut off by Xandru's hot mouth crashing on mine.

I hadn't even seen him move. One moment he was leaning against the rental car, and a nanosecond later, he had his hands on my cheeks and his body pressing me against the door, his mouth devouring mine. His lips were firm, demanding, urgent. Delicious. His tongue swept over my bottom lip, and my mouth parted, letting him in. Delectable. My entire body lit up with such an aching need, I truly thought I might die if it wasn't met.

Xandru's hands left my face, landing on the wall on either side of my head. He pushed himself away, breaking contact, but only enough to rest his forehead against mine. We breathed each other's air as we stared into each other's eyes.

He cocked his head to the side. "What ever made you think I wouldn't be all in?"

I scoffed. "Are you serious? Maybe because I feel like you've been avoiding me?"

"I thought you were going to break up with me. Yes, I was admittedly avoiding that."

The corner of my mouth turned up in a half-smile. "I wasn't sure we had anything to break up. You're always so busy, and I know there's real reason for that, but sometimes I can't help but feel like maybe you were looking for excuses . . . that you didn't like this new version of me but couldn't bring yourself to tell—"

He cut me off again with another kiss. Softer this time. Almost careful. *Caring.*

He slowly pulled back. "Michaela Petran, I fucking *love* you. I have since I was nine years old. Nothing will ever change that. I am yours for as long as you want me. But I was trying to give you space. I could never force you into something you don't really want. You've had enough of that."

His piercing gaze held mine, as if to make sure his point was driven home, all the way through my heart and into my soul. Finally, I nodded.

"I love you, too," I murmured. "I have never wanted anything—anyone—more than I want you. This. Us. I choose us."

I slid my hands into his hair and pushed myself up against him, while pulling him to me. Our mouths crashed together with renewed desperation and urgency. Our tongues met and tasted, stroked and taunted. His hand cupped one side of my head as his other slid slowly down my back and to my ass. He squeezed and lifted at the same time, pulling me up his body until I wrapped my legs around his waist. My center rubbed against his arousal, and I moaned into his mouth. Moving to do it again, I pulled my lips from his.

"No more waiting," I said. "I just can't anymore."

"You're sure?"

I grabbed his bottom lip between mine and sucked, slowly releasing it. "I'm positive. There's no such thing as the perfect time. I don't want to waste another minute without you." I gave him another teasing kiss. "Inside me."

He sucked in a breath, and I felt him grow harder between my legs. "Here?"

"Gabe's dead to the world for three days, right?"

"Kind of literally."

"No more waiting, Xandru." To prove my point, I sucked on his lip again, harder this time as I moved my hips up and down, feeling his swollen head straining against his jeans. The friction of our clothing was already about to send me spiraling.

We crashed through the front door and across the living room as he carried me to my bedroom. He kicked the door shut, and we landed on the bed, me on my back, his entire body pressed into mine. My hips bucked up against him, eliciting a moan from both of us. His lips moved from my mouth along my jaw and down my neck. My back arched, and I turned my head, exposing my throat. He paused at my carotid and sucked. Just the thought of his fangs sinking into me as his erection rubbed against me had me escalating toward an orgasm. He pulled back just in time.

"Not yet, love," he murmured as he stood and kicked off his shoes.

I kicked off my own, then sat up and grabbed the hem of his shirt. I stood as I lifted it up and over his head. Then I froze, taking a moment to admire. *Holy. Hard. Chest.* My fingers trailed over his smooth skin, my palms skating over his nipples. *Holy. Ripped. Abs.* His muscles twitched under my touch as my hands slid lower. I'd seen him shirtless a couple of times over the summer, but I'd had to look away so I wasn't tempted to jump his bones. Now I could stop and truly appreciate, because I sure as hell *was* going to jump his bones. I pushed my hands up again, over his broad shoulders, around his large biceps and triceps, and down his thick forearms, worshipping every inch.

As my hands came to his, our fingers danced together, twisting against each other, but never quite intertwining and holding. Xandru leaned in, his hot breath fluttering over my ear and down my neck, as I watched our hands teasing each other, fingers brushing softly, tips stroking over palms. Barely touching. Yet so very erotic.

A shiver ran through me.

Breaking the contact, his hands moved to my waist, under my T-shirt, and slid upwards, taking my shirt with them. His thumbs paused beneath my breasts, slipping under my bra, softly stroking back and forth. Then they continued upward, slowly sliding over my bra, pausing again to tease my hard nipples, before finally pulling my shirt over my head. Reaching behind me, I undid the clasp, letting the lacy material fall down my arms and to the floor. Now it was Xandru's turn to stop and admire, and his gaze was tangible as it slowly swept over me, causing my breasts to tighten and ache.

He leaned forward, and I dropped back to the bed, laying back as he came with me. His mouth lingered on mine before traveling over my jaw and down my neck. Stopping at the base of my throat, his tongue swirled over my pulsing vein, and I gasped when I felt his fangs scrape over my skin. But then he continued on, kissing his way to my breast, his hand caressing the other. My fingers dug into his shoulders as he took my nipple into his mouth, sucking and flicking it with his tongue. Heat pooled between my legs, and my pelvis lifted, needing to feel him against me. We still had too many damn clothes on.

As though reading my mind, his hand moved to the button of my jeans shorts. As soon as it was undone, his open mouth trailed down my stomach, his tongue swirling along its path, dipping around my belly button as he removed my shorts and panties. Then he started at one ankle and worked his way upward, the stubble of his facial hair rough in a pleasurable way.

I felt the tips of his fangs when he reached the top of my inner thigh and sucked, while his hands lifted me up, opening my legs. His eyes rolled up to watch me as he slid his tongue out, and ever so slowly, stroked me once up the center. I nearly came undone. Another slow stroke had me moaning and thrashing. A third one, and I groaned his name. His tongue flicked in circles, closing in on the nub of nerves. Then his lips closed down, and he sucked. I couldn't breathe. I gasped for air anyway.

When I thought I could take no more, his thumb replaced his tongue against my clit, his fingers slid inside me and curled, and his fangs sunk into the flesh of my inner thigh.

"Oh my fucking . . . *Xan*." I clawed at the bed, at his head and shoulder, anywhere I could latch on to keep me somewhat grounded. "Please," I begged. "Please." I tugged at him, not wanting to completely unleash yet. "I want you *inside* me."

His tongue swirled over the wounds, ensuring they were closed, before he rose slowly, his gaze locked on mine. How the fuck did he still have pants on? I sat up and unbuckled his belt with vampire speed. In a flash, he was back over me, free now, his swollen, hard length pressing against my belly.

"Make love to me." I wrapped my hand around his cock, stroking him as I shimmied into place under him. I ran my thumb over his silky tip, eliciting a moan, before positioning it against my opening. "Please," I breathed.

He hovered over me, his weight supported on his elbows and forearms, as he appraised my body. Memories suddenly flashed in my mind, many that had been locked away until now. Our first real kiss. Not the little pecks we'd giggled about in elementary school. Our first passionate kiss, tongues and awkwardness and everything, when I was twelve and he was fourteen. The first time I'd let him touch my boobs when I was a freshman in high school, his hand slipping beneath the vest of my cheerleading uniform. The first time he saw me naked, appraising me like he did now, as though not only seeing but worshipping. All of our firsts came rushing back, including the first time he'd entered me.

"This is what you want?" he asked me now, just like he had then.

I replied in the same way. "*You* are what I want."

He closed his eyes, like he had then, as though I'd just answered his biggest prayer. Then he leaned his forehead against mine, and our gazes locked as his hips tilted, pushing his way in. We both inhaled sharply. We stared at each other, relishing the feeling, before he slid deeper inside. Our eyes fell shut. My hips rose, taking him in more. Our mouths crashed together, and we became a desperate frenzy of kissing, licking, and sucking while our hips rocked and rolled, our momentum building.

His hand moved between us, cupping my breast as he thrust into me. He squeezed as he pulled out, pinching my nipple then pulling it as he drove back in. I moaned in ecstasy. My hands grasped at him, desperate for purchase, in his hair, on his shoulders, the muscles of his back, massaging and kneading, until eventually my nails dug in.

"Michaela," he moaned. "My Michaela. *Mine*," he growled, pumping harder into me and sending me to the edge of an orgasm.

"Yours," I screamed as I thrust my hips up, taking him in deep and squeezing.

"Fuck, oh, fuck," he groaned. Then, "Get ready, love."

His fangs let out, and so did mine.

He clamped his mouth down at the base of my throat, and I did the same to him. We bit into each other's skin at the same time as he rocked into me. Euphoria shot through me, from the taste of him flooding my tongue to the delicious pain of his teeth digging into me. From the sensation of my blood singing through my veins toward his hot mouth to the explosion of orgasm at my core. He pulled up onto his knees, taking me with him, so I straddled him, driving him in deeper. I wrapped my arms around his shoulders, my hand cradling his head as we continued to consume each other. We clung to each other with desperation while at the same time coming completely and fully apart.

Shouting.

Exploding.

Shattering.

Gone.

Spent.

Trembling.

"HOLY SHIT," I breathed as we collapsed onto the bed. "That was not at all like the first time."

Xandru laughed breathily. "Fuck, I hope not. I'd like to think I've learned something since then."

Giggling, I turned my head toward him, unable to move the rest of my body. His eyes had always affected me, but the look in them now slayed me. I hadn't thought it possible for a gaze to hold as much love and adoration in it as Xandru's did now. For me. *Me*. And I'd been so worried he didn't want me anymore.

Reaching out, I wrapped my pinky around his, my voice dropping to a whisper. "That was not like any time. Ever."

He rolled over so his face hovered over mine, our lips nearly brushing. "But there will be more times like this. A lot more. Yeah?"

I smiled. "Damn well better be."

He sealed the promise with a kiss.

∾

"WHAT THE HELL is Tase doing in my conservatory?" I asked Xandru that afternoon as I sat on the cottage's front porch, imbibing the nectar of the gods, aka coffee. If I was ever in a life-and-death situation and forced to choose between coffee and the sweetest human's blood, I'd probably die from indecision.

Especially after the day I'd had yesterday . . . and the morning we'd spent together.

Xandru came out to join me with a freshly brewed mug in his hand and sat on the chair next to me. "He was there yesterday, too. Says he's helping Mike with the metalwork."

"With a shovel?"

"Maybe the steam pipes run underground?"

"Hmm . . ."

"Would you rather I do the work? I know you don't like him here."

Sighing, I turned to face the love of my life. "Xandru, we still need to talk."

His face went blank. Not even a deer-in-the-headlights look, because there was no fear this time. He cleared his throat. "Er, right. Are you sure? I was hoping last night . . ."

"Last night was a start." I patted his hand. "I want you to know what I mean by all in, though. I mean *that*." I gestured toward the conservatory, where Tase was doing whatever kind of metalwork required a shovel. "What he's done to my family was . . . reprehensible. But on the other hand, I wouldn't be here if he hadn't. I wouldn't be back home with my family. I wouldn't be with you. I've forgiven him. And while that doesn't mean I actually like him, he's your brother. He's part of your life. So . . . he's part of mine."

"Kales, you don't have to take him on. He's a mess. And it'll only get worse."

"He's family."

"Not yours."

I had to inhale a deep breath to calm my frustration, because at that moment, I wanted to beat my chair over his head. I exhaled slowly, reining myself in, until I could speak calmly. I stood and moved over to his lap so I could be close enough to capture his full attention.

"Do you not get what I'm saying?" Holding his face in my hands, I looked him in the eyes. "All. In. *All*. As in everything and everyone. If it's part of your life, it's part of mine. And vice versa. I want to do this life with you, Xandru. Not just share the parts we pick and choose, leaving those we don't like for the other to deal with on their own."

"I understand. Everything but Tase, though. At least for now. You don't deserve to have to deal with his bullshit. One moment, he seems perfectly fine. The next, a switch flips, and you can see the monster he's about to become. Right there, clawing at the surface. I don't want you part of that. I don't want you near him."

"Are you making a decision for me, Roca?"

"Just wanting to protect you."

"I'm not a helpless damsel."

"That's not what I mean." He closed his eyes and groaned. "Please, Michaela."

"'Please, Michaela, will you support me and your best friend in helping my brother?' Why yes, Xandru, I will."

"Kales."

"Xandru." I leaned in and kissed his pouty lips. "I want to be there for you. You don't need to go through this alone."

"I'm not. I have my brothers and sisters and Addie."

"And they can give you the same kind of support I can?"

He furrowed his brow. "Not exactly."

"So let me be there for you, whatever that means. And I'll need you there for me, especially with Gabe now. I need to know that I'm also a priority in your life."

"You always have been."

I snorted. I knew he meant it. "Okay, I need you to *show* it. Don't run away. Don't push me away. Don't hide your feelings anymore. Because, Xandru, you really did almost lose me."

He brushed his knuckles across my cheekbone. "I'm sorry. From now on, I will show you how important you are to me. You are *most* important. You, whatever you need, will always come first."

I kissed him between the eyebrows, then tried to explain better. "I don't need to always come first. That's setting an expectation that can't be met. But I would like to come first a lot of the time, you know? And when I can't, when something—or someone—must come first at that moment, I can still be with you. I guess that's what I'm trying to say. We deal with all the other stuff together. As one."

"As one?" he asked, tilting his head back as his fingers played with a lock of my hair. "So—business, family, everything? We deal with it all together, as in one brain, one voice, one person?"

"No." I sighed. "As in, we don't shut each other out. Obviously, we'll have things we have to do on our own. And we may not always agree and will have to make our own decisions. But that doesn't mean we can't talk to each other about everything. We should be able to rant and vent and celebrate and talk through things. We need to be open and honest with each other. We can't hold things back because we think the other can't handle it. Or because we don't want to burden each other. I want to share your burdens. I hope you will share mine."

"Even Tase?"

"Even Tase. Even Gabe."

"Okay," he said on a heavy exhale. Pushing his hand back into my hair, he cradled my head and pulled me in for a brief kiss. "Open. Honest. In it together."

ELSMED FAIRCHILD, in all his fae glory that revealed he was not at all the elderly human he presented to the public, glared down his flat nose at us with frosty blue eyes, and I just knew he was trying to read my mind. He had the ability, and I was sure he used it whenever he could.

Old Man Mills also seemed intensely interested in us, even as the rest of the Court members talked amongst themselves. Well, except for the witch hunter Lilith Blackstone, who was understandably distracted, staring off into space as her fingernails tapped the arm of her chair. Her teenage daughter, Macy, had taken off days ago, and as far as I knew, there had been no word of her since.

They were all seated at the table on the dais at the head of the main room of the Court of the Sun and the Moon, with the Petran seat still empty, as I hadn't officially taken it yet. I sat in the row of folding chairs in front of them, Gabe next to me, his leg bouncing up and down as we waited for their decision.

He'd woken up four days ago, on the day of the solar eclipse, and exactly as Xandru had predicted, with eyes that were no longer brown, but the moroi gray-green, and with an uncontrollable thirst. Xandru and I had stocked up on blood from Sanguine Elixirs, the local liquor store with its special section for supes, and Sindi had brought more from Denver when she, Aurelia, and Addie arrived back in town. We kept Gabe's need satisfied while teaching him how to maintain control. So far, he'd done quite well.

But he was still a newborn vampire. He had no bites, which meant this was all about being moroi and not shifter, but nobody could figure out why this had happened. I'd asked if old aether could have caused it, but Saundra and Addie quickly dismissed the theory. After doing magical readings and other witchy stuff, the Court had finally concluded it must have been something biological—basically, that his hormones had been whacked-out. At twelve years old, he was the youngest moroi and the only to initiate his own triggering, as far as anybody, including Mammie, knew.

All of this meant he was an unknown—unpredictable.

And school started on Monday.

A gavel hit the table, and everyone quieted, resettling into their seats to face us.

"We've made our final decision," Saundra Beaumont, Addie's grandmother, announced. While she normally had a severe look to her, with her white hair pulled back in a perfectly coifed chignon and always wearing a business suit, she looked at Gabe with warm brown eyes, one side of her mouth tilting in a sad smile. She and her daughter Lyra had helped Mammie care for Gabe and Aurelia after Mom passed, often taking them into their homes. Saundra had a soft spot for him. "I'm sorry, Gabe, but you'll need to attend the Sun and Moon Academy, at least for this semester. Maybe the full year."

"No!" Gabe jumped to his feet. "That's not fair! I didn't do anything wrong!"

"Not yet," Old Man Mills muttered.

"But I won't do anything! I promise. All of my friends are at the regular school."

"This is in your best interest, son," Elsmed said. "None of us know what to expect, and we can't take any chances."

Odette Alverson tilted her head so her blond hair swung against her shoulder, and said much more kindly, "You'll learn a lot at the Academy, and you'll be able to drink whenever you need to. If something happens, you'll be surrounded by people who will be able to help you."

"It only has to be temporary," Saundra added. "If that's what you want. You may find that you like the Academy."

Gabe was about to protest again, but I stood next to him and took his hand, squeezing him into silence. "We understand. But he will be reassessed at the end of the first term, right?"

"Yes," Roman Bishop said in a bored tone. His lids hooded his blue eyes, and with a heavy sigh, he waved lazily toward the door. "He's dismissed."

"We still need you, though, Michaela," Saundra reminded me. "You can walk him out."

I led Gabe to the back of the room and out the doors to the small reception area, where Addie was redoing Sindi's tattoo. She'd given her a quick visitor's mark as soon as they arrived from Denver, but the plan had always been for Sindi to stay a while to help at the inn. She needed the magic given to residents, and while she was at it, had Addie elaborate on the Celtic design.

"Who would have thought we'd be going to school together?" I asked Gabe as I opened the door for him.

He looked at me sideways. "You're going to the Academy?"

I made my voice as enthusiastic as I could. "Yep! I have to learn some things, too. Things nobody else in this town gets to know. Because that's what happens at the Academy."

As hoped for, this piqued his interest. "Really?"

"Really."

"Hey, dude, check this out." Sindi showed off her updated tattoo. "I hear you get one, too."

This excited Gabe even more, and I was sure he had no problem with me leaving him with the two pretty women so I could return to the Court. I slipped back into the dark basement room and closed the door behind me. Roman flicked his fingers toward me—well, the doors, I realized—and a hiss sounded from behind me.

"The room has been silenced," he drawled.

"Michaela, you can take the Petran seat." Saundra motioned toward the empty chair on the dais. "You won't be officially sworn in until Founders Day, which gives you nearly a month to learn what you need to. This includes sitting in on the meetings and proceedings so you can come up to speed with current events. You just won't have any voting privileges."

I climbed the three steps to the dais and gingerly took my seat at the end of the table. Elsmed pierced me with his creepy eyes, leaning forward on his arms on the table and slanting his head toward me.

"Young lady," he said, "sitting where you are is an automatic oath to maintain all confidentialities of the Court and to protect all secrets. Everything we do is in the best interest of this town and the protection of its people. Most of what we do cannot be disclosed to anyone. Not a single soul. You do understand that what is discussed here stays within these walls unless otherwise directed?"

I gulped and nodded. "Yes, I understand."

"So, then," Saundra said, "the rest of today's agenda includes Macy Blackstone, Founders Day festivities, and the Rocas."

Well, shit.

CHAPTER 10

XANDRU

"Something's going on with Tase," Adrian, our next oldest brother, said as he helped me load some metal pieces into the back of my truck.

"Ya think?" I replied.

"Not the strigoi shit. Something else." He shoved a beam a little too hard into the bed.

"Bro. That's my truck."

"Sorry." He stopped working and dropped his hands on his hips as he watched me. He was a younger version of both Tase and myself —dark hair, gray-green eyes, tall, and broad. As the eldest three of the Rocas and born closely together, some days we were best friends, and others, each other's biggest competitors. Adrian was just enough younger, though, to have a slightly different perspective. "Do you remember before pot was legalized and Tase was into dealing?"

I nodded. "Dad was, too, you know."

"Yeah, I know. He had me take over when you wouldn't." Then he shrugged, as though it were no big deal. And they wondered why the Rocas had the reputation that we did. "Anyway, so when you're dealing, you have to hang out with people you normally wouldn't. We didn't know what Tase was doing then, so we couldn't figure out why he was suddenly all buddy-buddy with people he made fun of.

And he was always sneaking around. Didn't want anything to do with us."

I nodded. "I remember. Some of that was about the Order of Castor, though."

The Order was a secret society made up of seniors in high school who were mostly from the Old Families. Sort of a younger generation of the Court, although the Order actually let Rocas in. Probably as rebellion against the actual Court, because that's how the Order rolled.

"Yeah, but now?" Adrian asked. "Because he's doing it again."

"Sneaking around? That's just Tase."

"The people he's in with, though? What are *they* doing? It's not drugs anymore, unless it's big-time shit. And I wouldn't normally give a flying fuck, but Tase needs to keep his nose clean before the Court comes up with a reason to off him. You know they're looking for one."

Yeah, I did know. Especially if they sensed what Addie had.

I dropped a bundle of metal rods in the bed and looked at him. "So who do you think he's in with?"

"I saw Ronan Bishop's name pop up on his phone screen the other day."

"Uh-huh." That didn't surprise me. I knew it was no coincidence that I'd seen him in Vegas, in the same hotel at the same time. "Who else?"

"The Bishops, Xan. Isn't that enough?"

The Bishops were like the shinier version of the Rocas. Just as bad, probably worse, but they could get away with more because they were the Bishops. While we're both Old Families, they're actually revered as such. It didn't hurt that their magic was some of the most powerful in town. And that Roman Bishop was one of the most powerful people in town, with a seat on the Court *and* the High Council of the Luna Coven.

If something went bad between Tase and Ronan, Tase would most definitely be the scapegoat, even if he didn't already have a death sentence.

I slammed the tailgate shut. "I'll see if he'll tell me anything. Try to talk him out of it."

"And what about Michaela?"

I lifted a brow. "What about her?"

"You can't tell her. Not if she's about to be sworn into the Court."

"Michaela is on our side. She's family."

Adrian barked out a humorless laugh, then leaned toward me and growled, "She will *never* be family."

"She will be officially soon enough, if I can help it. Get used to it."

"No! I don't trust her. Tase doesn't. None of the family does. Except you. Which makes you a fucking moron." He turned on his heel and strode off toward the house.

I watched him leave, abandoning the work that I'd once again have to do by myself.

Michaela and I had finally been able to forge a real relationship, seeing each other every possible moment over the last few weeks, but the closer we grew together, the further my family grew apart. At least, from me. At one time, I wouldn't have cared. I'd never wanted the Roca way of life, anyway. My family brought on their own troubles. But we were all in this now, and by no fault of our own. Not even Tase's. Not entirely. The curse went back nearly two centuries, before any of us were a thought in our parents' minds. We were all tied into it, though. I just didn't know how to convince my siblings that the Petrans—those who remained—were not our enemies. Dad's beliefs were too deeply ingrained in them.

Adrian never returned, so I hauled the load to the ski resort and unloaded it myself so we could begin prepping for the ski season next week. Then I headed to the Sun and Moon Academy to pick up Michaela. The driveway to the private-school campus wound for more than a quarter mile through the trees until it opened up to a circular driveway in front of an old two-story building that looked like it belonged in another century in the Old Country—any old country. The grounds were vast and well-kept, ending on the far side near the great falls themselves.

Although in a different school and parking lot, sitting in my truck with the windows down and music playing took me back to the days when I'd picked Michaela up from Havenwood Falls High, after I'd graduated. I didn't realize I was smiling about the memories until the grin slid off my face as my gaze focused in on two people standing on the sidewalk that led from the parking lot to the school, in what appeared to be a heated discussion. Tase. And Gabe.

What in the actual fuck?

Jumping out of the truck, I strode toward them. Gabe looked at me, blanched, then turned and hurried back into the school. Tase casually meandered toward me.

"What the hell are you doing here?" I asked when we were face-to-face.

He lifted his chin. "Looking for someone. What's wrong with you?"

"Who would you be looking for at the Academy?"

He rolled his eyes. "Rowan Bishop, if you must know."

Another Bishop. And he wasn't even trying to hide it. "Why?"

"That's for me to know and you to fuck off."

I grabbed him by the collar and wrenched him toward me. "The Bishops will bring you down, Tase. All of us."

He shoved me off. "Thanks for the confidence, brother."

"What's going on?"

He started walking toward the parking lot, where I hadn't noticed his car before, parked over by a passenger van with the school's logo. "Business. Not yours. Just trust me."

"Trust you?" I scoffed. "You keep asking me to, but then you won't tell me shit. How deep are you in with them?"

"Don't worry about it. It'll all be fine." He opened his car door, gave me a salute-wave, then dropped inside. After starting the engine, he rolled down the passenger window and leaned over to look up at me. "Just keep it between us, though, okay? Don't be blabbing your mouth to your woman."

Bending over, I rested my forearms on the door and leaned into the window. "If any of this, whatever you're involved in, comes down on Michaela . . . if you hurt her or her family again . . . you won't have to worry about the Court. I will bury you myself. Do you understand that, *brother*?"

"I'm only trying to help her and her family. Brother."

I cocked my head as I stared at him. "What were you talking to Gabe about?"

He narrowed his eyes briefly, then played innocent. "Just asking him if he'd seen Rowan, but he hadn't. Later, bro."

Gunning the engine, he squealed out of the parking lot, leaving the tang of burnt rubber in the air.

As I turned back toward my truck, Michaela came striding toward me. The afternoon light angled over Miles Mountain to the west, lighting up her face and eyes. I met her halfway and scooped her into my arms. She returned the greeting with a deep kiss.

"Mmm . . . I missed you." I set her back on her feet and brushed my knuckles over her cheek. "Did you have a good day at school?"

She laughed. "I'm not going to school. It's just studying up on history and stuff, before I can take my seat on the Court."

"Does that mean you won't dress up in the schoolgirl uniform for me?"

Trailing her finger down my neck and chest, she smiled coyly. "Is that your fantasy, Roca? To see me as a schoolgirl again?"

I leaned in and kissed her. "We do have some pretty great memories of that time . . ."

"I never wore a school uniform."

My mouth trailed up her jaw until it reached her ear. "No, but you were pretty fucking sexy in that cheerleading getup."

My fingers ran up her thigh, and although she wore pants now, I had no problem imagining her in her short blue-and-silver skirt.

She shivered under my touch. "I might still have that." She paused, and her voice lost its playfulness as her eyes grew dark. "At the house, though."

The moment over, she broke away and walked to the truck.

"Do you plan to avoid the place forever?" I opened the door for her. "Because we could try to sell it. That'd be a lot of money you could use."

"I can't sell our family home," she said flatly.

I shut the door and walked around to the driver's side. I'd expected her response, but on occasion, I tried coaxing her into thinking about the family's estate. Ignoring it—and everything else about her parents—wasn't healthy. I didn't want to push her too hard, but Addie and I had agreed we wouldn't let her play ostrich forever.

Now that I was sleeping with her—actually sleeping—I knew her subconscious never stopped dwelling on everything. She woke up regularly gasping for her parents, begging mine to stop, or just plain screaming. If Alina knew how much guilt Michaela carried over our parents' deaths, she'd probably lay off. Maybe. Then again, it was Alina. Being mean was a sport to her.

"I do need to check on it soon, though," Michaela said once I joined her in the truck. "I haven't in a while, and we probably need to do stuff before winter, right?"

"I can help," I offered.

"There's also something I want to look for. Something of my dad's. The reading I've been doing for the Court has been really interesting, about our history—the moroi's and the town's."

"So school was good." I turned the engine on.

"Yeah. But I'm ready to be sworn in next week. I have way too much to do, like finishing up the inn and reopening for good. Our reservations are already starting to fill up," she said excitedly. "Sindi's been great, and she and Addie have talked me into putting my education to work, so I'm planning some special events at the inn, just like Mammie used to do. I want it all ready and beautiful before the holiday season kicks off."

I laid my hand on her thigh and gave it a squeeze, receiving a giggle in return. I smiled. This was my Michaela—coming out of school, talking about friends, and planning parties and the future.

This was what I'd missed for five years. What I thought I'd lost forever. What I couldn't live through losing again.

"So, was that Tase I saw leaving?" she asked as we turned onto First Street.

Damn. I'd hoped she hadn't noticed.

"Uh . . . yeah," I admitted. "Hey, is Gabe okay?"

She gave me a puzzled look. "Yeah. I saw him as I was leaving. He said he needed to talk to a teacher, but he seemed fine. Why?"

I shrugged. "Just wondering. Is he adjusting any better?"

"I think so. He still misses his friends, but he's made new ones. Hasn't tried to eat anyone yet, so that's good." She stared out the window as we passed the cemeteries, and I hoped I'd succeeded at changing the subject. "So what was Tase doing at the Academy?"

Shit. We'd promised each other no secrets, but Adrian had made a point. Michaela was about to become part of the Court, tying herself to the most powerful people in town. In a very different way than Tase had. Her knowledge of any connection between Tase and the Bishops could put us all at risk. I'd have to convince him to sever that tie, but in the meantime, I wouldn't put Michaela in such a difficult position.

"I don't know," I finally said. "He said he was looking for someone, but didn't say who. He was in a hurry . . ."

I felt her give me a sideways look as I watched the road and turned up the radio. A few minutes later, as we approached town square, she reached over and turned it down.

"I don't want to go home yet," she said. I glanced over at her, and she gave me a smile with a gleam in her eye. "Let's go to our place."

I returned her grin with a knowing one of my own and turned left on Eighth Street toward Havenwood Heights. Before we reached her property, though, I turned off one of the cul-de-sacs onto a maintenance road and climbed up the mountain until we were about even with the top of the falls. I parked where we used to in our high school days, at a point that looked over the whole town. It had a similar view to Fallview Tavern, but offered privacy that was difficult to find as teens—or as adults when our homes overflowed with people and responsibilities.

As soon as I cut the engine, Michaela turned and slid onto my lap, straddling me, just as she used to do. My cock immediately jumped to life. Unlike when we were younger, when I never knew how far she'd let me go, I was pretty certain today what she wanted. Her body heat poured off her as she ground against my lap.

"Fuck, Kales," I murmured right before she leaned in and nipped my bottom lip.

"Yes, you should." She gazed into my eyes, rocking her hips against me while pulling her hoodie over her head. I was admittedly disappointed to see that she wore a T-shirt underneath it. But when she lifted my hands and placed them on her breasts, I realized it was the only layer left—she wore no bra. Her nipples pebbled under my palms as I squeezed the soft flesh. My cock grew harder. She shifted against it. Now I was almost in pain.

"What's gotten into you?" I asked, as she cupped her hands over my cheeks and rubbed her palms against the stubble.

She answered by leaning in, her tongue swiping over my lips before pushing its way in. Not that I gave any resistance. I could never deny her. I couldn't deny myself, not when it came to tasting her. She kissed me hard, and I devoured her in return, until both of our lips were sore and swollen and neither of us could breathe. She pulled back and slipped her hand between us, under the waistband of my jeans, and then my boxers. Her warm hand wrapped around me and gently squeezed. My head fell back, and I watched her smile sexily through hooded lids as she stroked me. It only took a few times before there just wasn't room for her to move anymore.

She leaned to the side, sliding her leg off of me, but still holding me in her hand, taking me with her. I undid my button and zipper, and she moved the fabric down until I was free. She lay back on the seat, stroking me with one hand while removing her pants with the other. Naked from the waist down, she bent the knee closest to the seat while letting the other fall open. I swallowed hard, appraising her beautiful body, not knowing where I wanted to touch her first. She moved her hand between her legs, showing me.

"Fuck, Kales," I murmured again.

"Yes . . . please," she said breathily, as her hand slid down to the base of my shaft, squeezed, then slid back up.

I dove in at her neck, nipping and scraping my fangs over her smooth, soft skin. I could practically taste her blood as her vein pulsed against my tongue. She tasted like coconut, and smelled both sweet and spicy. I had to keep moving, or I'd take her too soon. I pulled her shirt up enough to expose her breast, lifting it and appreciating its full heaviness in my hand as my thumb rubbed over her rock-hard nipple. I flicked my tongue out, tasting her again. She moaned throatily. I curled my tongue around it, and she pumped my cock harder. My mouth closed over her breast and sucked, and she squeezed and pulled in response. I was about to come all over her fist.

My other hand joined hers between her legs, moving it to the side. My fingertip brushed over her as I sucked on her breast again. She bucked against me. I stroked downward and slid inside her wet opening, my thumb pressing and circling her clit as I curled my fingers.

"Fuck, Xandru," she whispered.

"Yes, please," I responded against her breast.

She suddenly pushed me up, back into sitting position. She straddled me once again, and I was barely ready when she came down hard around me. We both gasped. She was so fucking soft. So fucking wet. So fucking perfect.

Her breasts pressed against me as she kissed me hard while lifting up slowly and slamming down. My hips moved with her, thrusting deeper within. Our rhythm picked up quickly, and I palmed the flesh of her ass, moving her ever faster. We didn't even have a chance to draw blood before we both suddenly came. I threw my head back, barely feeling the *thunk* against the back window, and squeezed my eyes shut as I exploded within her. Her voice moaning my name echoed in my ears as she quaked around me.

I opened my eyes as I came down from the high, finding her watching me with a small but satisfied smile. She leaned in and delivered a slow kiss, sucking on my bottom lip as she pulled away.

"Sorry," she whispered, as a sweet blush filled her face.

"Don't *ever* apologize for that." I cupped her cheek and pulled her back in for another kiss.

"I just . . . I had memories of you picking me up from school and coming up here . . . and, well . . ." She pulled her lip between her teeth. With her hair a little disheveled and her shirt halfway up her stomach and the rest of her naked, she looked sexy as fuck. My dick was already responding again. "It made me horny as all get out."

I chuckled as I brushed my knuckles over her breast. "Like I said, don't ever apologize for that."

She slid her hand around my neck, cupping it as her fingers teased my hair. As she watched me, her expression changed to one I wished I could capture forever.

"I love you always, Xandru Roca," she whispered.

My throat tightened, and I tried to swallow, but couldn't. I hadn't heard those words, exactly like that, in years. I wasn't sure I ever would again. And they, along with this perfect image before me, were too much. My lungs seized, needing air.

She tilted her head, studying me. "And he says . . ."

Somehow, I managed to breathe, then swallow, and then finally find my voice. To give her the response I'd always given before, since the first time she told me she loved me. I'd never thought the phrase big enough for how I felt.

"You are my world, Michaela Petran."

CHAPTER 11

MICHAELA

*T*he smell of old books, leather, and lemon engulfed me as I sat at a polished mahogany table under the domed ceiling of the Academy's library, a twenty-pound monstrosity of a book laid open in front of me. "A little light reading," as my favorite witch would say. Well, my favorite after Addie and Saundra and the other Beaumonts. Oh, and Gallad Augustine, who sat across from me as my Court-appointed tutor. Okay, so my favorite fictional witch has been known to say that. Gallad was quickly becoming my favorite male witch.

Although still a senior in high school, he probably knew more about the supernatural and the big secrets of Havenwood Falls than ninety-five percent of its residents. He'd only been studying it all since he was a kid, part of being groomed to eventually take the Augustine seat on the Court and the Luna Coven's High Council. Basically, he was the younger, male version of Addie, which made sense since he was her cousin. He had a heart of gold and a brain to match, but with his leather coat and combat boots, he kept those attributes camouflaged by a bad-boy persona. In that way, he was pretty much a younger version of Xandru.

It had been awkward at first. Addie and I used to babysit him, and now he was tutoring me in the supernatural and town history.

But when I managed to distract him from the heavy weight on his mind, he'd been a great help.

"You're doing it again," I whispered, nudging his jeans-clad leg under the table.

He tore his gaze away from the far wall of stained glass windows and blinked green eyes at me. "Huh?"

"Haven't figured it out yet?" For weeks, he'd been working on a way to find his missing girlfriend, Macy Blackstone, but so far had been unsuccessful.

His face fell, as did his gaze. He pushed a hand through his already mussed-up dark hair. "No. And I'm running out of time. Macy left on the new moon, and it's back around in two days. The town's wards will make her forget everything about her home, her family . . . me."

The despair in his voice broke my heart. "The entire coven's working on it, right?"

"They're taking a whole different angle than what I've been trying. If I could only get through to her . . ."

"I'm sure someone will figure it out, and she'll be back in time for Founders Day on Friday."

A sad sigh escaped him as I went back to my reading.

"This moonstone is pretty serious shit, isn't it?" I muttered out loud.

In a bit of a delayed reaction, Gallad's head suddenly snapped up. "Wait. What did you say?"

I slapped my hand over my mouth. "Oops. Sorry, kid. I meant serious *crap*."

"No . . ." He gave me a bewildered look, then squinted and cocked his head. "What are you reading?"

"Uh . . . this history book you gave me." I shrugged, trying to be nonchalant, because history and I normally didn't get along. I could never stay awake through the classes in high school. But this was different. Leaning forward, I whispered, "Don't tell anyone, but I'm kind of digging it. Especially this." I tapped my finger on the heavy book. "Who knew there were so many magical tools and artifacts?

This one, the Eye of Valerian, is part of the moroi history. *Our* history. It's inlaid with moonstone, which I looked up, as you taught me, because stones and gems are probably present for a reason. And it has all kinds of magical and energetic attributes. For—"

Gallad jumped up from his chair, sending it crashing to the floor.

"Michaela, you're a genius!" He paced, rubbing his hands over his head. "I'd totally dismissed moonstone because it's more of a feminine stone. Works for the females better, you know. But Macy's a female. I mean, of course she is, but I wasn't thinking in that way, because she's not doing the spell. I am, but we're a couple, which moonstone's great for, and . . ." He must have realized he was rambling, because he stopped and turned back to me, a big smile on his face—the first one I'd seen since we began working together right after Macy left. "Freaking moonstone—that *has* to be the missing component. I could kiss you, Michaela!"

I jerked back. "Um, save it for Macy."

"Yeah, for Macy. I'm gonna prove we're soul mates and get her back. Fucking *yes!*" And with a fist pump into the air à la *The Breakfast Club*, he ran out of the library.

"Okay, then." Smiling, I went back to my studies, focused on this Eye of Valerian.

Gallad didn't know it, but I'd been returning to this page after finishing his assigned reading for the last several days. There really wasn't much written about the special object, just a vague description, but the name tickled a memory I couldn't grasp. I didn't know whether it was something I'd heard in passing and quickly forgotten, or if it was another one of my lingering memory holes, which was infuriating. Considering it was important enough to be in this history book and was part of moroi heritage, I felt like I should know more about it.

I didn't expect Gallad to return, so I ended our session early. I gathered the books and reshelved them, then headed out. I'd left my car for Sindi, and Xandru was supposed to pick me up again, so I texted him to let him know I was headed to the house in the

Heights. I had time to spare, which wouldn't be the case soon with my responsibilities to the Court and decorating at the inn, now that the renovations had been completed. Besides, the Eye of Valerian bugged me, and I felt sure it had something to do with our home or family.

I took my time on the walk as I enjoyed what was probably the last of the nice weather. The autumn equinox was in three days, which meant cold and snow would soon follow. Already the days were growing shorter and the nights chillier. At least I could look forward to skiing again.

Havenwood Heights was an upscale, gated community that crawled up the side of Mt. Alexa not too far from the falls. Mostly Old Families owned the grand estates here, the properties separated by acres of pines, aspens, maples, and oaks, providing seclusion and privacy. The mage families had built their manors closest to the falls, which, according to my readings, contained a wealth of magical energy. The mages denied it in public, but they had to. Otherwise, our little town would be flooded with magic wielders—real and wannabe. But that would explain the draw our box canyon and the falls had for supernaturals, many of whom stumbled upon the area accidentally, just like the Old Families had back in the 1850s.

As I crossed through one of the wooded areas, I recalled Addie and me running this same path when we were kids, because it was the shortcut between her house and mine. Our parents warned us not to, because the woods could be dangerous, but we couldn't be bothered with following the winding main street. Although we were both aware of differences between us and other kids at school, we didn't really understand that there were real animals in the forest who'd love to chomp on little girls.

Xandru's truck pulled into the driveway just as I stepped onto the front walk to the family estate. Stopping in my tracks, I stared at the massive gothic manor that looked like a small castle, and all the happy thoughts drained right out of me, as though a plug had been pulled. I'd been distracted by the good memories and had forgotten to brace myself for seeing my childhood home and the emotions that always flooded over me when I did so. Pushing the feelings back down, I tried to focus on thoughts that were lightyears away from the heavy ones, such as memories of arguing with my parents about my relationship with Xandru. Or trying to fathom their feelings when they chose to send me away, thus ending their own lives in the hopes of giving me and my siblings normal ones. As normal lives as orphans can have, anyway.

Do better than this, I ordered myself, squeezing my eyes shut and focusing on tuning out those thoughts. I drew in a deep breath, forcing the tightness in my chest to loosen, before reopening my eyes and making myself see the home from a stranger's perspective. *Step back and observe.* That was one of Addie's suggestions for coping with overwhelming emotions—to pretend I was an observer of my life, not attached to the dammed-up feelings nor to what I was experiencing.

So I observed the mansion and pondered.

Now that I knew our parents had built the house nearly a century before they knew they could have more children, I wondered what they did with all the space before. Even with the three of us kids, there was enough room for a family five times our size. I knew why they'd built it so large, though—it was a statement. Of wealth, but more importantly, of standing in the community. That was also why our house was close to the top of the entire Havenwood Heights subdivision.

The Petrans weren't only Old Family, but were one of the very first of those who'd wanted to establish a sanctuary for the supernatural. They'd been driven out of their homeland after the massacre by their first round of children, bringing the Rocas with them. All of them were cursed, as a result of that massacre, but determined to find a new home, a haven for their families and others who wanted to join. Eventually, they met the Beaumonts and then the Augustines, both of whom had come from Salem, and from there, the group grew as they made their way south and west.

Yes, I did quite enjoy learning the *real* history of Havenwood Falls.

Xandru's hand rested on the small of my back, and we walked up to the massive front doors together. He unlocked the door for me and let us in. My nose twitched as we entered, and not just because of the dust layered on every surface.

"Do you smell that?" I asked. "Someone's been here recently."

"Smells like Gabe."

I sniffed again. "Yeah, and Aurelia. But there's something different . . ."

His nostrils flared, and his eyes tightened for a brief moment, but then he simply shrugged. "Probably because Gabe smells different now."

Really? I hadn't noticed, but I was around him a lot more, which probably resulted in nose-blindness. "Hmm . . . that must be it. I wonder what they've been doing here."

"You want me to check everything out to be sure?" Xandru asked. "I can also see what needs to be done before winter."

I smiled up at him. "Would you mind? I need to look for something in my dad's office." I paused. "Just, um, check in on me every once in a while so I know you're okay."

Leaning down, he gave me a quick kiss. "Sure thing."

Making my way to Dad's office at the back of the house, I managed to suppress older memories, but had to shake off the ominous feeling settling over my shoulders from more recent ones. Residual memories of when I'd been here before and Mr. Roca, transformed into a large white man-bat, had kidnapped me. That was when I'd come across some of my mother's old diaries on the shelves lining the walls of the office, and I'd learned about my older brothers, born in the early 1800s. They'd purposely wanted to become strigoi, so they massacred dozens in the area around their small town in Romania. Several covens of mages had to band together to stop them, and that was how the curse was put on my parents, Mammie, and the Rocas—to prevent such tragedy from happening again. The same curse that jumped to the Rocas when Tase turned me.

I went to those diaries as soon as I entered the wood-paneled room. I thought I'd lost the one I'd been holding when Mr. Roca had swooped me away, but we'd found it later on the living room floor by the shattered windows in the back of the house. I flipped through them all again, thinking I might have read about the Eye of Valerian on that fateful day when I'd learned more about our family history than I'd ever known. But there was nothing in Mom's diaries.

I circled the large mahogany desk, sat in Dad's leather chair, and swiveled around, taking everything in. I dug through his drawers and filing cabinets, then scoured the bookshelves again.

The whole time suppressing the sadness that tried welling in my chest and stung the backs of my eyes.

"There you are." I plucked a tome off the shelf. I knew my father had also kept a journal. People did that sort of thing back then, since there were no cameras or social media to keep track of life.

The journal started with entries about discovering and settling into our box canyon, and beginning to build the inn. I turned the pages quickly, finding a few here and there had been ripped out. Finally, the Eye of Valerian was mentioned on a page dated July 1854.

I have finally been able to take care of the Eye of Valerian, hiding it away for good now that we are settled in our new safe haven. Valerian himself, a practitioner of the dark arts and the original moroi, created the piece, and it has been passed down our family bloodline ever since. It appears at first glance to be a pocket watch, but is so much more than a simple timepiece, powerful in many ways, as Valerian himself was. It is not a piece I wish to possess, nor one I can release to anyone else, but it remains indestructible. Therefore, I enlisted the help of two mages I trust to protect the timepiece by trapping its powers, and I have hidden it where only I know to ensure the power it holds can never be used—or abused—again.

Well. That was a bit disappointing. I'd been hoping to learn more about it—maybe find the piece itself. I flipped through the pages, but found no more written about the Eye of Valerian, such as where it was hidden. Here at the house? Or maybe at the inn? But the inn had been under renovations, and nothing, as far as I knew, had been found.

Unless Gabe had discovered it? He'd shown me everything he'd found, though. Right?

Bumps somewhere else in the house jolted me out of my own head, and chills ran up my spine. Leaving the journal behind, I crept out of Dad's office, down the hall, and into the large chef's kitchen.

"Xandru?" I called, though it only came out in a whisper.

Afternoon sunlight flooded through the windows, reminding me that this was not that night, but I couldn't help but feel a sense of déjà vu. Especially when Xandru didn't respond, just like Addie, Aurelia, and Gabe had never answered that night. My gaze swept the kitchen and the great room beyond, falling upon a knife block on the marble counter and the fireplace poker by the hearth. Poker it was—it had a longer reach. I twitched my hand in the air, and the sharp metal stick flew across the room to me.

"Xandru," I whisper-shouted again as I tiptoed past a formal dining room and into the foyer, holding the poker up, ready to swing.

"Hey!"

My heart leapt into my throat as I spun around and looked up, cringing at the thought of finding another man-sized bat hanging from the ceiling. But no. It was only Xandru, standing at the top of the stairs. He jumped all the way down, landing right in front of me and sending my heart racing again. The poker dropped and clattered to the floor, my hand flying to my chest.

"Look what I found." He grinned widely, holding up a blue vest with a silver dragon on it in one hand and a matching skirt in the other—my old cheerleading uniform.

"Are you kidding me? You scared the shit out of me!" I gave him a light shove.

"Sorry, but *look*."

Humoring him, I studied the uniform, and then frowned. "It's so . . . *small*."

Turning the pieces over, he eyed them. "Well, you *were* small."

One hand went to my hip as I jutted it out. "*Were?* And what am I now?"

He looked up, his eyes flickering with an oh-shit moment. But only briefly, before he grinned and pulled me into an embrace, his hand slipping down to my butt and giving it a squeeze. "Now, you have luscious boobs and a nice round ass."

I laughed. "Good save there, Roca."

"Yeah?"

"Yeah." My head craned back to look up at him. "*Luscious* boobs, though? I didn't know you even knew that word."

"Mmm . . . lickable came to mind first, but I do have a filter. Sort of."

Leaning up on my toes, I kissed him before turning for the door. "Let's get out of here."

I'd have to deal with this place another time. I still wasn't ready.

I couldn't even care that Xandru's idea of looking for ways of winterizing included going through my old closet. I hadn't noticed he'd brought the uniform with him until I was sliding into the truck's seat.

"Are you kidding?" he asked when I said something about not fitting into it. He held the two pieces up to me. "You looked sexy before, but I can't wait to see those luscious boobs and that round ass in this now." He tossed the pieces at me and added before he closed my door, "But only for me. Nobody else will see that, not even at Halloween."

Like I'd ever wear my old cheerleading uniform as a Halloween costume in my own hometown. Examining it, I knew I'd look like a porn star, with it barely covering my lady parts.

"Are you sure this isn't some cult kind of thing where they're going to make you drink the Kool-Aid?" Sindi sat on my bed, watching me get ready for my official swearing in. "But, you know, blood Kool-Aid?"

My eyes widened. "Blood Kool-Aid. We should try that! Gabe will probably like it."

She rolled her big blue eyes. "You're a sick bastard, Kaela."

I smiled at the name. And not just because it wasn't Kaekae. She'd known me for many years in Atlanta only as Kaela Peters, so adjusting to me being Michaela Petran still hadn't happened. The rest she'd taken pretty well—once she got over being mad at me for not telling her sooner. Until she'd physically come to Havenwood Falls, though, I hadn't been able to tell her anything about it except that it was nice and I liked my new job, especially when I was promoted to general manager so quickly. Not until she agreed to move here and the Court gave me permission was I even allowed to tell her about my family here.

She was thrilled for me, but I thought she was even more excited about being able to go out in the sun. I couldn't blame her, because she'd been a vampire for over a century, forced to avoid daylight all that time. She also enjoyed all the hot men in town. Nobody specific had caught her full attention, but she didn't mind the eye candy.

"You have to admit, it's weird, this Court thing," Sindi continued. "We can't even be there for you to be sworn in. How do we know it's all legit?"

Shrugging, I wrapped a lock of hair around the curling iron. "It's part of Havenwood Falls. The Court makes it all work. Without it, this place would be chaos. Or nonexistent. And I guess I'd rather be a part of the decisions than have them made for me. I've had enough of that, thank you."

"You have a point, I guess. I still think it's bizarre." She stood to her full height, towering over me. "I'd better go get ready myself. I'm looking forward to this Founders Day. It sounds so charming and quaint. Maybe there will be a lumberjack competition!"

I smiled and shook my head as she left the cottage for her own next door—the one I'd stayed in when I'd first arrived back in town. She seemed to be enjoying small-town life a little too much. I wondered how long it would last, especially once the snow began to fall. Would she stay, or would I have to say goodbye again?

As I crossed the town square for City Hall, people were already gathering in groups, preparing for the Founders Day games to begin. Most groups consisted of family members, or, at least, the same supernatural types—fae in one group, the McCabe mountain lion shifters in another, etc.—all to prove a point of who was faster and stronger. Although a couple adult teams were mixed, I was surprised to see a group of mixed teens, and I decided they'd be my pick for the winners, simply because of their courage. According to Aurelia, the supernaturals had become very cliquish since we'd been in school.

"That Kasun girl doesn't know what she's doing," Irene Beckett gossiped as I passed by her on the corner of Town Square Park. "I know teenagers. I taught them for thirty years and could never get the different kinds to cooperate as a team for more than a few minutes. And she thinks she can get them to win? Foolishness, I tell ya."

"Ah, give her a chance to prove herself," I said. "You never know."

The old woman lifted a silver brow. "Are you defending a *wolf*, Michaela Petran?"

Ugh. I hated to admit it, but I was. "I'm defending a girl boss. One girl boss supporting another. Maybe if you'd done that back when you were teaching, you'd have had more success." I held back the *cranky old bitch* part as I walked off to cross Stuart Street.

After all of the studying and buildup about the power of the Court and keeping secrets and everything, the actual swearing in was more of a letdown than episodes one through three of *Star Wars*. Saundra Beaumont did some magical thing that made my skin tingle and said a few words, I recited the vows I had to take, they gave me a special phone, and then it was over. No letting of blood or drinking of it, Kool-Aid flavored or otherwise. As soon as we were done, everyone took off for the ribbon cutting at the new library.

"That was lame as shit," I said to Addie as we left through the metal door and stepped out into the sunshine.

"They rushed through it, being Founders Day and all." She stopped to switch out her regular glasses for shades.

"Why would they schedule my swearing in for today then?"

"Magic of the new moon combined with the equinox strengthens the spell. Trust me—the ritual may have seemed lame, but the magic binding you was not. Tonight will be freaking insane. I can't wait."

A chill ran down my spine, and I couldn't help but wonder if Sindi had been right in her paranoia. On the other hand, I hadn't heard Addie this excited about something in a long time. All that magical energy must have been crackling through her veins.

Sindi waited around the corner for us, and we all walked over to the library for the ribbon cutting. I was excited to see Graysin Ravenal in all her awkward gloriousness when she checked into the inn the other night. Not just because we had a lot of design work to do with the inn, but because I genuinely liked her. She'd been responsible for the library's interior design, and I hoped her return to town for the ribbon cutting meant she was staying.

Although, I didn't think anyone could miss the awkward tension between her and Everett, the guy she'd left behind, up on the porch as Mayor Barbie cut the ribbon. She stood slightly angled away from him, using her dark hair as a curtain between them. His normal, laid-back demeanor was replaced by a stiff stance, a clenched scruffy jaw, and dark eyes scanning over the crowd, but every once in a while, darting toward her when he thought Mayor Barbie's bouffant hair hid him.

"What the hell?" Addie hissed from my side.

I looked at her to see what had her attention and followed her gaze. Across the street in Cook's Corner Park, standing within one of the walled gardens, were two tall males, their heads just above the wall's height. They appeared to be in deep discussion. One was unmistakably Tase. The other glanced up, and I sucked in a breath.

"Is that Ronan Bishop?" I whispered.

"It sure as hell looks like it."

I glanced around the dispersing crowd, searching for the peasant top and flowy skirt that was signature Callie Montgomery. "I don't see Callie. I wonder if she knows he's back."

"*I* want to know what the hell Tase is doing talking to him." Addie stomped off in their direction, but Ronan saw her and immediately took off.

I looked up at Sindi, whose bright red lips were pulled into a smirk as she watched Addie.

"I kind of feel sorry for Tase," she said.

"Don't," I muttered. We waited for Addie to rejoin us, but she and Tase disappeared behind the garden's walls, and I wasn't about to go see what they were doing. "So, I guess it's you and me now. Addie will meet us there, and we'll catch up with Graysin and Callie. We'll need to distract Callie, if Ronan's back."

By the time we reached the square, though, we were too late. We crossed Eighth Street just in time to see Callie's eyes connect with Ronan's. I stopped in the middle of the street as they glared at each other, Callie in yoga pants and layered tanks, a pile of bracelets adorning her wrists, and her waist-length, dark hair pulled into a loose ponytail, and Ronan dressed for a night at the club. After one long, intense moment, she took off running toward her store, leaving Graysin standing there in bewilderment. Ronan sauntered after her.

"Oh, shit," I breathed.

We hadn't known Callie too well growing up because she'd traveled a lot with her family, so she hadn't really been part of our crowd. After I left, though, she came back permanently to manage her family's consignment store, and she and Addie had become closer friends. We'd hung out since I'd returned, and I'd learned just enough about her love life to know I didn't want to be anywhere around when Ronan finally caught up to her.

"We need to rescue Graysin before she gets in the middle of something bad," I said to Sindi as we finished crossing the street.

"I don't think we need to worry about her."

Graysin had already moved, but away from Callie, Ronan, and

the sure disaster that was coming between the two. When I saw her headed toward Everett, I decided we didn't need to interrupt that reunion, either. In fact, considering the tension between those two at the ribbon-cutting and the possible explosion about to take place at Callie's Consignments, we probably needed to grab a bucket of popcorn and a seat for the show.

"So, what now?" I looked up at Sindi.

"Whoa." That single word came out in a totally Sindi way—breathy and horny. "Who is that fine specimen of sex on legs?"

My gaze followed hers. "Oh, hell, no!"

Her tongue swiped over her lips as she stared at him, not even looking at me as she spoke. "You said Xandru didn't have any other brothers besides Tase, but there's no mistaking that's a Roca."

Grabbing her arm, I tried pulling her away toward Coffee Haven. "I said he didn't have any you needed to be involved with."

"Oh, I totally need to be involved with every *inch* of that." Jerking her arm free, she strode away, making a beeline for Adrian Roca.

Crap. Of course, with Sindi being who she was . . . if anyone could handle a Roca, she could. I just wished she wouldn't.

She glanced over her shoulder at me, batting her baby blues. "Aren't you going to come and introduce me?"

I shook my head. "Nope. I will in no way be a part of this. You're on your own."

She threw me a stern look, then shrugged and smiled, flipping her red ponytail over her shoulder and continuing toward the biggest mistake of her life. Which was saying a lot.

I looked around town square, saw the teams were starting to prepare for the first races, and realized I was alone. "Well, so much for making this a girls' day."

I made my way to Coffee Haven to grab a special coffee made by Harlow, the witch barista. The shop's owner, Willow, who was a fae, offered up a secret menu that contained special ingredients for the supes. Harlow could make the drinks, as long as Davis, the new human manager, wasn't around. For me, she topped my whipped cream with a sprinkle of what looked like red sugar crystals, but they weren't made of sugar. The drink—coffee with a sprinkle of blood—was my personal heaven. When I saw Gabe standing alone outside, I ordered one for him, too.

I hurried past Callie's Consignments, cringing at the sounds coming from inside the closed store, to where Gabe stood in front of Madame Tahini's place.

"I don't drink coffee," he said when I held the cup out to him.

"Trust me. You'll like this one."

His eyes lit up when he took a sip.

"Right?" I smiled. "Just don't tell anyone. So what are you doing out here alone? Aren't you supposed to be helping for your volunteer work?"

"I did earlier with setup. Ms. Howe told me to take a break." He took another swallow of coffee, licking the whipped cream off his upper lip. "So are you officially a member of the Court now?"

"Yep."

"So you can get me back into regular school?"

"I'll try after this semester. As long as everything goes well."

He frowned. "I'm trying as best as I can."

"I know you are. Hey, I've been meaning to ask you. When you found all that stuff while they were working on the inn, you didn't happen to find any pocket watches, did you?"

"No."

Was it me, or did he answer that a little too quickly?

"None? Not even a timepiece for that leather cuff you found?"

He shifted his weight. "Well, yeah, there was one, but it was junk. Didn't work."

"What did it look like?"

He shrugged. "Like an old-fashioned pocket watch."

"Was it decorated with moonstone?" He didn't reply at first, and I thought maybe he didn't know what moonstone was. "White but kind of pearly?"

"I don't know," he finally said, more of a growl than spoken words, though. "I mean, no. It was just plain. Old and boring."

He started to walk off. Something wasn't right, though. His entire energy had shifted. I didn't need to be a witch to sense that.

"Gabe, are you sure? You didn't find anything like that?"

"I think I'd know, Michaela! I don't have anything like that," he shouted, throwing his half-full cup in the trash can. "I have to get back to help."

He hurried off, leaving me frowning.

"What did you find in that old inn of yours?" a raspy voice asked from my right. I turned to find Old Man Mills's lanky frame standing in front of his pawn shop on the corner, his wild white hair, pale green eyes, and snowy skin making him look like an elderly version of Jack Frost. "Anything you want to sell?" He shuffled closer, and I inched away. "Maybe that timepiece that doesn't work?"

"Gabe found it all. It's up to him."

"I'd be very interested in seeing what he found."

Something in his tone made the hairs on the back of my neck rise. "Why?"

"Could be worth something, young lady. I'd pay him handsomely for it."

"Do you think the timepiece is valuable?"

His white brows lifted. "I don't know without seeing it, but I have a good hunch there was something valuable lost—or hidden— in that inn."

The strange feeling intensified. "I'll, uh, let him know."

"Be sure you do. I *insist.*"

I took a bigger step away, not at all liking his tone or the way he looked at me. As if he wanted to eat me. Considering he was a dragon shifter, that could have very well been in his thoughts.

"Like I said, it's up to him."

"Just remember, one man's junk is another man's treasure." His tongue seemed to slither on the word treasure.

Nodding, I turned to hurry off, only to crash into Addie.

"He's so creepy," I whispered as we crossed the street back to the park.

"What did he want?"

"He thinks we found treasure while renovating the inn."

"Treasure, huh? As in *dragon* treasure?"

I snorted. "You're such a dork. That's a myth."

"Is it?"

I looked sideways at her, and she rolled her eyes.

But perhaps she was on to something . . .

Based on my father's journal, the Eye of Valerian could have been hidden somewhere in that inn. The date of the entry had been right around the time they'd been building it. And the more I thought about it, I couldn't imagine Dad hiding a family heirloom, especially one with magical powers, anywhere else besides the inn or the house—the two places he had complete control over.

Until he died.

If Gabe hadn't found the pocket watch, I wondered if someone else had. It definitely could have been valuable, considering Old Man Mills's interest.

And then I recalled a certain somebody digging in the conservatory during the renovations. Somebody who'd already proven how far he'd go for money.

CHAPTER 12

XANDRU

"Why do I feel like I've been hit by a Mack truck?" Tase asked from behind me.

I turned from the kitchen window that looked out on the backyard and the mountain behind us, which looked like the gods had dropped a million golden coins on it. It was a magazine-worthy picture of October in the Colorado mountains—the golden leaves of the aspen trees flickering in the breeze, the oranges and reds of oaks and maples scattered among them. The first snow could come any time.

My older brother walked into the kitchen wearing sweatpants and rubbing his wet head with a towel.

"Not a Mack truck, but you were hit by my fists a few times," I answered.

He squinted at me. "Why?"

I chuckled. "You really don't remember?" He shook his head and cringed. "I guess you were a lot drunker than I realized. You don't remember the fight at Fallview?" He gave me a blank look. "Simon breaking us up? Almost falling over the railing and into the falls?"

"Shit. Wish I did. Sounds like fun." He wrapped the towel around his neck, then opened the fridge and started digging around.

"A lot more fun than this hangover bullshit. I can't even remember the last time I had a hangover."

"Probably the last time we got in a fight." I was sure the pain he suffered was more from the blows we exchanged than the bourbon. My own body wasn't feeling too great, and I hadn't had much to drink. "And it wasn't fun. It was stupid. I guess you don't have any idea what the hell got into you?"

I'd moved past being angry, because the whole reason for the fight was ridiculous. I knew he hadn't been in his right mind.

"Considering you don't sound like you still want to hit me, must not have been too bad."

"You accused me of messing around with Addie."

Tase poured himself a glass of orange juice. "Oh."

"Oh? That's it?"

"What else should I say?" He turned around and leaned against the counter, taking a drink of his OJ. Then he walked over to the bar and added a dose of bottled blood and a shot of vodka. "Need a bit of the hair of the dog, methinks."

"Tase, why in the hell were you possessive about Addie? You have no claim on her."

He pulled a long draw on his drink, staring at me with that cocky look our whole family had mastered. Then he shrugged. "Don't know, brother."

"You're lying. What's going on? Wait. You're not together, are you?"

Tase didn't reply at first, and my chest tightened as anger built within. Then he scoffed. "Of course not."

"Good. Because after everything she's doing for you, she doesn't deserve to be broken, which you know you would do."

He nodded slowly. "Right. Because that's all I *can* do."

Turning, he walked back toward his bedroom. I watched him retreat, knowing he held something back. Again.

"Oh, hey," I called after him, almost forgetting, not for the first time. Tase paused at the top of the stairs and looked down on me. "Michaela's been riding my ass for a few weeks now to ask you if you found anything when you were working in the conservatory. Something that didn't really belong there?"

He cocked his head and narrowed his eyes. "Like what?"

"Like a pocket watch or timepiece. She has a crazy idea it might have been buried out there, and since you were in there with a shovel . . ." I let my sentence trail off.

She hadn't told me much about it, except that she'd learned about a family heirloom that might have been hidden in the inn somewhere. She was concerned that someone might have found it and sold it—that someone being Tase.

Tase shook his head. "Nope. She should ask that little brother of hers, though. Didn't you say he'd found all kinds of things?"

"She already did. He had no idea what she was talking about."

He stared, his nostrils flaring, his jaw muscle ticking, and a green glow flickering in his eyes before he forced a smile. "Then I don't know what to tell you."

Liar. I lifted my chin. "Another question. Have you been to the Petran estate in the last month or so?"

"Why the twenty fucking questions, man?"

"Have something to hide?"

"Always." He gave his famous wicked grin. "But why would I have any reason to go there?"

"You tell me. I could smell you there."

"Don't know what to tell ya. I haven't been there in years. I think you're letting that woman get a little too deep into your head, little brother."

I had no proof it had been him I smelled that day in Michaela's family home. The scent was old, barely noticeable, so I had no real argument. But it had definitely been a moroi and of my family, so if not Tase, then one of my other brothers. None of whom belonged in that house.

Heading to my room to dress for the day, I paused when I heard Tase across the hall, speaking quietly. I moved into my room and stood at the cracked door to listen.

"The little shit says he doesn't know anything." Pause. "Yeah, he's gotta be lying about it." Another pause. "I'll see if I can, but we could be back at square one. Mihail wasn't an idiot . . . Yep, still got it . . . All right, meet you there."

I ran my hand over my face, thinking. Tase had lied right to my face. No surprise there. I was surprised, though, that he'd barely tried to hide the phone call. Either he wanted me to hear, or the strigoi within was strengthening, making him more arrogant than ever, and more careless. Which was not fucking cool.

Mihail Petran had hidden the timepiece, according to Michaela's findings, and considering we'd just been talking about it, I was sure that was the subject of Tase's phone call. Which only confirmed he'd been at the estate, looking for it. Did he find it and was he trying to sell it? Michaela said it was possibly valuable. Had Tase been speaking to a potential buyer?

Only one way to find out. When Tase left, I followed. He went to the ski resort, which was closed, so I slowed down, watching to make sure he parked and exited the car before I pulled into the Dirty Knuckle and parked. Rather than going into the bar, though, I stood out of sight and watched a sleek BMW sports car pull into the ski resort—Ronan Bishop. The mage remained in his car, and he must have used a silencing charm, because I couldn't hear them with my vampire senses. They talked for a few minutes before he took off, but Tase stayed. Just as I was pondering leaving, an unfamiliar, older sedan rolled into the ski resort's parking lot.

That driver stayed in the car, as well, as Tase walked up to it and spoke through the window. I could hear him say something about money, but the other person's voice was too soft for me to hear. A moment after I shifted, trying to gain a better perspective of the driver, Tase looked up and right in my direction. I ducked around the corner of the bar, but a second later, my phone rang.

"I see you, motherfucker."

"Want to join me for a beer?" I asked casually.

"Nah, come on over. There's someone I want you to meet." A sharp edge laced his tone. He didn't sound like he really wanted me to meet this person—more like he was cornered into it.

The feeling running through me as I walked over to the resort was similar to when we were younger, and I'd busted him doing something he wasn't supposed to. Except this wasn't as fun, probably because I knew the stakes were higher. Whatever trouble Tase got into now could be deadly.

So I strode over to the car on guard, not expecting to see the young blond woman sitting in the front seat and a dark-haired kid in the back.

Tase leaned sideways against the door as I walked up. "You remember Shelly Martin, Xandru? She worked at the Haven Saloon for a year or so, about five years ago."

I peered at the woman, probably in her late twenties, not bad looking at all. She smelled human. A vague memory danced at the back of my mind, but the time right after Michaela had left was somewhat lost in a drunken and drugged-up haze. I knew we'd spent a lot of time and money at the Haven Saloon, drinking and smoking with the owner, Bent Brent, before Rhys took over the Dirty Knuckle. I was about to apologize for not remembering her, when I looked in the backseat again at the kid, who was about four or five years old. Dark hair, eyes like . . . My head snapped up, and I glared at Tase.

"That's Carter." He loosely crossed his arms over his chest. "You wouldn't remember him. He was born about eight months after Shelly took off. She didn't know she was pregnant, and then forgot about Havenwood Falls after she left. Bent Brent called her up a few months ago, and as soon as she returned, she remembered . . ."

I cocked my head, my heart stuttering. What the hell was he trying to say? Had I fucked up? Or had he?

He smirked. "Don't worry, bro, he's not yours."

Shelly made an annoyed sound.

"I'm sorry," I said to her, "but I need to talk to my brother for a minute."

"I need to go anyway. Tase?" She looked at him with wide, expectant blue eyes.

He dug in his back pocket for his wallet. He pulled out a wad of cash and handed it to her. "I'll take care of the rest. Don't worry, okay?"

"Thank you," she said with sincere appreciation, before shifting the car into gear.

Tase gave the kid a wave as she drove off.

"What. The. Fuck. Tase?" I shouted.

"Calm down," he growled.

"You're kidding me, right?"

He grabbed his head and paced in front of me. "No. He's definitely mine. Eloise Sinclair did a reading, and Dr. Underwood confirmed it. You can't deny those two. But it was just a fling."

"Does Addie know?"

"Why would she need to?"

"Maybe because she's your *friend*."

He shook his head. "She doesn't need to know. Neither does Michaela."

"Tase—"

"You can't tell her!" he roared, his eyes glinting green and his fangs letting out. He immediately stepped back and drew in several long, calming breaths. "Addie and I aren't together. Not then, not now. It has nothing to do with her."

"She'll find out eventually. How do you want that to happen?"

He jabbed a finger at me. "Better not be you. Or Michaela."

"It needs to be you."

He stared at me for a long moment, then groaned. "Fuck! I know. But I've already screwed up in so many ways. I don't know *how* to tell her."

"How long have you known?"

"A while. A month or so."

I shoved my hands into my pockets, exhaling a sharp breath. "Fine. It's not my secret to tell. But you need to."

"All right."

"Soon."

"When the time is right." I lifted a brow, and he sighed. "Look, this is one of the reasons I'm still working with the Bishops. Ronan and I have this thing going, and I can't pull out yet, but I will soon. The money is insane, and I'm just trying to get everyone financially set up as best as possible for when . . . I'm gone. All of you guys, as well as Shelly and Carter."

"Stop talking like you're dying."

"Come on, Xan. You know as well as I do that I will be soon. It's just a matter of time until the Court has to put me down."

"We'll find a way to break the curse. Addie will."

"Like I deserve that," he muttered. "Look, I need to be prepared. *We* need to be prepared. That's why I thought you should know about this. Just in case something happens, and they take me down sooner rather than later. I wanted you to know that I want Carter taken care of. I can't be much of a dad to him, but I can at least take care of him financially."

I nodded. "He's family. But you need to tell everyone."

"I will. I will."

"And tell me what's going on with the Bishops. What kind of shit are you into?"

His eyes tightened, and I could practically see within them his internal debate whether to answer. "To be honest, I don't know everything about it. Ronan sends me shipments or has me meet with contacts, and I bring the shit into town. I leave it at a warehouse, and it gets picked up. Money's left for me."

"By who?"

He shrugged. "Don't know."

"You don't know?" I was only mildly surprised.

"It's the kind of business where you don't ask questions." That's why I was only *mildly* surprised. It was one of Dad's business lessons. "Sometimes it's the other way around—I take the money or the package out of town, leave it somewhere, and pick up something later in return."

"So you've never looked at these shipments? Never even peeked to have an idea what you might be risking your life for?" I knew my brother better than that.

He made a face. "Of course I have. Sometimes I already know because Ronan and I plan it all out."

"And?" I asked, when he didn't continue.

He hesitated. "They're mostly collectibles."

"Like art?"

"Art. Jewelry. Weapons. It varies."

"You mean the artifacts."

He cocked his head. "You know about them?"

"I was in the Order, too, dipshit." I rubbed my jaw. "And you don't know who's picking these shipments up?"

"I leave that up to Ronan and Roman."

I turned and leaned against his car. "So Roman's involved, too?"

"I'm assuming so, but I don't know for sure. Why all the questions?"

"Well, like you said, you could be taken down at any time. We have to be prepared, and that means someone should know what pies you have your fingers in."

"Ronan and I have already discussed it. That's why he's back in town more, to protect the business in case I lose it. One reason, anyway. The gargoyles' presence is another, especially now that Graysin came back. They can cause us problems."

"Ah. Now I know why you and Everett aren't buddy-buddy."

"Exactly. So . . . now you know. Between us only. None of this goes anywhere else."

I hesitated, thinking of the promise I'd made Michaela. But this really wasn't my secret to share. "If this blows up in my face, I'll kill you myself."

"Yeah, you keep threatening that." He walked over to the driver's side of his car. "Wanna grab a beer?"

I jumped in the Camaro for the short ride back to the bar. "I can't believe you're a fucking dad."

He grunted. "I'm not. I'm a sperm donor." He paused as we pulled up next to my car, and he cut the engine. "I wish I could be a dad, though, Xandru. I honestly do."

CHAPTER 13

MICHAELA

*G*raysin, Callie, Addie, and Sindi followed me as we toured the first floor of the inn the night before we fully reopened to guests—just in time as the weather was calling for a good snowstorm next week, and Tase would be opening the ski lifts soon. The girls oohed and aahed as we entered each room, although they'd all seen the place at one stage or another since they'd each helped it come together in their own way.

"Thanks to Addie and a little touch of magic—and the crew, of course—the hard stuff was finished quickly," I said, as we returned to the lobby with its newly redone wood floors that shone beautifully. "And thanks to Graysin, the décor is simply perfect."

"Don't forget my nineteen percent friends' discount," Callie added.

"Yes! Thank you so much for that," I gushed.

"And my excellent crew management skills," Sindi said.

I laughed. "If you call watching their asses management."

"Hey." She pouted. "I made sure those asses were constantly moving."

"By grabbing them," Addie teased.

Sindi smirked. "I couldn't let Madame Luiza have all the fun."

"Speaking of, where is Mammie?" Addie asked.

"I don't know. She said she didn't want to miss girls' night. She must be in the ghost world." I laughed at how bizarre yet normal for us that sounded as I walked over to the front desk, where a tray of champagne flutes waited. I handed a glass to each of the girls. "All of you deserve so much more than a toast. You went above and beyond to return this inn to its former beauty, but with enough modern touches to make it perfectly nostalgic and luxuriously comfortable at the same time—and in record time. I wish I could give you more than this simple toast or even this night, but I raise my glass and say cheers to you. I'm so happy to call you my friends!"

I beamed at the girls who stood in front of me with blank stares. Addie raised a brow. Graysin and Callie exchanged a look. Sindi burst out laughing.

My shoulders sank. "Too much?"

"Uh . . . well . . . sweet. It was sweet," Graysin attempted. Sindi laughed even harder.

Callie rolled her eyes. "It definitely conveyed your *luuurve* for everybody, if that's what you were going for."

Addie joined Sindi in more fits of laughter.

"Oh my god, you just brought back memories of when you accepted the homecoming crown," Addie gasped out between giggles. She removed her glasses to wipe her eyes as she mimicked my voice. "Thank you all so very much. I am so *honored* that you think so much of me, and I promise not to let you down . . ." She trailed off, tilting her head. "Oh, wait. No, I think that speech was when you were elected student council vice president."

Sindi's laughter halted as she peered at me. "It's like I don't even know you!"

I rolled my eyes, then blew out a breath of relief. "Thank god you were all honest, because I kind of made myself gag with that speech. I mean, I *am* grateful, but no need to embarrass us all."

"Thank you," they said in unison.

"So no Grand Reopening?" Callie asked, her bracelets clinking together as she lifted her flute to her mouth. One drunken night at the bar, she and Addie had a competition about who was wearing the most. They were too drunk to count correctly, so they decided it was a draw.

I shook my head. "Nah. We were really only fully closed for a few days at a time, so it seems kind of weird to have a big party. It's just the Thanksgiving feast for all of you next week. Besides, with all the events around town during the holidays, I didn't see a need to add another. We're participating in pretty much everything, so there will be lots of opportunity for people to check out the inn."

"And it'll be all decked out for the holidays," Graysin said, her dark eyes lit up with excitement.

"We start tomorrow, right?" I verified with her, and she gave me a nod.

"Thank fuck you didn't add another event," Callie blurted. "I don't know what's worse—the holidays or summer around here. There's always something obnoxious going on in this town. At least Music on the Square is over for a while."

"I kind of like Music on the Square," I said.

She grimaced. "It wouldn't be so bad if it weren't every freaking Thursday."

Addie gave her a funny look. "It's not."

"Yeah, it is," Callie argued.

"It's called Third Thursdays Music on the Square," Addie said. "Because it's the third Thursday of the month."

Callie's brows scrunched together. "Really?"

Addie and I both nodded.

"Wow." She shrugged. "It certainly feels like it's every week. Probably because there are never decent bands."

"Can't argue with that," I said.

"Can't the Cult, er, I mean the Court do something about that?" Sindi asked, looking at me pointedly. "Now that you're on it, maybe you can bring change. Like some kickass bands."

She loved goading me about the Court, but I had to keep warning her about calling it the Cult. She was going to get her ass banished if she wasn't careful.

"Events like that are for the fake council," Callie said flippantly.

Sindi's auburn brows rose. "There's a fake council?"

"It's not fake," Addie said.

"May as well be," Callie scoffed.

"What the hell is the fake council?" Sindi demanded.

"It's the City Council," I explained. "The mainly human one that does all the normal city stuff, like making decisions on building codes and garbage collection. They oversee the parks and the community events."

"They *think* they're in charge," Callie said, "but it's a ruse. Even Mayor Barbie knows it is."

"So, uh, let's check out the conservatory," Addie quickly said, before the conversation veered off in a direction that put us in a precarious position with Court secrets and other taboo subjects.

I led the girls past the front desk to our left and the dark wooden grand staircase to our right, with the piano sitting under it. Mike McCabe and his men, with Everett's help, were able to restore the wall of stained glass images that rose behind the stairs from the bottom of the ground floor all the way to the ceiling of the third floor. When the sun was in the western sky and shone through, the colors that played on the stairs and the bench seats on each landing whisked you away to another realm. Well, not literally—which, in Havenwood Falls, could be possible. I would have said the staircase was one of my favorite places in the inn, but there were too many to name a true favorite.

"So, what's the Court like?" Graysin asked, rather innocently, as we passed through the library, another room I adored, with its floor-to-ceiling wooden bookcases and fat-cushioned chairs. When nobody answered, her steps faltered. "Oh, is that something we're not supposed to talk about?"

Part-gargoyle, she was aware of the supernatural side of Havenwood Falls, but was a relative newcomer. Not just to town, but to the whole underworld the human race believed to be myths. She was bound to have questions.

"It's basically just taking care of the town, and making sure our secrets stay safe," I said.

"Just like the brochure says," Addie quipped.

"There's a brochure?" Surprised, Sindi gave me an accusatory glare for not sharing it with her.

I rolled my eyes. "She was being snarky. But that really is all we do, at least, in my experience so far. Discipline those who get out of hand. Make sure situations are cleaned up. Argue about *how* to clean things up."

"Miss Mary Beth mentioned how you stood up to Roman Bishop during Rowan and Julianna's case before the Court," Graysin said, a hint of awe in her voice. "She's kind of pissed at you, but I hope you knocked him down a few pegs."

"He's an asshole," I blurted before I could stop myself.

"All the Bishops are," Addie quickly agreed, then we both looked at Callie.

"Sorry," we said at the same time.

She growled—actually *growled*—and for the first time, I could believe there really was a demon in her. "I know better than anybody what a bunch of assholes the Bishop boys are. No apologies necessary."

"I have a feeling Roman and I are going to clash on everything," I said as we passed through the dining room and approached the French doors at one end that opened to the conservatory.

"Just be careful," Addie said, dropping her voice to a whisper as the others walked behind us. "He's a fucktard, but he really is powerful. In all kinds of ways."

"Yeah, well, so is my best friend."

She let out a harrumph. "Not even Grandmother Saundra likes taking on Roman Bishop, if you haven't noticed. Not that she can't. There's just too much at stake. Be careful, Kales. You don't want him on your bad side."

I gave her a small nod, then turned to the others as I opened the doors. "And you all are the first to see the conservatory."

The large space off the side of the banquet hall-slash-ballroom also competed for one of my favorite places, especially since the weather had changed—winter came early in the mountains. I had to admit that Tase had done fantastic work in fixing and cleaning up the metal frame, and all the glass pieces had been replaced. During the day, guests could sit out here and feel like they were out in the snow, but without the freezing temperatures. At night, it provided a stunning view of the stars through the glass ceiling.

We sat in one of the seating areas Graysin had arranged, and where I had set out some cheese, crackers, and wine. After pouring us each a glass, I joined the others as we all leaned back on the cushioned lounge chairs to gaze at the sky—a glittery sight not too many places in the world could compete with.

"I thought this would be my favorite part," Addie said, disappointment lacing her tone.

"Me, too. Nature, stars, and the moon are your thing," I said. "It's not your favorite?"

Sitting up, she glanced around. "I don't know. I just feel . . . something."

Callie sat up, too. "I sense it, as well."

"Dark magic?" Addie asked, and Callie nodded.

"Just a faint trace," Callie clarified. "Like it had been here once, a while ago."

"Exactly." Addie gave me a look of concern.

We didn't stay out there long, but moved back to the front parlor, or the circle room, as it had come to be called by all the workers. The woodwork on the walls had been restored, but painted a light cream color to brighten the room. The formerly dark wood had made it feel closed in, and hardly anyone had ever sat in it. The ceiling was sectioned off like pie pieces with cream wood trim separating the slices and an image of the sun with the moon at the center, a chandelier dangling from it. The panels of the ceiling pieces were painted a deep blue with yellow stars. A couple of faux tropical plants sat among the comfortable wood and upholstered furniture. Graysin and I loved how the room was like a mirrored reflection of the conservatory on the opposite corner of the building.

Three bottles of wine later, our conversation became silly and full of giggles. Aurelia had come in at one point, and we'd actually managed to embarrass the crap out of her, scaring her off to the cottage. Mammie never did make an appearance, which was just as well. She'd be busy with her hauntings once the rooms started filling up tomorrow, so she needed to gather all the energy she could.

Callie and Graysin stumbled out of the inn, and I was grateful they lived within walking distance. Addie stood, much steadier than the rest of us, but rubbing her arms. She hadn't been the same since we'd been in the conservatory.

"Are you okay?" I asked as I walked her to the door.

She shrugged. "Yeah, I'll be fine."

"Should I be worried about the conservatory?"

"Nah. Whatever might have been there before is gone now. I think I'm just extra sensitive tonight. Some insane shit happened earlier today with Harper Sinclair."

"I heard. The whole Court was alerted. Poor girl can't even sign her name without Hell breaking loose. Literally."

Harper was Eloise's niece, and she had her own psychic scribing abilities, but they were of a much darker nature than her aunt's. Today at the real estate office, she'd scribed a threatening message from a demon.

"It has me a little wigged out, I guess," Addie said.

"Saundra said she contacted this Lucas guy." His name was specified in the message that threatened him and anyone who helped Harper, which was pretty much our whole town. I hadn't been on site today, but I could understand why Addie was freaked out by it.

She nodded. "Yeah, but I don't know if that's a good thing or not. I feel a shitstorm brewing in the energy surrounding this town. We have some rough times ahead."

I stepped outside with her. "Well, if that's not a buzzkill."

I threw my arms around her in a hug.

"No kidding," she murmured over my shoulder.

She'd been right. Over the next several days, the energy tangibly changed.

I AWOKE WITH A START, my heart racing with fear even as guilt washed through me. Xandru's arm snaked around my stomach, and he pulled me into him, tucking me into the curve of his half-sleeping body. He tried to comfort me, but his touch, his love, his compassion only made the guilt worse. This was why I hated sleeping. I loved lying in bed with him, though. If only I didn't always nod off. If only I wasn't mortal with a physical need for rest.

As soon as Xandru's breathing resumed a deep rhythm, I slipped out of bed and padded out into the sun-drenched living room. I blinked against the brightness, wondering why the curtains were pulled back.

"It's about time you got up," Aurelia said from the kitchen, making me jump. "Do you always sleep this late?"

Joining her, I pulled a coffee cup off a hook while glancing at the clock that read a little before noon. "I forgot you're out of school. You scared the crap out of me."

"We've been out all week."

"Give me a break. I just woke up. And it's not like you've been around much."

"Well, don't worry. I won't be in your hair for long today, either. Laurel, Alicia, and I are meeting up—"

"Didn't you just spend the night with them?"

She shrugged. "Well, yeah, but what are breaks for, if not spending it with friends?"

"And what about Lena?" Lena and Laurel were twins, and Aurelia had been friends with both of them for years. Lately, though, I rarely heard anything about the quieter sister.

Aurelia huffed out a breath. "She's . . . not like us. She's just not into the same things. She'd rather stay at home, like an old lady."

"She sure was there for you when you needed her most, after Mom died. Was Laurel?"

Turning her back to me, Aurelia dumped the contents of her cup into the sink. "I have to go. They're waiting."

I stepped closer. "Aurelia."

She lifted her head to look out the window, still avoiding me.

"Laurel and Alicia are *fun*. Yeah, it's dumb stuff like boys and clothes, but their silliness makes me laugh. I just want to laugh. To live. I don't want to sit around and dwell. Lena's great for stillness and peace. I needed that then. But not now."

"So you were using her."

"Michaela . . . no." She sighed. "Maybe."

"Don't be an asshole friend, Aurelia. You know what Mom would say about that."

I could only see her profile, but her eyelashes fluttered rapidly, blinking back tears, I was sure. Then she spun on her heel and pushed past me, grabbing her coat off the rack by the front door.

"Well, Mom's not here," she snapped. "I wouldn't be such a mess if she were!"

"You don't have to be a mess now."

"I have to go." She threw open the door. "I'll be back later."

"You promised to help with last minute preps for tomorrow's dinner," I reminded her.

"I will. Don't worry," she huffed as she stomped outside, slamming the door behind her.

I leaned against the counter, coffee cup cradled in my hands, the steam rising into my face. I closed my eyes, but the tears still came, leaking under my lashes. Time had made coping easier, but some days . . . some days, I just wanted my mom. Those days seemed to come out of nowhere, slamming into me like a speeding bus.

I couldn't say this one had come completely out of the blue, though. I'd been feeling it creeping up for days, maybe part of that dark energy Addie had warned about. It began about the same time as the inn was officially reopened and preparations made for tomorrow's Thanksgiving feast and the holiday season. Mom would have loved how the renovations turned out, and how Graysin and I had decorated the entire inn for Christmas, like it was straight out of her favorite holiday movies.

She should have been here for it all.

After I finished my first cup of coffee, I slipped into the bedroom and quietly pulled on my jeans and a hoodie. By the door, I stuffed my feet into my snow boots, pulled on my thick gray coat, a purple, slouchy knit cap, and mittens. I crunched through the snow on the inn's lawn, poked my head inside to tell Sindi where I was going, and made one more stop at Coffee Haven. A fresh cup of nectar, complete with whipped cream and special sprinkles, steamed in my hands as I walked across town to the cemetery.

Snow blanketed the front section with its precise rows of headstones, well-placed benches, and clusters of neatly trimmed trees. The sidewalks were shoveled and salted, all the way to the back of the human, public part of the grounds. From there, I followed the path already dirty and packed down with footprints to the stone-pillared, arched tunnel that went under Blackstone Road. The other end opened up to an older section that wasn't cared for in the same meticulous manner as the front, but in its way was much more beautiful and solemn and reverent. This was the section for the Old Families and the supernaturals.

Some of the oldest graves had metal cages over them, to keep the dead in if they should rise again. Runes and other magical symbols were engraved on many tombstones. Colored glass balls and crystals hung from tree branches. One section was a maze of mausoleums, similar to the cemeteries in New Orleans. It was toward the front of this section that I headed, for the Petran family columbarium, but I stopped in my tracks when I saw a tall, broad figure standing in front of the stone building next to it—the Rocas'.

For a moment, I wondered how Xandru had beaten me here when I'd left him sound asleep back at the cottage. Then I realized it wasn't him.

Tase leaned on one gloved hand pressed against the wall, his other hand tracing his mother's engraved name. His head hung low, his chin to his chest. A lump rose in my throat, and my chest tightened. I glanced around and over my shoulder, thinking I should leave. He didn't move, but I knew he'd heard me approach. Just as I heard his low whispers about family and wanting to make her proud and how she should have been around for her children and grandchildren.

My head dropped as renewed tears rolled down my cheeks, splattering onto the dirty snow at my feet. I brushed at them with my mittened hand and turned to leave. Tase deserved privacy for his mourning. Especially from the person responsible.

"It's not your fault," he said, causing me to pause. He didn't yell —he knew he didn't need to—but he spoke loud enough for me to know his words were meant for my ears. I turned back, but didn't approach any closer. Tase turned as well, his gaze sliding over me. "I know it's not."

I swallowed. "Not everyone believes that. I wonder myself if there was anything I could have done differently."

He walked toward me. "There wasn't, Michaela. Even if you had, they would have had to be put down. Xandru and I knew it was only a matter of time."

"But if the Luna Coven—"

"Our parents were too far gone to be helped. Even Mother." Tase stopped a few paces in front of me. "They'd hidden it too well until it was too late. All the Luna Coven could have done differently would have been to send them to the Infernum, but that would have been worse than death for them."

I'd only learned of the Infernum recently—a purgatory worse than Hell where they trapped those supernaturals who were too difficult, or impossible, to kill.

The look on his face . . . the sadness filling his tone . . . I'd never seen this side of Tase before. A more human side. A side that missed his parents as much as I missed mine.

"I'm so sorry," I whispered, not knowing what else to say.

"Don't be," he said softly. "You did what you had to do to save yourself, and Aurelia and Gabe. The man and woman . . . who knows how many others? Because of you, my brothers and sisters won't face our parents' fate. They won't all admit it out loud, but they know deep down that you saved them. You were a hero that day, Michaela."

My breath plumed out on a sharp exhale. "I'm far from a hero."

"We all know I'm the one to blame. If I hadn't turned you, your family *and* my family would be whole right now."

I shook my head. "Not exactly whole. I wouldn't be here. I'd be living an entirely different, *fake* life. I like my life now, Tase. A lot. I like what I see for the future. What Xandru and I talk about as we lay in bed."

His smile didn't reach his eyes. "That's good to know. It really is."

"The inn is part of that future. Thank you for everything you've done for it." I dropped my gaze, staring at our boots in the snow. "It really was so much more than you needed to."

He cleared his throat. "Trust me. You deserve it all and then some."

I looked up at him, into eyes so similar to Xandru's, yet so much greener than they used to be. Hesitating for only a moment, I reached out and squeezed his arm. "I've forgiven you, Tase. I hope someday you can forgive yourself. I hope you have the chance to, before it's too late."

His smile deepened. "Thank you. That means a lot to me. More than you could ever know."

"Family forgives, and we're family. Maybe not by blood or marriage—"

"Yet," he interrupted.

I smiled. "Maybe. But even if that never happens, we've known each other since birth. Even with all the feuding and grudges, we've been in each other's lives forever. And while our parents had their issues, we don't have to. We don't have to carry on with the nonsense."

"Family, huh? You really want to claim us as family?"

My shoulders lifted in a shrug. "Why not? You'll certainly keep things interesting. You really want to claim the Petrans?"

He laughed, the sound strange among the silence of the dead. "You're something else, Kales. Xandru's lucky to have you. You really would do anything for him, wouldn't you?"

He gave my shoulder a return squeeze, then brushed past me, headed toward the tunnel. Before I realized what I was doing, I half turned and called over my shoulder, "You know, Addie would do anything for you. You might want to think about giving it a chance."

He waved two fingers in the air, acknowledging that he'd heard me, but otherwise didn't respond. Which was probably for the better, because I had no idea where that had come from. If anyone ever asked, I'd plead temporary insanity.

Then I realized he hadn't answered my question about accepting the Petrans as family. That was probably answer enough.

"Well, I tried," I muttered, as I trudged over to our family's plot. "I hope that didn't make you roll over in your graves. Of course, you're cremated, so you really can't roll over." I snickered at my stupid joke. "Anyway, I'm trying, Mom and Dad. I know this isn't the life you wanted for me, but it's the life *I* wanted. I'm still so mad at you for what you did, but . . . I hope I can still make you proud, even with the Rocas . . . and with Gabe . . . The inn looks amazing, so there's that . . ."

I spent over an hour pouring out everything about our lives, and my hopes and fears, and while it wasn't close to being the same as having Mom's shoulder to lean on, the release helped. As I left, I thought I saw Aurelia standing on the far side of a tree in the distance, as though waiting her turn.

This part of the cemetery certainly was busy today.

CHAPTER 14

XANDRU

*M*ichaela stood with Anne McCabe, Mike's wife, at the entrance to the inn's newly redone dining room, a long room that spanned the entire back of the building, ending on the east side with French doors that led out to the conservatory. Dressed in black pants, a dark gray sweater, and sexy as hell knee-high boots, my gorgeous woman flipped and waved her hands, gesturing about, as she told Anne about how the space converted to a ballroom for larger functions. She only talked with her hands this much when she was passionate about the subject.

I was about to approach when I heard the words Cupids & Cuties, and decided to hang back a minute, not wanting to be at all involved in a discussion about the party the inn was hosting for Valentine's Day.

Anne gushed about how much she loved how the old and the new combined seamlessly throughout the inn, and Michaela introduced her to Graysin, the brains and talent behind the look. As Anne and Graysin walked off, I strode up to my girl and wrapped my arms around her from the back. She leaned into my embrace.

"You've outdone yourself," I murmured against her ear. "The food smells amazing."

She laughed softly. "Well, don't venture into the kitchen.

Mammie's giving them hell in there. I'm not sure what she misses more—decorating town square or cooking."

Everett Weston walked up beside us, wearing, like me, jeans and a button-down that was close enough to dressy. "I've been hoping to meet her. I haven't had the pleasure yet."

And then he suddenly jumped and growled as his eyes bugged out.

"Mammie!" Michaela gasped, slapping her hand over her mouth as the ghost made herself visible next to Everett. "No getting fresh with our guests. We *like* this one."

"I'm sorry." Mammie batted her eyelashes. "But I just couldn't help it. I like this one, too."

Michaela reached out, closing her hand over the leather cuff on Everett's wrist. "I'm really sorry. She has this new outlook on . . . life."

Mammie nodded. "The dead don't have to be proper. Besides, it's a compliment. You have no idea how much energy that takes."

Everett rubbed the back of his neck, then gestured toward the bar. "Um . . . I think I'll get Graysin a drink."

I chuckled as he hurried off toward the far side of the room. "I don't think that was quite the pleasure of meeting you he'd expected."

Mammie giggled. "It was certainly a pleasure for me. That man has quite the ass."

"Maybe you should go back to giving the kitchen staff hell," Michaela muttered.

Madame Luiza's image disappeared before Michaela could admonish her any further, and a few nearby hotel guests gasped. Murmurs scattered across the room, asking who else had seen the ghost.

Turning to face me, Michaela rested her arms on my shoulders. "So everything looks good? Do you think separating our personal guests at different tables is okay? I was going to sit us all at one big table, but then I thought the inn's guests might feel left out, so—"

"I'm probably not the best person to ask these things, but it looks perfect to me." I leaned in and gave her a kiss. "Stop worrying so much. Try to enjoy yourself. You worked hard for this."

She pushed up on her toes and gave me another kiss, this one longer. Just as our lips parted, she pulled away. "I should probably go mingle before I convince you to leave early. Which wouldn't be cool, considering I'm the hostess."

I grasped her chin and stroked my thumb over her lips. "Let me know if you need anything at all."

"I think we have it under control. Sindi is seriously a godsend. I'd better go check on the kitchen, though, before Mammie makes them all quit."

According to my untrained eye, the feast went off without a hitch. Which was saying a lot, considering the mix of guests. Rusty, a wolf, and his mate, Sherry, a human, had come for dinner after a small food disaster at their cabin, and sat with Savannah Bast, who was the high school's new history teacher and something not human that I couldn't pinpoint. At another table sat Elias, a fallen angel who'd lent a helping hand with some of the inn's work; Addie, the witch; Tase, the vampire and the only other Roca in attendance; Everett and Graysin, the gargoyles; and Callie, a gypsy demon. I had to give it to Everett for putting up with my brother. The McCabe construction crew, a mix of species, were scattered across a couple of tables, except for Mike and Anne. The mountain lion shifters sat with Michaela, the kids, Sindi, and me—aka, the vampire family. Even Aurelia was on her best behavior.

As we finished dessert, though, it quickly fell apart.

Most of the inn's guests had already left for an evening stroll around town or to their rooms. As the last ones trailed out, including a high-school-aged girl who was staying with her parents, something about the way Gabe watched her go caught my attention. It could have been normal adolescent hormones . . . or it could have been something more sinister.

He suddenly jumped up from the table. "Can I go?"

Michaela motioned toward his untouched pie. "You don't want to finish your dessert?"

He made a rude face. "I don't like pecan pie."

"Well, you can still sit here a little longer with our guests," Michaela said firmly, giving him the mom-eye. She was already learning to perfect it.

She was a lot better at this parenting stuff than I was. Of course, she'd had better role models, and her charges were younger. Andrei and Aurora were a lot closer to eighteen and had pretty much been on their own long before our parents died. As long as I could get Andrei to finish school this year, I was counting it as a win.

"I'm done, and I'm bored," Gabe argued. "These are your friends, not mine!"

"Gabe," Michaela started.

He ran off before she could say anything else. She huffed in exasperation, and Tase and I stood at the same time.

"Let me," Tase said, glancing from me to Michaela. "It's what family does, right?"

I cocked my head at the bizarre statement coming from him, of all people, to her, of all people—I knew full well he'd never consider the Petrans family. But Michaela simply nodded, distracted by her buzzing phone—the special one, from the Court. Addie picked hers up at the same time.

Tase strode out the same way Gabe left, while Addie and Michaela both jumped up, exchanging a look before Addie whispered, "Harper," and ran toward the front door.

"I'm sorry," Michaela said to her guests. She spoke quietly, probably to avoid scaring any of the inn's guests still lingering. "We have a town emergency. I have to go. You should all probably get home quickly. Everett and Graysin, you might be needed."

"We'll be at my place on standby," Everett said as he took Graysin's hand.

Just as they all left and Michaela was on her way out the front door, a muffled scream sounded from behind the inn. She looked at me with wide eyes.

"Go," I said. "I'll check it out. You do what you need to do."

She hurried over and gave me a quick kiss before running out.

Glad to have an excuse to follow Tase, I went the opposite way, crossing the dining room in a handful of strides and exiting through a set of French doors, into the night. My eyes scanned the rear lawn and didn't see anything out of the ordinary, but my ears caught a commotion behind the cottages and my nose smelled blood.

"You let it get out of hand," Tase's voice growled as I approached.

I jogged around the corner to find Gabe and Tase standing over an unconscious girl, Tase handing Gabe a small package.

"What the fuck, Tase? You bled her out?" I demanded, dropping down to check on the girl. Her pulse beat steadily. Only a small amount of blood stained the snow.

"No. I knocked her out so I wouldn't want to kill her," Tase bit out. "A little of our blood and glamour, and she'll be no worse for the wear."

"God damn it. This isn't cool." Standing, I looked at Gabe and the small package he held—displaying a logo I was quite familiar with. My gaze bounced to Tase, then back to Gabe. "What the hell's going on?"

"You need to turn around and walk away," Tase said quietly, but firmly. "You don't want to get pulled into this."

"Hell no! What are you doing?" I snatched the package out of Gabe's hand. The logo of Circle J, Adrian's pot dispensary, was emblazoned on it. "Edibles? You're giving a twelve-year-old *edibles*?"

"I'm giving a *vampire* trying to control his *bloodlust* edibles," he snapped. My brow shot up. Tase sighed. "Seriously, you should go."

I stood my ground. "No, *you* should really start explaining what the hell is going on. Does Michaela know about this?"

"No!" Gabe shouted. "She can't know."

I shoved my finger in Tase's chest. "Explain yourself. Now."

He shook his head slowly. "I tried to warn you. I didn't want to put you in this position, but if you insist . . . Gabe's struggling. He's only keeping it together because of the cannabis."

My head snapped toward Gabe. "What do you mean, you're struggling?"

"The cravings . . . they're hard to control. It's getting worse." He motioned toward the body on the ground. "It was like her blood begged me to drink it. But the cookies and brownies help. They're the only things that help."

"Fuck," I whispered, pushing a hand through my hair. "Why didn't you tell your sister?"

"She can't know! She's on the Court. She'll tell them. Then they'll make me stay at the Academy."

"You obviously need to. Why didn't you at least come to me?"

"Because you'll tell Michaela. So would Sindi."

"That's why he came to me," Tase said. "He knew I'd help without burdening either of you or causing problems between the two of you."

"You can't tell her," Gabe pleaded. "Please, Xandru. Just let me learn to control it."

I threw my arms out, toward the girl. "But you're not!"

Tase shifted on his feet. "Yeah, well, that's my fault. He ran out, and I didn't give him more."

"Yeah, because you want the stupid watch," Gabe accused.

"Excuse me?" I said.

Gabe ignored me. "You know what? You can have the dumb thing. It's not worth it. Then I won't need your stupid cookies, either. If Xandru promises not to tell Michaela about this, I'll tell you where it is."

Tase and I both stared at Gabe. Was this little shit really giving the two of us ultimatums? I wasn't sure if I was more pissed or impressed at the size of his balls.

"You found it? You know where it is?" Tase finally asked, and shock replaced both pissed and impressed. Because he sounded *excited*.

"Of course! What do you think did this to me? It's because of that dumb watch that I attacked Michaela. It made us wreck, almost killed Aurelia. And now my life is ruined! You can have it. I hate that thing!"

He shouted loudly enough to cause lights to blink on and a wolf to howl in the distance.

"Lower your voice," I said through a clenched jaw. "The last thing we need is Rusty or one of the Kasuns to show up."

"So where is it?" Tase's tone was both cautious and demanding at once.

"I buried it. But it doesn't matter. I can still *hear* it."

"What the hell does that mean?" I asked.

"It *speaks* to me," he said, his voice haunted. "It tells me what to do to be strong and powerful. To be better than everyone. But its words are . . . *evil*." He lurched toward Tase and grasped his hands, begging. "Please, just take it away. Far away, Tase. Promise me you will if I tell you where it is."

What the hell? Michaela hadn't said anything to me about the timepiece being dark. Just that it was old and possibly valuable. Were we talking about the same thing?

"I swear on my mother's grave," Tase vowed, and I knew that tone—I could practically hear him doing the *cha-ching* sound in his head. Yeah, we were talking about the same thing. Gabe was just a kid, who'd probably freaked himself out with some made-up stories about the old watch.

The kid looked at me. "And you promise not to tell Michaela?"

I glared at him. For once I knew the best parenting move to make, except he wasn't my kid to parent.

"Xandru, please?" he begged.

I dropped my hands to my hips. "I promise I won't tell Michaela . . . as long as you do."

"*Xandru*," the boy wailed.

"It's the grown-up thing to do," I said. "If you don't want the Court treating you like a baby vamp, then step up and be a man when it counts."

He scowled.

"Look," I said, "tell us where the watch is, and I'll give you one week to get yourself under control and come clean with your sister about the edibles. That's my final offer. Deal?"

Gabe groaned. "All right, fine. Deal."

"One week," I said again. "I'm serious. If you don't tell Michaela or if you don't get better, I *will* tell her. And you better be upfront with me about how you're doing."

He nodded so hard, I thought his head might bounce right off his neck.

I turned to Tase, an uneasy feeling crawling down my spine at the thought of letting him retrieve the heirloom. The kid had to be imagining the evil voices. Right? Blowing things out of proportion? On the other hand, Tase smuggled artifacts, and he seemed especially interested in this one, because of its value. Which meant it might have held some kind of power.

"What do you want with it?" I asked my brother.

"I'm sure you already know." He held his hands up. "I want nothing to do with any power it might have. This is the last piece, Xan. It's what I've been needing to finish the job. It'll set us all up, and then I can be done with what we talked about. I swear."

"It's their family's, though, so the money goes to—" I cut myself off as realization dawned on me.

"I prepaid her," Tase said. "Handsomely."

Son of a fucking bitch.

This was the real reason Tase had paid off the inn's mortgages and covered all the renovation costs. He'd even paid for furniture and fancy throw pillows. All as a cover so he could gain access to the inn and claim ownership of this timepiece. I'd known all along there had to have been an ulterior motive.

"We'll talk about this later," I growled through a clenched jaw.

"So we're doing this?" he asked.

My head fell back, and I stared at the sky as thick snowflakes swirled downward. To be fair to Tase, he'd shelled out nearly two hundred grand for the inn's mortgages and renovations. I knew Michaela had been searching for the timepiece, but she'd given up a while ago, believing it was long lost. She might have let Tase have the thing, if he'd been upfront with her. But if it was truly hurting her brother, then maybe it was best she continued to believe it unrecoverable. And if Tase could extract himself from the business with the Bishops, that would be good for all of us, including her.

But I sure as fuck hated keeping another secret from the woman who trusted me more than anyone. The woman I planned to make my wife one day soon.

I sighed, my breath pluming out like smoke as I lowered my head.

"Go get the watch and meet me at home. We'll discuss the rest later." I looked down at the tourist girl. "Gabe and I will take care of her."

"I got this, bro," Tase promised me.

He glanced at the girl, and the slight glow of green in his eyes didn't make me feel any better. I had to rely on his greed—and possibly that he actually did want to be a good dad—to overcome whatever power the timepiece might possibly possess. I gave him a shove to send him on his way.

After he jogged off, I turned to Gabe. "So, are you ready to heal your first victim?"

"Will you teach me how to compel her, too?" he asked excitedly.

I snorted. "Not on your life. I'd say you have a few years before you get to learn that power."

CHAPTER 15

MICHAELA

I didn't have to worry about nightmares after Thanksgiving —I didn't have time to sleep. Snowfall after snowfall had Tase opening the slopes early, and then the visitors' bureau hauled in the tourists by the busloads. Holiday events filled up the calendar, including the Cold Moon Ball.

And then Heidi Bennett went missing.

This was when I discovered just how hard the Court worked at keeping things hidden from the public. I'd already learned about the sirens and how the Court gave them names of men who deserved death sentences, such as the recently demised Dr. Nance, and nobody else in town had a clue. I'd helped with disaster recovery at the homecoming dance and altering teens' memories (a tool certain Court members, like Roman Bishop, liked to abuse, in my personal opinion and experience). The battle on Thanksgiving night between angels and demons had been relatively easy to keep quiet, since it involved only a handful of people and had been contained to the other side of the mountain.

But when a teenage girl disappeared in the woods the night of one of the largest parties in town, people noticed. And they talked. Especially the high schoolers. Aurelia pretended not to be bothered, but I could smell the fear on her. What if she was next? Parents all over town wondered the same thing about their own kids. Before worry could escalate to widespread panic, the Court soothed everyone by having Sheriff Kasun deliver a public story that his men were investigating, but all initial evidence and firsthand accounts pointed to the belief that Heidi had run away.

That wasn't true, though. We had her phone—stained with blood. A child harmed, possibly killed, by a supernatural was the Court's worst nightmare. We quietly formed and executed a search party of supes, and we scoured the woods surrounding the entire town two nights in a row. We'd found nothing so far. We fed the public the runaway story while continuing a secret investigation, questioning all possible suspects.

"School's about to let out, so we'll be over to the inn to question Gabe," Sheriff Ric Kasun told me on the third day of her disappearance as we closed the second emergency Court meeting of the day. The first one had been to discuss Dr. Jared Lewis, who was expected to arrive in town this weekend and start at the medical center after the first of the year, replacing the late Dr. Nance. The second meeting had been to discuss updates on the Bennett case.

I about choked on my coffee. "I'm sorry?"

"We have to cover all our bases," Roman said from Kasun's side. "Question all suspects. We discussed this only minutes ago, Ms. Petran."

"Well, I know, but he . . . Gabe . . ." I spluttered. "Why would he be a suspect?"

"From my understanding, he might be struggling with control," Kasun said.

"*What?*" I nearly shouted. "He's fine!"

Kasun pierced me with silver eyes. "Are you sure about that?"

"Of course I'm sure. I've been keeping an eye on him. I make sure he gets plenty of bottled blood to keep him satiated. He's doing well in school. What makes you think he has control issues?"

Roman arched a dark brow and said in his arrogant, sarcastic way, "You might want to check his backpack, Ms. Petran."

165

He brushed past me as he strode for the door, leaving me with my mouth gaping.

"Don't take it personally," Kasun said. "We'll be questioning Atanase, as well."

I snorted. "At least that makes sense."

Kasun dipped his chin. "See you in a little while, Michaela."

It took all of my control to not make a childish face at his back. I had a feeling Roman instigated this questioning of Gabe, probably in retaliation for my vote on his brother's case last month. Kasun, of course, loved any chance he had to harass vampires. At least that was just natural instinct and not necessarily vindictive.

"You want me to curse him to smell farts the rest of the day?" Addie whispered in my ear.

I nearly spit out my coffee again. "You'd do that?"

She shrugged. "It's one of my favorite ways to handle asshats. And Roman is the epitome of an asshat. It wouldn't be the first time."

Another laugh burst out of me as I imagined his smug face sniffing, trying to figure out the smell. "Did he know it was you?"

"He's an asshat, but he's not dumb. He figured it out almost right away and said, 'Very mature, Adelaide.'" She mocked his arrogant, uppity voice perfectly. "But then, for the next week, every time I put on clean socks, I stepped in a wet spot. I'm positive he cursed me back."

"So that's why not even Saundra Beaumont messes with Roman Bishop?" I mused.

"Oh, no. He'd kill you in a heartbeat," Addie deadpanned. "But usually worse."

"Worse than murder?"

"He'll make your life a living hell, so you'd want to die. And I'm not talking about wet socks your whole life. I'm talking about making a loved one go barking mad with a twist of his hand. Delivering the name of someone you love to the sirens. Seizing all your business assets and bankrupting your entire family with a phone call. He's powerful in many ways, and won't hesitate to use that power if it benefits or protects him, his family, or his business interests."

"He's done all those things?"

She tipped her head. "The worst part is that nobody can ever prove it was him. He's always one step ahead, which makes him even more dangerous."

"I'll keep that in mind." I glanced at my phone screen for the time. "I'd better get home."

I texted Gabe as I crossed the square on my way back to the inn, ordering his butt home right after school. As soon as he walked in, I snatched his backpack off his shoulders before he could put up a fight.

"Hey! What are you doing?" he demanded, trying to grab it back.

"As your guardian, it's my job to check up on you," I said, walking around the front desk. "To make sure you're doing your homework and handing it in . . . keeping your work organized and taking care of your books . . . and, you know, not carrying around weapons or biting classmates."

I'd unzipped the large pocket while I spoke, and I looked up to see Gabe had frozen in place. Xandru had walked in, and he paused next to my brother as I dumped the backpack contents onto the desk.

"And apparently I do need to check on you more." I stared at the pile in shock. There were two textbooks, a few spiral notebooks, wadded up papers, pens and pencils, and . . . three wrappers and two unopened packages with the Circle J logo on them. I held them up. "Are these what I think they are?" His face told me everything. "Gabe, how could you?"

"You never told her?" Xandru asked.

My eyes widened with another punch in the gut. "*You* knew?"

"I kept meaning to," Gabe said, "but you're always busy, Michaela."

Oh, my god. Was this my fault? Had I been too wrapped up with the inn and Xandru to know what was going on with my own brother? Made myself too unavailable for him? I suddenly didn't know with whom I was more upset—Gabe, Xandru, or myself.

This parenting gig sucked.

"We'll talk about this later." I gathered the wrappers and edibles. "Come clean up the rest of your stuff, sit in the parlor and do your homework, and no video games or friends." I looked at Xandru. "Can I talk to you?"

I didn't wait for an answer, but turned and walked to the back offices, to my private one in the corner. I dumped the incriminating evidence on my desk and spun around to face him.

"Why didn't you tell me?"

"I was giving him the chance to tell you himself. To do the right thing. I thought he would have by now. That was the deal."

"How long have you known?"

He stuffed his hands in his jeans pockets and rocked back on his heels. "Since Thanksgiving."

"That was almost two weeks ago! What happened to telling each other everything?"

He stepped up to me and wrapped his hands around my upper arms, gently holding them. "I'd given him a week, but the time got away from me. I really thought he would have told you. I'm sorry."

I shook my head. "Would you have told your parents without being forced to? Wait. Never mind. Your parents wouldn't have cared. But I do care. Why is he eating edibles? Does he really have control issues?"

I leaned my forehead against his chest.

"He did. He went to Tase—"

"Tase?" I let out a harsh laugh. "He went to Tase before me or Sindi or you?"

"I know. It's a little scary. But look at it from his perspective. If he was feeling a loss of control, he may have seen Tase as someone who'd best understand." Xandru lifted my chin with his finger, dropping his voice. "He didn't want to disappoint you. He cares about what you think. That's not a bad thing."

"It is if it means he won't talk to me about the important stuff." I sighed, stepping away. "Kasun's men are going to be here any minute to question Gabe in Heidi's disappearance. And then they're going after Tase."

"Tase has an alibi. Trust me—I already questioned him. Gabe does, too, remember? We were all at the ball when you found out about Heidi."

My brows scrunched together as I leaned my head back to look up at him. "That's right. So why— They're just harassing us." And then another thought occurred to me. "Roman knew about the edibles. He was the one who told me to check Gabe's backpack."

Xandru's forehead wrinkled as his brows rose high. "Well, that's no good. He's up to something."

"When is he not?" I muttered, but as I thought about it, the idea that he'd go this far as vengeance for my vote over a month ago seemed ridiculous. There had to have been another reason. Something he wanted? I stepped back from Xandru's embrace. "Did Tase ever tell you who the witch was who paid him to turn me?"

He shook his head.

"Could it have been Roman?"

"He referred to her as a female. Didn't the Court investigate?"

I gnawed on my lip. "Yeah, but the suspect left town. They haven't been able to trace her anywhere, like she vanished off the face of the earth. They think she could be dead. But now I wonder if she had ties to Roman. Addie said he'd brought her before the Luna Coven, but nobody wanted her in. He could have covered for her with the Court, and he seems to have it out for me. For my family."

Xandru cocked his head and narrowed his eyes. "I'll talk to Tase."

Sheriff Kasun, his deputy son Conall, who was basically a younger version of Kasun but meaner, and Roman showed up a few minutes later, giving me just enough time to warn Gabe and prep him. I hadn't actually expected Roman to come for something so mundane, which only furthered my suspicions that he was targeting me and my family. I took Gabe's trembling hand and led them all into our small meeting room.

"Mind if I look around?" Roman asked as he leaned against the doorway. "I haven't been here since the renovations. I'd like to see Graysin's work."

Peering at him, I wondered what his interest in Graysin's work was. Sure, he'd been married to her sister, but I didn't think they had any kind of relationship. I was about to say I minded very much when Sheriff Kasun spoke up.

"Roman, go do what you need to do," Ric said.

"I'll give him the tour," Xandru volunteered from out in the hall. Thank god. He wouldn't let Roman out of his sight.

I turned to Ric. "What does Roman need to do?"

He shrugged. "He said he needed to do an energy reading for traces of unknown magic. We're here to talk to Gabe, but Roman thought it . . . what did he say?" He looked at Conall.

"Sagacious." Conall rolled his eyes.

"Yes, that was the word." Ric nodded. "Roman thought it *sagacious* that he ensures there are no unregistered guests staying here."

I pulled back. Unregistered meant supernatural visitors who hadn't informed the Court they were in town, which was required within twenty-four hours of arrival. "Don't you think I'd say something if there were?"

"Some types—like that skinwalker you had last spring—not even my nose can detect, but magic may be able to." He gestured toward Gabe and me and then to the seats as he took one for himself. "So, Gabe, how have you been?"

Gabe answered their questions in the short and direct way I'd advised him to, not adding any extra information. Since Roman had known about the edibles, I told him to come clean on those, but I lied through my teeth when I said I'd known about them.

"That's why I was surprised that you mentioned he was having problems," I said. "We're doing everything we can to manage the urges."

Ric nodded, but Conall only glared at me.

"We don't normally condone giving kids marijuana," Ric said, "but we know this is an unusual situation. The real addiction to blood is much more dangerous than any side effects of the cannabis. But we do have rules, Michaela. This should have been reported to both the Court and the school."

I nodded. "The school I understand. But why does the Court need to know every detail about our lives?"

"In this case, it's to ensure that if we find him in a suspicious situation, we know the full background. We'd know why he'd be exhibiting certain types of behavior. As is everything with the Court, which you should know by now, our rules are for the best interest of *all* of our residents. Including Gabe."

Roman sauntered in at that moment.

"I assume you found that our guests are what they say they are," I said, after Ric nodded for him to join us.

He stayed just inside the door, slightly behind me. "I did. Are you aware there's a trace of black magic in the conservatory?"

I stood and faced him, crossing my arms. "I am. Addie felt it, but said it's old. Whatever it was is long gone."

He lifted his chin. "Gone, yes, but not too long ago. Only in the last six months or so. I noticed the flooring is new. Were any unusual objects found buried under the old floor? Old family heirlooms?"

His question caught me off guard. Why would he ask that? Did he know something about the Eye of Valerian? Did he know where my father would have hidden it? Or was he referring to something else?

"I assume you're knowledgeable about the Eye of Valerian, since it was part of your required reading for your Court seat," Roman said, answering my silent question. A thick tension suddenly filled the air at the mention of the trinket. "The last known whereabouts was in your father's possession. He hid it, for very good reason. The timepiece wasn't found, was it?"

Gabe gasped behind me. "Does it have black magic?"

I looked over my shoulder to find his eyes wide. "Gabe, do you know where it is?"

He'd shown me the plain, old watch I'd already known about,

but it really was plain—no moonstone inlays—and only "old" to a twelve-year-old. Probably not even as old as I was, a replica of the old-style pocket watches.

Gabe blinked, slowly, then shook his head.

"Are you being honest, young man?" Roman asked.

I wanted to snap at him for calling my brother a liar, but it wouldn't have been the first time Gabe had lied to me recently.

"I . . . I don't know where it is. Honest." He hesitated as he looked around the room before his gaze eventually fell on me. "But I found that leather brace, remember? With the place for a timepiece? Are . . . are they connected?"

I had no idea, so I looked to Roman, who seemed to know more than anyone.

"I know nothing about a bracelet," he said haughtily. His hard gaze narrowed in on Gabe. "The Eye of Valerian is a very powerful piece. If it is found, it must be handled with care. In the wrong hands, especially unprotected, it can be extremely dangerous. Even deadly."

"And I assume yours are the right hands?" I dared to ask.

He turned those deep blue eyes on me and smirked. "You know what they say when you assume, Ms. Petran."

With that, he strode out of the room and a few seconds later, out of the inn, leaving me to figure out that riddle. I mean, I knew he meant the word assume "makes an ass out of u and me," but which part was he saying I assumed inaccurately? That he wanted the piece, or that his hands were the right ones?

I'd practically forgotten Sheriff Kasun and Conall were still in the room, until I turned back to face Gabe.

"Are we done here?" I asked them.

They both stood.

"For the time being," Sheriff Kasun said. "If you know anything about Ms. Bennett's disappearance, please don't hesitate to call me." He paused and looked over my head for a moment. When his gaze dropped back to mine, his eyes were softer than I'd ever seen them. "As far as the Eye of Valerian goes, let's just hope your father hid it well. But if you do find it, hide it again, Michaela. While it probably has uses for good, it's too dangerous. In anybody's hands."

"It has that much power? Do you know anything about it?"

Kasun's eyes returned to their normal hardness when he dealt with vampires. "Only that your father hid it for good reason."

He nodded at Conall, and they both vacated the room. Gabe and I followed them out, then I turned in a circle, surveying the lobby and front parlor.

"What happened to Xandru?" I wondered aloud.

"No idea, but I'm going to the cottage," Gabe said as he grabbed his backpack from behind the front desk. Something sounded off in his voice.

"Are you okay? Don't let Roman get to you."

He shook his head. "It's not that. I'm just really tired and want to get my homework done."

I grimaced. "Do you need a cookie or brownie?"

"No." He rolled his eyes. "That would make me even more tired. I just didn't sleep well last night. Bad dreams."

I knew what those were like.

I followed him to the back of the inn, but while he exited through a set of French doors in the dining room, I checked out the conservatory, and then every other room on the first floor. I came back to the bar, where Sindi was preparing for the evening dinner crowd.

"Have you seen Xandru?"

She looked up from the golden napkins she was folding into pretty Christmas stars. "He was on the phone when he left Tall, Dark, and Handsome in the lobby, and then he hightailed it out of here."

"Huh." Frowning, I watched her go back to work.

She paused again. "Don't think for one minute I'm enjoying folding fabric into cutesy shapes. This shows how much I love my job and what I would do for you."

"Don't worry. Your reputation is safe with me."

She smirked before her hands started flying again.

"And Sindi?" She looked up at me again. "Thank you for everything."

Now she offered a real smile. "No worries. But if you want to do something for me, you can introduce me to Tall, Dark, and Handsome."

"Since when did you need to be introduced to a guy? Oh, and *absolutely not!* Anyone but Roman, Sindi."

She made a face, then smiled again. "Okay, fine. Adrian it is, then."

I groaned. "Out of all the men in this town, those are your two picks?"

"Oh, I still have my eyes open, but only because you insist on no Rocas."

"Well, any Roca is better than Roman Bishop."

"I might have to test that theory," she teased. She stopped folding again and pulled the collar away from her neck, displaying a new tattoo, another Celtic design, with an edge. "My early Christmas gift to myself. What do you think?"

"I like it. Honoring your Irish heritage even more. Did you talk Addie into doing it?"

She pouted. "No. But I decided to give that Gwen girl at Tragic Ink a try. She does great work, but she's an odd duck, isn't she?"

I snickered. "She's all right, though. Just not a people person."

"I can't blame her, if all her customers are like the bitch who was leaving when I turned into the alley, ranting and raving . . . I thought Gwen was going to close up shop and cancel my appointment."

"Who was it?" I asked, curiosity piqued. Sindi described the brunette woman who looked like she came out of old-time Hollywood. "Must have been Ada Daryn. Huh. I wonder what kind of tattoo Ada would be getting and where." I shuddered at the thought—the rumor that she practiced black magic wasn't the only nasty one floating around about the old witch. "Never mind. I don't want to know."

Sindi shrugged. "All I can say is if that hag treated me the way she was treating the guy with her, she would have been my dinner. Except . . . she probably tastes like a used jockstrap."

"Ew! And yes, probably." Wrinkling my nose and giggling at the same time, I turned and headed back to the front of the lobby so she could get back to work and I could call Xandru.

"Sorry, babe, had to find Tase ASAP," he answered.

"Oh, everything okay?"

Silence.

"Xandru?"

"Uh, yeah, of course. Just wanted to get to Tase before Kasun did. Talk later?"

"Yeah, sure. Love you."

"Love you, too, babe."

CHAPTER 16

XANDRU

"*Y*ou'd better be up here," I muttered as I ended the call with Michaela and continued the hike up Mt. Sousa behind our family home, the sun setting behind me.

I'd already checked the ski resort and the Dirty Knuckle, but nobody had seen Tase for hours. I drove by his place before coming to the family home, but he was at neither. I even checked the workshop. I hadn't been able to reach him by phone, which wasn't unusual considering our unreliable service, but Michaela's call came through, which told me Tase was likely ignoring me.

I'd caught his scent behind the workshop and followed it up the rocky climb toward an old hunting shack Dad had built back before he had money, as a place of escape from the town's bullshit. Or Mom's temper, depending on the day. The scent grew stronger as I approached the one-room, dilapidated log cabin that was no bigger than our smallest bedroom at home.

"This must be important for you to track me here," Tase said from the doorway, and I stopped about twenty-five yards away. "I already know Kasun's looking for me." He shrugged. "I have an alibi, remember?"

"So why are you hiding?"

"I'm not. You know me, though. I'd like to approach him on my terms, not vice versa."

I peered at him through the descending darkness. An owl hooted from the bare branches above, and another answered in the distance.

"You're making yourself look guilty."

He smirked. "All the more reason—so when my alibi vouches for me, I can watch Conall's smug grin fall right off his face."

"You're willing to put her through that?"

"Well, that's the other thing. Shelly's not in town right now, and knowing the Kasuns, they'll arrest me just because they can."

I rocked back on my heels. "So this isn't about delaying the fact that Addie's going to find out?"

He scowled. "I don't care what she thinks."

"Yeah, right," I muttered. "I actually needed to find you to discuss that pocket watch."

Narrowing his eyes, Tase's gaze scanned the area. Then he motioned for me to come inside.

As I closed the distance between us, my mouth suddenly grew dry from the hike, and I pulled my flask of blood out of my coat pocket. I drained it before I even hit the door, but it did nothing to quench my thirst.

Inside the shack, an old oil lantern sat on a small table, barely illuminating the threadbare recliner and a bookshelf filled with an eclectic collection of "how to get rich quick" books and extremely old, leather-bound tomes, as well as a scattering of metal doodads. Little figurines and gadgets Dad had made out of boredom with scraps lying around—among them, a stag with shavings forming its antlers, a solitaire game made with a piece of two-by-four and nails, and a small metal skull, with one enclosed eye socket and one open, vacant one. I didn't remember seeing that last one before. Tase must have made it. I didn't care enough to ask, distracted by the empty blood bottles and bags that were littered everywhere.

I looked at Tase with brow raised, but instead of interrogating him, I simply asked, "Do you have any more blood?"

Maybe it was the scent from the bags that had obviously been stolen from the medical center, but a strong desire for human blood slammed through me. My stomach began to ache with the need.

"All out," Tase said. "Sorry, brother. Now what about the timepiece?"

"What did you do with it?" We hadn't been able to talk about it since he'd found it—he'd conveniently been too busy.

He shifted his weight, studying me.

"Tase?" I tried to make his name sound like a warning, but the hunger distracted me too much, so it came out as a question instead.

"I'm meeting the buyer tomorrow."

"So you're selling it, without us talking about it?"

"I *have* to. I'm committed. I've already told you what this means. Why the sudden interest?"

"Because Roman Bishop had a few things to say about it today while we stood in the inn's conservatory, mostly wondering if it'd been found." I folded my arms over my chest. "It felt like he was fishing for info, but since you're partners with his brother, I figured he wouldn't be so curious if he knew where it was."

"He doesn't. This trade has nothing to do with the Bishops, not Ronan and definitely not Roman."

"I thought the artifact market was your and Ronan's thing. It is an artifact, isn't it?"

"It is, but this is a separate deal."

I licked my lips, which felt like sandpaper. Or my tongue did. I wasn't sure which was worse. Fuck, I needed a drink.

"So you're going behind the Bishops' backs? What the hell? Who *are* you dealing with?"

He smirked. "It's not really going behind their backs. They know nothing about it."

"Obviously, that's not true."

"They know the artifact exists. But they know nothing about the deal I have with this buyer. It's Magda . . ." He blew out a harsh breath before he continued. "The witch who paid me to turn Michaela."

The already tight space felt like it was closing in on us. Between the bloodlust and my rage at Tase's simple statement, the shack suddenly became too small for me, let alone both of us.

"You're still in contact with her?" I roared.

"I was trying to reel her in. Trying to be the hero. At first."

"At *first*?"

"Then that shit went down with the girl in Montrose."

I cocked my head. "That was her? The witch who wanted Michaela turned set you up to kill?"

"She was sending me a message with the girl. That she knew about the curse. And if I cooperated, she'd take care of me. If I didn't cooperate, she'd ensure the curse took over fast."

"How did she know?"

He lifted his hands. "Got me. But she does."

"So what else does she want from you? Haven't you done enough?"

"The timepiece," he said as though it were obvious. "It's called the Eye of Valerian. It's a moroi-specific artifact. With powers."

Shit. Michaela hadn't told me that. Did she know? I should have never let Tase be the one to dig it up.

"That's why she wanted to take the Petrans down," he continued. "So she could buy out their property and find it."

"And that's the real reason you covered the costs of the renovations."

He nodded. "It allowed me access."

"I should have known it wasn't out of the goodness of your heart." I'd already figured this out, but shook my head in renewed disgust.

"Hey. It was a win-win situation. Michaela got everything she needed out of it, and her business is booming now."

"So why does this witch want this Eye? You said it's a moroi artifact, right? What can a witch do with it?"

"I've told you, this isn't the kind of work where you ask questions. But it must be more than that, especially if Roman was asking about it. It's . . . it's powerful, Xandru."

"So it's talking evil to you, too? That's just great," I scoffed.

179

He shook his head. "Nah, not like that. I don't know what the kid was flipping out about. You can just *feel* it has power, but nothing like good or bad. It's not like I walk around with it in my pocket, though."

I huffed out a breath, and that only made my mouth drier. "So where is it now? You're not actually going to sell it to her, are you?"

"It's hidden. But I have to."

"What the hell? No! Not to her."

"I. Have. To," he growled.

"Why?" I demanded, leaning into his face. "Surely you can find another buyer."

"Because I value my kid's life," he spat. "And yours and our brothers' and sisters' lives." He peered at me for a long pause, and then added, "As well as the Petrans."

"*What?*" I seethed.

He nodded. "She's threatened all of you. I give her the Eye, she spares everyone's lives. If I don't, we're all dead."

"Who the fuck is she to threaten us?"

"She's a witch! And not afraid to use black magic. She can take us all down at once from fifty miles away."

"Son of a bitch." I scrubbed my hand through my hair. "You're meeting her tomorrow?"

"In Montrose."

"Are you serious? Were you going to tell me?"

He squinted. "Why would I?"

"Because you can't leave town unescorted, remember, dipshit?"

"Adrian's taking me. He needs to make a supply run anyway. And you need to stay here so nobody suspects me being gone."

I stared at him with disbelief. He'd made all these plans without consulting me, even after our agreement on Thanksgiving. "You'll set off the wards. The Court said I must go with you."

"Adrian can handle it. And the Abbadons have the wards handled. Setting off a distraction from me."

"For shit's sake," I muttered with a sigh. "Now you're tied up with demons, too?"

"Oh, please. Now *you're* being the dipshit. You know Dad's been doing business with the demons for decades. They owed me a favor."

I rubbed at my burning throat. "Damn it, Tase, I don't like the sound of this. And now Roman's breathing down Michaela's back about Gabe and that fucking artifact. I swear, if anything happens to her or her family because of you—"

"I know, I know. You'll end me yourself. You've already told me that."

"I'm serious. Don't fuck them up any more than you already have."

"As of tomorrow, the artifact will be far away, and nobody will ever have to know what happened to it. That bitch witch will be gone, and everyone will be safe and sound. I'll make sure the Rocas *and* the Petrans are set up comfortably. It'll all be good, brother. I promise." He jabbed a finger at my chest. "As long as you can keep your fucking mouth shut about it."

My eyes kept darting toward one of the empty blood bags, the bloodlust desperate for even a lingering taste. "I have to get out of here. I need a drink."

I burst out of the shack and blurred down the mountain toward the lights of home and a fridge full of bottled blood. It wasn't human, but a six-pack or so of bear blood, and a couple hits off a joint, should take the edge off enough to push through the ache. By the time I opened the back door, though, the desire had already faded almost completely.

"That was fucking weird," I muttered as I headed to the fridge, just in case the urge returned. I hadn't a need for human blood like that in ages. Not since we'd been at the hospital after the wreck, and before then, it had been over a year. I'd mastered that part of me a long time ago.

Tase and Adrian returned the next night without the Court knowing he had left, and he assured me it was all taken care of.

And then he began to avoid me.

I saw him a couple of times, including once when I picked up Gabe from the Academy and he was talking to Rowan Bishop. But every time I approached him, he managed to disappear from my sight before I reached him. Then he seemed to vanish altogether, not going to work or taking care of business, leaving it all for me to do. Again.

He avoided Adrian and Andrei, too, so we sent Alina after him. He always had a soft spot for his baby sisters, and she was at least able to get close to him. But then she disappeared, as well, sending a single text saying she was okay but staying with Tase. She refused to say where they were.

The only time I was able to see Michaela during this time was at the special town holiday events and once for drinks with everyone else. Except Tase, of course. I felt a wedge driving between us once again and knew I had to do something big to ensure she knew my inability to spend time with her was not by choice. That if I had my way, we'd spend every day of forever together.

CHAPTER 17

MICHAELA

*X*andru and I never got to talk. Not really. Not about Gabe and the edibles. Not about the artifact. And not about Tase. We were too busy for more than a shared drink and a kiss hello and goodbye for the next couple of weeks. I became all wrapped up in the Homes for the Holidays light tour charity event and the Hot Cocoa & Cookie Crawl, both of which the inn was involved in; dress shopping with Aurelia for the Yuletide Ball, then arguing with her about why she no longer wanted to go; an influx of skiers and other vacationers keeping the inn nearly full; the investigation of Heidi's disappearance, which was quickly becoming a cold case; and, of course, gift shopping and wrapping.

On top of it all, Gabe's being "a little tired" turned into utter exhaustion, and I had to keep him home from school for the last two days before break. Which wasn't good, because vampires didn't get sick, not even mortal ones like us. Because he was more energetic at night, we thought his vampire nocturnal instincts were overpowering the magic of his tattoo, giving him daylight sickness. So Addie came over and redid his marking on the day before Christmas Eve.

As for Tase, Xandru couldn't tell me what was going on, but he was constantly running around, once again taking care of Tase's businesses, including the busy ski resort. He still had the metal works company to manage, as well, which was busy with custom gift orders. When I pressed him to let me in, he'd only say that Tase was being Tase, and he was trying to figure it out himself.

Thinking that Gabe might have been more comfortable in his own bed, Aurelia and I discussed staying in the family home, moving Christmas there and everything. But then we started talking about the holidays when we were younger and she told me about last Christmas, their first without Mom or Dad. We decided we'd follow Mammie's lead and start new traditions at the inn, which would also allow our aunt to be a part of the festivities.

Supporting our suspicions that his tattoo needed to be redone, Gabe rallied the next day, on Christmas Eve, just in time to join us on the slopes in the afternoon, one of our new traditions. Aurelia wasn't sure she could be bothered at first, but we talked her into it, and once she saw me on skis, she was glad she came. She and Gabe both enjoyed making fun of this one-time ski bunny returning to the slopes for the first time in five years. At least they were nice to Sindi, who was popping her snow-skiing cherry.

"You make fun of me and not this one?" I asked, as we helped Sindi back up on her feet after her eighth face-plant in a single run. So much for gothic vampires being good at everything and more graceful than the Russian ballet.

"I don't remember Sindi strutting around for the last month bragging about how she couldn't wait to hit the slopes and show everyone how it's done," Aurelia said pointedly.

"Yeah, she's new," Gabe said. "Give her a break."

"Okay, fine." I looked at Sindi as I dropped my hands to my hips. "But if you're still like this next year, we're totally mocking you."

"Totally," Aurelia and Gabe agreed.

"Who says I'll ever be doing this again?" the Southerner muttered as she cleaned off her goggles.

"Maybe because Adrian sometimes works the lifts?" I suggested.

Sindi shrugged. "Eh. I'd rather be in the control room keeping him warm anyway."

"Ugh!" Aurelia and Gabe groaned.

After several hours skiing and snowboarding, which turned out to be Sindi's forte, we gathered by the fire in the inn's media room, Aurelia with her hot cocoa and Gabe, Sindi, and me with warm blood. A few hotel guests joined us as we watched Mom's favorite Christmas movies. Mammie didn't make herself seen, but I could sense her watching from the shadows.

Since the Rocas never celebrated the holidays, Xandru gave all ski resort duties to Adrian and finally claimed a day off so he could spend Christmas Day with us. It was a lazy, laid-back day. The inn had only begun to start making money again, but we still had a lot of catching up to do on personal bills. So there weren't many presents to open. We simply enjoyed each other's company instead. By early evening, the kids grew bored and went outside for a snowball fight while Xandru and I stayed in by one of the fifteen Christmas trees in the inn (not counting those in the cottages).

"Good day, yeah?" Xandru asked as we watched the flames dance in the hearth. I sat sideways on the sofa, my head leaned against his shoulder and my legs draped across his lap.

"The best. For you?"

"Any day with you is a good one."

I snorted. "Cheeseball."

"Okay, any day away from my fucked-up family is a good one. Is that better?"

I fingered the button on his gray Henley. "Are you ever going to tell me what's going on?"

"Yes. But not today. This is a good day. Let's not ruin it with my family drama."

"Fine." Not wanting to fight about it, I sighed as I moved my hand from his shirt to his scruffy jaw, loving the abrasiveness of it against my palm. "I know Christmas isn't a big deal to you, but thanks for making it one for me."

He rubbed circles with his thumb over my thigh. "You really

went all out this year, with the inn and everything. I figured it was important to you."

"Mom loved the holidays, so a lot of it was for her." I laughed at a memory. "It wasn't just about us kids, though. She didn't fool me. Year after year, I came home from school and caught her watching cheesy romantic Christmas movies."

"Uh . . . isn't that what you did last night?"

"Only in honor of Mom," I lied. I secretly enjoyed the movies myself. "You probably don't even know what they are, do you?"

"I'm assuming not *National Lampoon's Christmas Vacation*?"

"Uh, no. These are even dorkier, but in a different way. They're all about these single people, one is often a widow or widower with a kid, and/or their business is failing, or they have to prove themselves worthy of the family business . . . Anyway, they pretty much have the same plot and even a lot of the same actors in all of them. And they always have a happily-ever-after ending, either on Christmas Eve or Christmas Day." I sighed. "Mom was such a romantic. She and Mammie both."

"Perfect. Maybe she'll appreciate this then, even if it is me doing it." Xandru removed my legs from his lap and set my feet on the floor, then scooted off the sofa to kneel in front of me. He stuffed one hand in his front pants pocket and cupped my face with the other.

I tilted my head to lean into his hand. "What are you doing?"

"Michaela Petran," he started, his voice thick. He cleared his throat. "Michaela . . . I thought I lost you once, but you returned. I can never lose you again. You are mine, and I am yours."

Oh. My. God. Was Xandru proposing?

A sound came from the distance, and somewhere in the back of my mind, a small voice told me to pay attention to it, but the rest of me was entirely locked on to the man in front of me. We'd talked about marriage for years when we were younger, but hadn't really discussed it at all since I'd been back. After we made our big turning point back in August, I admittedly thought he would have asked by now. And here he was, on his knees, extracting something from his pocket.

He held out a small velvet box in his hand. "I want to make this official and final. Michaela—"

A scream cut him off, followed by Mammie soaring into the room. "Michaela, it's Gabe! It's bad!"

Xandru and I jumped to our feet and rushed to the rear lawn of the inn, forgetting to hide our speed from guests' eyes. Aurelia and Gabe were both on the ground in the snow, Aurelia sitting and crying, blood leaking from a small cut above her eyebrow, and Gabe on his back, convulsing. I fell to my knees by his side and tried to hold him so he wouldn't hurt himself. His fangs were out, red veins webbed across his face, and his eyes were rolled back, so only the whites showed.

"What happened?" I demanded as Xandru held a small snow-pack to Aurelia's wound.

"I fell and hit my head on a planter under the snow. I was trying to get inside, but Gabe . . ." She trailed off.

"Gabe what?"

Aurelia shuddered. "It was like we were back in the car when we wrecked. He attacked me. I think . . . I think he wanted my blood."

Xandru and I exchanged a look as Gabe's body stopped seizing beneath me.

"Take her inside," I said to Xandru. "Aurelia, stay in one of the vacant rooms. Let Mammie know."

I picked Gabe up and carried him to the cottage. He stirred some, but remained unconscious as I lay him on the bed and removed his coat and boots. Once I tucked him under the covers, I hurried to the kitchen and grabbed a couple of bottles of blood. He was only semi-conscious when I returned, but at least able to drink. After finishing one bottle, he passed out.

I paced his room all night long, waiting for him to wake, but it wasn't until the following afternoon that he finally did. Sort of. He was incoherent, thrashing about and growling, and his fangs protruding as the veins popped again. I fed him more blood, he passed out again, and we repeated this a few times throughout the following day. His coloring grew porcelain white, except for the dark purple circles around his eyes. His skin stretched taut over the edges of his cheekbones and jaw, making it appear as though his eyeballs were sinking into his head. Neither blood nor regular food helped.

I called Dr. Jasper Underwood, a fae with supernatural healing abilities, and he made a house call, but couldn't figure out what was wrong. There was a young shifter in a coma at the hospital, one of the Blaekthorns, but Dr. Underwood was certain the cases were unrelated. Completely different energies, he'd said.

None of the other special healers in town could figure out Gabe's illness, either. For three days, supes of all kinds traipsed into my cottage, trying to solve the mystery. Saundra Beaumont didn't understand it, not able to identify any form of witch magic. Eloise confirmed a dark energy, but it blocked her from reading anything more. They all believed it was magic of a dark sort, although none used the word "curse."

Still, I recalled Addie's claims about Roman Bishop.

"What did you do to my brother?" I asked him after his housekeeper finally let me in and led me to the front room of his estate in Havenwood Heights. On the outside, it had a similar gothic castle look to ours. I'd never been inside before, but I barely paid any attention to the interior except to note it was designed with elegance and luxury—I was solely interested in the man's answers.

Roman lifted a highball glass toward me. "Drink?"

"What. Did. You. *Do?*" I ground out.

I hadn't wanted to confront him alone, but I needed Sindi to stay at the inn, and I couldn't get a hold of Addie or Xandru. Addie once said that one of the few things that could take a witch down was a pissed-off vampire. So on the way over, I reminded myself that I was a badass vampire and mustered all of my anger into a hot ball of rage burning within me. If things went sideways, I'd have to move faster than Roman could shoot off a spell, and break his neck. If he truly was behind my brother's illness, I'd have no problem doing it.

Roman lowered the glass in his hand. "You do know, Ms.

Petran, that it is quite rude to come barging into a person's home, especially at such an hour, and immediately start making accusations?"

"I'm all out of patience as well as fucks. Something is wrong with Gabe. I think he's dying. And I'm pretty sure you have something to do with it."

"He may be."

"Tell me what the hell you did! *Why?*"

Roman took a slow sip of his drink, watching me over the rim of his glass, before he spoke to me as though I were an ignorant child. "Did you ever find the Eye of Valerian?"

I tilted my head. "Is that what you want? Is that why you're doing this?"

His dark eyes narrowed. "I'd be careful if I were you, throwing accusations around. Especially when they are directed at someone like me. Regardless of who your family is." He lifted his index finger from his glass and pointed at me. "Find the Eye of Valerian and your problem is solved. You do know one of its powers, don't you? That it creates bloodlust in an untriggered moroi? That it provokes a mature moroi to kill and become strigoi?"

"What? Wouldn't that be dark magic?"

A sigh of boredom escaped him. "I didn't expect you to be so ignorant. What do you think drove Gabe to attack you and trigger his own gene?"

"No." I shook my head in disbelief. "He said he didn't find it."

"By the state of his current condition, I'd say that he lied to you, Ms. Petran. Find the artifact," he snarled. "And return it to its cage."

"Cage? What cage?" I asked, bewildered. I didn't care that he was losing patience with me. I needed answers. I needed to save my brother.

"A piece like that needs protection. Now I'm done answering your questions." He flicked his hand, and the doors banged open.

"Wait. If I find it, if I bring it to you, will it fix Gabe?"

He rolled his eyes. "The cause of a curse is often also the cure."

"So that's a yes. Can't you do some kind of locator spell?"

"It's been done. Goodbye, Ms. Petran." He ushered me toward the door.

"But why don't you just go get it?" I persisted as we moved.

"It is not me who is interested in obtaining it."

Like I believed that. But whatever. If it could cure Gabe, I needed to find it. "Then at least tell me where it is."

He stopped at the door, one side of his mouth curling up in a smirk. "Why don't you ask your boyfriend?"

CHAPTER 18

XANDRU

*W*hen Tase and Alina finally walked through the front door of our family home three days before New Year's, I took one look at them and flew at my brother, my fist pulled back. He was faster, though.

And much stronger.

Tase's fist slammed into my stomach, making me double over and soar backwards into the railing surrounding the sunken living room. He'd gained more strength, which wasn't a good sign of what he'd been up to for the past few weeks since I'd last seen him. But that wasn't what pissed me off the most. I straightened, one arm across my stomach, the other jabbing a finger at him.

"We agreed, you fucker!" I spat. "We weren't going to turn Alina until we knew the curse couldn't affect her."

He shrugged and rolled his eyes. "We were running out of time."

"We had nearly a year!"

Alina stepped between us and glared at me with gray-green eyes —eyes that had been brown the last time I'd seen her. "It wasn't his fault."

"Alina," Tase warned.

"What?" She threw her hands in the air. "I'm sick of him blaming you for everything."

"So who did it?" I demanded.

"I did. I was tired of waiting on your controlling ass, so I cut him while he was sleeping and drank his blood." She lifted her chin, but a flicker of fear in her eyes and a faint scent coming off her skin told me she was lying.

It took me nearly a full minute to realize the truth.

"God damn it, TASE!" I roared. "You didn't fucking sell it, did you?"

I lunged at him again. My resolve to beat the living shit out of him made me more of a competitor. We threw punches, ducking some and taking others, until I dove at Tase's legs and took both of us down, where we grappled on the floor. At some point, we rolled down the stairs to the basement, fists still flying.

"Settle the fuck down and let me explain," Tase said, once he was able to pin me in a chokehold.

I stilled, and he let go. We both jumped to our feet, facing each other.

"How many?" I demanded.

"How many what?"

"How many humans have you killed?"

He growled. "None."

"You did not gain that much strength on animal blood."

"I didn't say I didn't *drink* human blood. But I didn't kill any. Thanks to Alina. It's probably a good thing she did turn."

"You have no idea how wrong you are." I swiped at one of Mom's old ugly vases, sending it flying and crashing into the wall. "You still have the fucking Eye of Valerian, don't you?"

Tase didn't answer, only peered at me as though deciding what lie to tell me.

"Don't fucking lie. I know you still have it, because it did to Alina the same thing it did to Gabe. Am I right?"

Tase lifted his chin and smirked. "As a matter of fact, no, brother, you're not. That was entirely her doing."

"Truth," Alina called down the stairs. "All my doing. We had our own little ceremony without you losers."

I glared at Tase. "So you weren't asleep? You really did turn her?"

He shrugged. "A little lie."

"God damn it." I dropped my hands on my hips, shaking my head at the floor. I looked back up at him. "So *did* you sell the artifact?"

He grimaced. "Well . . ."

"Shit! What else have you lied to me about or gone behind my back and done?"

"Do you really want to know?" He smirked again. "It's powerful as fuck, Xan. More than I realized."

I clenched my fists, suppressing the urge to swing again. "Exactly why you were supposed to get rid of it!"

"No. It belongs with us. With the moroi. Xandru, it can break my curse."

I rocked back and glared at him. "How do you know?"

He shrugged. "I feel it."

"You *feel* it? You're risking everyone's lives based on that?"

"It's the artifact of our people, bro. I asked the current Order of Castor to research it. It goes back to the original moroi and contains the very magic that created our kind. You've been around Addie and other witches enough to know what that means."

I rubbed my clenched jaw. "It means it can both cause and counter what harms us."

"Exactly. And since strigoi is part of being moroi, it can counter the strigoi curse."

"How?"

He tilted his head from side to side as he made a face. "I haven't figured that part out yet."

Closing my eyes, I shook my head in disbelief. "Have you asked Addie for help?"

"Hell no! Nobody can know I have it, especially anyone tied to the Court."

"And what about the witch you were supposed to sell it to? What about everyone's lives you were so worried about?"

He waved his hand with indifference . . . arrogance even. "I'll take care of her."

"Tase."

"Its power is only meant for us! Not for her, and especially not for the Court. They'll want to use it against us. All of us. Including your precious Petrans."

"Hey, guys," Alina called down, "speaking of the actual devil . . . Michaela's coming up the front walk."

"Fuck," Tase and I muttered at the same time.

"She can't know," he said. "At least let me figure out how it can help me first. Give me that. If not for me, for my son."

"Damn it, Tase." I groaned, not knowing what pissed me off more—that he'd already used his son as leverage with me or that he was putting me in this position. "You want me to lie based on a fucking *feeling*!"

"It makes sense, though, right? You know it does."

The doorbell rang, followed by angry pounding.

"Get rid of her," Tase told Alina, and I didn't argue.

Alina smirked. "Gladly."

Knowing she was being lied to, Michaela wouldn't go easily. I heard her reaction to seeing Alina, followed by arguing, and then a scuffle.

"Stay here," I ordered Tase before I flew up the stairs. One family fight was enough for one hour.

Michaela saw me and jabbed a finger at Alina. "You fucking liar." She turned fiery eyes on me. "And *you*. What haven't you been telling me?"

Michaela advanced on me, so I wrapped her hand in mine and took her up to my room so we could have some semblance of privacy. I closed the door behind us, and we turned to face each other.

"What's going on?" I kept my voice low enough so only her vampire ears could hear, reaching for a stray lock of hair hanging in her face.

She swatted my hand away before crossing her arms. She was pissed. Off.

"Where's the Eye of Valerian?" she seethed.

Oh, shit. I swallowed. "No idea what you're talking about," I said after hesitating a second too long.

She shoved her hands against my chest, making me stumble back into the door. "Don't fucking lie to me, Roca! Roman did a locator spell and says you do know."

Ah, fuck.

I held my hands up in surrender. "I really don't. But Tase does."

Her expression changed to one of shock, and she gasped as though I'd just hit her. The way she looked at me broke me—betrayal, anger . . . pain. Pain I caused. Based on her reaction, she must have believed Roman was the liar. She'd put all of her hope and faith into me.

And I'd just let her down.

"Come sit and let me explain." Taking her hand, I led her to the bed. She did as I said, probably still in shock. I gently sat her down and told her the little bit I could.

Her face crumpled and then morphed. The previous look of betrayal was nothing compared to how she looked at me now.

"Gabe did find it?"

I nodded. "He handed it over to Tase, though."

"And this has been going on for . . . for *months*?" she asked.

"Before Gabe turned. It's what set him off in the first place." I'd already told her this, but it didn't seem to be sinking in.

"You knew about this all this time and didn't tell me?"

"No, not really. What I did know—they weren't my secrets to tell, Kales. I was just talking to Tase—"

Her eyes narrowed. "Just now? You mean when you didn't want to see me?"

I cringed.

She jumped off the bed, shouting, "You had Alina try to send me away, because you still weren't going to tell me, were you?"

"Michaela—"

"Were you?" she shrieked. "Were you ever going to tell me everything? *Anything?*"

"When I could . . . what I was able to—"

"Fuck you, Alexandru Roca. FUCK. YOU!" she yelled.

I reached out for her, but she pushed me away again. In a blink, she was at the bedroom door.

"This is over," she said flatly, her back to me. "You and me—we're done."

"Kales?" I didn't know what else to say. Now I was the one in shock.

She shook her head slowly as she scoffed. "And to think I thought you were proposing the other day and I was going to accept!"

My heart stuttered and dropped at her words. "Kales, please, just let me—"

She twisted around. "No! I've *let* you do enough. You say we're all family, but those are just words. When it comes down to it, you will *always* pick your own blood. Even if it means lying to me and keeping secrets. I can't live like that. Especially this time, Roca, because all of your fucked-up choices are going to kill *my* brother."

She threw the door open and stomped out into the hall and toward the stairs.

I hurried after her. "What do you mean?"

She spun on me. "That *thing* . . . that Eye of Valerian . . . as long as it's out of its cage or unprotected or whatever, Gabe will only worsen. But as always, in your fucking world, Tase comes first."

She flew down the stairs.

"It's not like that." I rushed after her. "There's stuff you don't know."

She paused at the bottom of the steps, but didn't turn around. "Are you going to enlighten me?"

I sighed. "I . . . can't."

She barked out a humorless chuckle and resumed her march for the front door.

"Hold on," I practically begged, and I didn't even care. I couldn't lose her. "Tase *can*. He's right downstairs. Let me get him."

Stopping, she turned and folded her arms over her chest again, tapping her foot. I started for the basement stairs, but Alina stopped me with a laugh.

"Did you really think he'd stick around?" she asked. "Tase took off the moment you turned your back on him, knowing you'd blab off to the bitch."

"I'll deal with you later," I growled, before I jumped down the stairs to inspect the basement for myself.

Alina was right. Tase was long gone. *Shit.*

"Of course he took off," Michaela huffed. "When the hell would Tase do anything for anyone but himself?"

"I'll find him, Michaela," I vowed. "I'll find him and get the artifact. I promise."

"Like I can believe your promises," she sneered. "I can't ever trust anything you say again, Xandru. But I promise you this: If my brother dies, you can bet the Court will know *everything*."

Tase could have punched me a million times in the same spot, and it still wouldn't compare to the pain in my chest as I watched Michaela stroll out of my house . . . and possibly my life.

I slammed the door and punched the wall before turning on Alina. "Where is he?"

She shrugged. "Hell if I know."

"Alina," I growled. "Where were you two hiding the past few weeks?"

"Like I'd tell you."

"Why *wouldn't* you? A boy's life could be at stake!"

My sister rolled her eyes. "She's being a drama queen, I'm sure."

I stalked toward her, and she backed away. "Tell. Me. Where. To. Find. Tase. NOW!"

She flinched, but then leaned forward and yelled back at me. "Why the hell do you care so much about them? Michaela's wrong! You're always putting *them* before *us*! Do you care at all about your own family?"

"I care about us all!"

"And that's your fucking problem! You've spread your loyalty so thin, you have none. Well, the rest of us don't give a shit about Gabe or any of the Petrans. We just want to protect our own, and that will *never* include any of them."

Rage boiled in my stomach, and it was all I could do to resist throttling my little sister. Her arrogance and lack of compassion, especially for the Petrans, had been taught, though. I reined in my anger and took a different angle.

"Fine," I said, my voice low, deliberate. "Then think of it this way. You heard Michaela. If this isn't fixed with Gabe, she goes to the Court with everything. What do you think will happen to Tase then? And to everyone who protects him?"

Alina snorted. "That bitch doesn't know shit. She has nothing to tell them."

One side of my mouth lifted in a smirk. "Don't underestimate Michaela Petran. Especially when it comes to family."

CHAPTER 19

MICHAELA

*E*verything hurt. My heart was shattered, my chest an open, aching wound. Tears I refused to shed stung my eyes. My throat burned from damming up the sobs, my head pounding with a million whirring thoughts. A vampire shouldn't hurt this damn much. But apparently our hearts and souls didn't heal as quickly as our bodies.

Trying not to think about Xandru's betrayal, I sat in vigil next to Gabe's bed every spare moment, pleading for him to wake or to show at least some signs of improvement. But if Roman had spoken the truth, Gabe wouldn't improve until we found the Eye of Valerian and returned it to its so-called cage. Whatever that was.

Tase, the only one who knew the Eye's whereabouts, had conveniently disappeared. Addie wasn't able to reach him. According to her, Xandru hadn't been able to find his brother at any of his usual places, either. At least, that was his story. He evidently had no problem lying and keeping secrets, so for all I knew, he was still protecting Tase.

As for the cage, we had no idea where it could be. Nobody even knew what it was or what it looked like. Roman denied knowing anything more about it, even when Saundra confronted him.

In the meantime, I researched everything I could to try to learn more about the artifact. Addie brought me books, but they lacked information about the Eye, and the top-secret tomes, which may have been the most helpful, couldn't leave the Court's restricted library. Enchanted, they couldn't even be snuck out. So late at night, Addie came over and slept in the chair by Gabe's side, and I bundled up and trekked through the snow to the back of the City Hall building. I spent two full nights poring over the books in the restricted section.

Not until early morning on New Year's Eve, six days since Gabe fell ill and three days since anyone had seen Tase, did I discover what I was searching for—on a torn piece of paper taped into one of the oldest books. The handwriting on it was my father's, the page one of those ripped from his journal, dated June 1854:

It has been confirmed. The Eye of Valerian possesses dark magic, just like the creator himself. I've witnessed what this kind of power can do. The blood shed. The lives lost. The souls blackened. I would have destroyed the piece by now, but it is indestructible. The power is seductive and a threat to the safe haven we are creating here. The other leaders and I have agreed that its existence cannot be known outside our small circle, but they do not know of its full power. Not even I do. It must be protected and hidden away for safe-keeping before it destroys again. I will do this, and only I will know its whereabouts, and that shall stay with me until the day I die and beyond.

Yeah, right. *Should have done better, Dad.*

I noticed he mentioned nothing about a cage, though, making me wonder if Roman had made that part up.

When I returned to the inn as the sun rose, Mammie was floating by the front parlor's window, the first time I'd seen her since Christmas. Since before Gabe went down.

"Where have you been?" I asked. "I've needed you."

She turned from her gaze out the window with eyes full of sadness. "I'm so sorry, dear. I didn't know how to tell you."

"Tell me what?"

She glanced away, frowning. Her image faded out, then back in again. "I'm having trouble. Being here."

"Here? As in our world?"

She nodded. "I'm trying, but . . . it's taking more energy than before. There's a darkness . . ."

"Is it what's affecting Gabe?"

Her eyes widened. "What's wrong with Gabe?"

She didn't know? "He's been in some kind of coma."

"Oh, no. Oh, dear." The news hit her hard, and her image disappeared.

"Mammie?" I called after a minute or two had passed.

"I'm . . . I'm here." Her voice came from a distance before she slowly reappeared. "I don't know . . . for how long . . . I can hold it."

Then I was running out of time. "What do you know about the Eye of Valerian?"

If a ghost could visibly pale, she just did. She clasped her hands together and held them under her chin as she shook her head. "Oh, dear, you do not . . . you do not want to discuss that."

"I need to know everything I can, Mammie. It's doing this to Gabe." I gestured in the general direction of the cottage. "Maybe to you."

"But . . . that's impossible. Your father—"

"Buried it under the conservatory to hide it. Gabe found it."

She gasped, then faded in and out again. "You are sure? But even so . . . it was . . . protected."

"How?"

She shook her head. "I don't . . . know. Only your . . . father does."

Of course. And my father was dead and inaccessible, even by Eloise Sinclair. Even after what happened last time, she'd tried again, before visiting Gabe, but to no avail.

"Roman Bishop called it a cage," I said, "like it's a physical object. But if that's true, apparently the Eye was removed from it. We don't know how. We just know that Tase has the Eye, or at least knows where it is."

Mammie's eyes widened with unmistakable fear, and rather than fading, she became more like a strobe light, flashing in and out. "Oh, no! That . . . no good. No good! Michaela . . . must . . . find . . . Protect . . . again! Oh no, oh no, oh no."

She drifted back and forth, blinking in and out, panic filling her voice.

"Tell me what you know," I begged, desperate at the thought I was going to lose her. "Why's it so dangerous?"

"I . . . not know . . ." She blinked out, then in again. "Only Mihail . . ." Out and in. "He'd . . . never tell . . . protected me . . ."

"I need to know what it's doing to Gabe!"

"My boy," she cried out. "My boy . . . my boy . . ."

Her voice faded away, her image diminishing into nothing.

"Mammie?" I turned in a circle, searching. "Madame Luiza? Please! Come back. I need you!"

But she didn't. Maybe she couldn't.

I rushed through the inn, looking for her by all of her favorite windows, all the while wondering what boy she'd been crying for. Gabe, who was almost like a son to her? Or her actual son, who died two hundred years ago?

"Damn it, Mammie," I cursed, and then I apologized. "I'm sorry! I'm so sorry. Please, come back."

More guilt and sadness swamped me, piling on to the load I already carried. What if she'd never be able to return? I didn't know what I'd do without her. But throughout the day, as I distracted myself with work, Mammie never reappeared.

Once Sindi woke for the night, she relieved me of my inn duties so I could go back to Gabe while she managed the New Year's Eve party I had no interest in being a part of.

"If you see Mammie, please tell her I'm sorry."

She squeezed my shoulder in a very un-Sindi-like gesture. "I'm sure she's fine. Are you going to be, though? You don't even want a glass of bubbly at midnight?"

I frowned. "I'm not in a bubbly frame of mind."

"How about some Jack or José?"

Despite everything, a soft chuckle escaped me. "I wish. But I need to be in my right mind. Just in case something happens."

Because eventually, *something* had to happen. Whether it was Tase or Gabe, someone would eventually give. I could only hope it was Tase.

Putting all of my hope into Tase Roca was stupidity at its finest.

But the alternative was unacceptable.

The closer we came to midnight, the more my mind drifted toward territory I'd been avoiding for days. The partiers at the inn grew louder, and I couldn't help but wonder what Xandru was doing. The revelers started the countdown, fireworks boomed overhead, music played, and people sang and cheered.

I sandwiched Gabe's hand between mine and leaned my forehead against the edge of the bed, tears rolling down my cheeks and plopping onto the carpet below.

I shouldn't have been sitting here with my unconscious brother, trying by sheer will to keep him alive. This was not how we were supposed to spend New Year's. We all should have been at the party, together. Xandru and I should have been sharing a midnight kiss at this moment, Gabe and Aurelia groaning in the background. Our friends should have surrounded us, champagne glasses raised as we toasted in the new year.

Instead, I no longer knew whom I could trust. Sindi and Addie seemed to make up that entire list now. Not that the list had ever been long, but there at least had been one other name that made up for the lack of numbers. I sobbed, a fresh wave of pain racking through me from Xandru's betrayal.

"Maybe we should leave town," I whispered to Gabe after I'd regained control. "I probably should have taken both of you far away last summer, and none of this would have happened. We can still go, though. I mean . . . what do we have to stay for?"

Fresh tears rose. The life I'd created was a ruse, built on a foundation of secrets and lies. It was not the life I wanted for Aurelia and Gabe. And for the first time, I could somewhat understand why my parents had sent me away. This was exactly what they'd been trying to protect me from—the dangers of living in this town.

The dangers of loving a Roca.

Swiping hard at the tears, I drew in a shuddering breath. "But I need you to fight this, Gabe, before we can do anything. I need you to come back to me. *Please*."

Silence answered my plea.

Hours later, a commotion outside the cottage woke me. I hadn't realized I'd dozed off, hunched over the edge of Gabe's bed. Blinking away the haze, I walked out to the living room, grabbed my coat off the rack as I shoved my feet into boots, and went outside to see what the ruckus was. I found Sindi standing at the bottom of my steps with her back to me, arguing with Addie and Xandru, who stood in front of her.

I sucked in a breath at the sight of him, feeling like I'd been sucker-punched in the gut.

His gaze flew up to me. He looked as broken as I felt. And yet, those eyes—they nailed me in place.

Always the fucking eyes.

Sindi glanced over her shoulder. "Damn it. Now look. We woke her up."

"Kales, we need to talk." Addie moved for the stairs. She was all bundled up in a beanie hat, black down coat, gloves, boots, and a thick scarf wrapped around her neck, as though she'd been out in the cold for a while, or planned to be.

Xandru moved, too, but Sindi stepped in front of him, shaking her head. "I told you. Addie, yes. You, no."

Scowling, he shoved his fists into his coat pockets, his gaze riveted on my face.

"We don't have time for this!" Addie snapped. I couldn't remember the last time I'd seen worry etched so deeply into her face as it was now. And was that fear in her eyes?

"What's going on?" Zipping up my coat, I went out to them, since Sindi was trying to protect me from Xandru, and Addie apparently wouldn't talk without him.

"I was with Harper Sinclair tonight," Addie said, a tremble in her voice so slight, I only detected it because I knew her so well. She glanced at the sky, which was starting to show a hint of lighter blue over the eastern mountains. "Well, earlier this morning, anyway. She scribed a message."

I tilted my head. "Like Eloise does? I thought—"

She cut me off, urgency filling her voice. "She's still learning to use her powers. They're a little different than Eloise's, but that's not important right now. I know what we need to do for Gabe, and we need to do it fast, or our whole town is at risk. But we need Tase."

"No shit," I muttered. "But he disappeared four days ago, remember? And what do you mean, our whole town is at risk?"

"We hoped he'd be here," Xandru said, ignoring my question.

I squinted at them. "Why the hell would he be here?"

"I've been doing locator spells ever since I left Harper," Addie explained, her words pouring out in a rush. "Xandru and I have been trying to hunt him down. If we don't find him and the Eye of Valerian . . . it could be bad. Very bad. Bad like what caused the curse on all of you in the first place."

I gasped. "*What?* As in another massacre? How do you know this?"

"I just do! I'll explain later. Right now, we have to find Tase before it's too late!" She paused, gathering herself. "Every time we get to where he is, he's gone again. He's always one step ahead of us. So we've been blowing up his phone with messages to meet us here." Dropping her gaze, she kicked at the snow. "I just hoped . . . I hoped maybe he'd actually do the right thing."

Tears pricked my eyes again, at both the heartbreak clear in Addie's voice and my own disappointment. A small part of me also hoped if Tase knew what was at stake, he would have stepped up. I'd tried so hard to believe in him.

I thought we'd made big strides at the cemetery, but apparently, he was just that good of a liar. Even when he'd seemed interested in helping Gabe at Thanksgiving, I now knew he'd had an ulterior motive—to corner my brother into handing over the artifact. As much as I'd wanted to believe that he'd done everything for the inn because he felt he owed my family, I'd always suspected there was another reason. I'd been right.

Tase only helped Tase. That's just who he was.

"So what, we try to trap him?" I asked.

"It won't be easy. He has this idea that the Eye of Valerian will end his curse," Xandru said quietly. "It's a moroi artifact. It goes back to the creation of our kind—both the moroi and the strigoi sides."

"And what creates may also end." I exhaled slowly, my breath puffing out in a white cloud. How had we not considered that before? "And that's what you mean about things going badly? Because it'll make him go strigoi faster?"

"Alina, too," Xandru added. "She's been exposed."

"And possibly Gabe," Addie said softly.

"Oh my god." The air whooshed from my lungs. Gasping for a breath, my gaze darted around, as though answers would appear in the snow-covered lawn. "So what do we do? Call the Court?"

"No!" both Xandru and Addie nearly shouted.

"You know what they'll do to him," Xandru said. "Maybe to Alina and Gabe, too."

My chest heaved again, my stomach plummeting to my feet.

"I'll do whatever I have to," Addie vowed, "whatever magic it takes, to get that artifact from him."

"If he gives it up to anyone, it'd better be me," an unfamiliar female voice called out from above.

Addie and Xandru both spun around, and my gaze snapped up to find a woman standing on the peaked roof of the inn's tallest turret—the one above the conservatory. She was tall and thin, dressed in a long black cloak, cinched at the waist, and black boots that reached up under the billowing hem of her cloak. Her face was hidden in the shadows of her hood.

"Question is, will he? He cares only for himself, and you know it," she said.

"Who the fuck are you?" Xandru demanded. "What do you know about my brother?"

She laughed. "He owes me, and I seek what is mine. Since he fails to honor his end of our bargain, I will take what I am owed— one brother for another is a good start."

A swirl of black smoke appeared from nowhere, circling her. When it dissipated, she was gone.

"Did that just happen?" Sindi asked.

"Who the hell was that?" Addie demanded. "She sounded a little familiar."

"I'll look for her." Xandru blurred from sight.

"What did she mean, one brother for another?" I asked. "If she was looking for Tase, do you think she meant Xandru?"

"Or Adrian or Andrei?" Addie asked, but neither of them felt right. Why would she have come to us about either of them?

Addie's gaze locked onto mine, and we both gasped.

"Gabe!" we said in unison.

Spinning, I ran inside, Addie and Sindi on my heels, and burst into Gabe's room. His bed was empty for the first time in a week. It took one second to search the bathroom and kitchen.

My hand flew to my chest, my lungs struggling for air. "How? Where? *Why?*"

Addie immediately started pulling objects out of her coat pockets and laying them out on the coffee table. "I've been doing locator spells all night. I can do another."

Sindi and I rushed back outside while Addie did her witch thing.

"I'll take the inn," Sindi said. "You look out here."

Xandru suddenly appeared, shaking his head. "I checked everywhere. There are no tracks anywhere. No footprints. She literally vanished."

"She . . . she took . . . Gabe," I choked out.

"Or she distracted us while a partner did," Sindi accused, arching a brow at Xandru. "Maybe your brother?"

He grimaced. "That doesn't make any sense. If she's who I think she is, my brother wouldn't have gone near her. He has what she wants." He moved toward me, his arms open as though to embrace me. "Kales, we'll find them. I promise."

I shoved him away. "You already promised you'd find Tase, and you broke that one. Now look! How do you expect me to trust you? Your promises mean *nothing* to me!"

His expression morphed into the same one he wore when I first broke up with him. Pure devastation. Good. He had an idea of how I felt.

Yet . . . my heart still felt a stab of guilt for hurting him.

Stupid heart.

"What do we do?" Sindi asked.

"Found him," Addie called from the doorway.

"Gabe?" I asked at the same time Xandru said, "Tase?"

All guilt for him vanished.

"Gabe," Addie said, throwing a violent look at Xandru.

"We need them both," he murmured. "I'll keep looking for Tase."

"You need to go with us," Addie said. "You're Tase's blood. Maybe . . . maybe it will serve some purpose with this bitch."

"Go where?" I asked.

Addie glanced down at the map in her hand. "The old Thawer Mines."

"Seriously? How?"

During the early years of Havenwood Falls, gold and silver had been discovered in the area, and several mines had contributed greatly to the wealth of the Old Families. Except for one that had become a museum and tourist trap, they were all now defunct, including the Thawer Mines, which happened to be the oldest and hardest to reach.

"I'll make a portal," Addie said. "We'll be there in no time."

"I'll stay here," Sindi offered. "Just in case . . ."

"If Tase shows up—" Xandru began.

"I'll kick his ass into submission," Sindi said. She shrugged at the look he gave her and smirked. "He's not strigoi yet, which makes him still mortal. I'm not. Which means I'm stronger than him."

Addie hurried inside to collect her tools and ingredients, and we followed her in so she could make the portal sheltered from any prying eyes, human or otherwise.

"Does this seem too easy?" I asked her before stepping through the portal.

"Yep. She's practically invited us in, not trying to cloak him at all."

I tried peering through the portal, but it was just a swirling mass of air. "Well, I don't have a choice."

"*We* don't have a choice." Xandru moved next to me, his hand brushing against mine. I fought the urge to curl my pinky around his.

With a deep breath, I stepped into the swirling air. Addie, Xandru, and I left Sindi in my living room and now suddenly stood in the snow, the front of a boarded-up doorway leading into the side of a mountain before us. Using brute strength, Xandru tore off the wooden slats blocking the mine's entrance, but then Addie waved her hand and mumbled something, and the entrance completely cleared. She produced an orb of light that flew up and led our way down the mine's tunnel.

Knowing the tunnels ran for miles down into the mountain, my heart sank. How deep had she taken him? Would we get there in time? Would I ever see my brother again?

Fortunately, we found them in the first widened area we came to, the space lit up with torches, throwing flickering light on the walls. Wooden beams crossed overhead and against some walls, supporting the mountain surrounding us. Railroad rails ran through the room, branching off to three other tunnels that disappeared into darkness. A rusted-out piece of machinery sat near the far wall. The wind whistled through the tunnels, whipping up a musty, slightly metallic odor.

Gabe lay in the middle of the room, on the hard stone floor. The woman stood over him, the hood of her cloak lowered to reveal a mop of dull brown hair and a plain face that appeared to be about forty years old, although looks were deceiving when it came to the supernatural.

"Good. You found us."

Too easy. Way too easy.

"Magda?" Addie asked with surprise, and I recognized the name —the witch who'd paid Tase to turn me. The witch who'd been turned away by the Luna Coven because she practiced black magic.

The woman smiled. "Alive and well, as you can see."

"What do you want with my brother?" I demanded.

She stepped over Gabe's body, turning her pale eyes on me. "I want him dead," she deadpanned. "And you, as well. My goal has been to destroy all of the Petrans. So here we are."

Xandru stepped protectively in front of me. "Over my dead body."

She sneered. "Oh, that's part of the plan, too. After what your kind did to my family, *all* of you filthy moroi will die. Tase was supposed to take care of that by triggering a Petran kid, but the fucking Lunas interfered. So it looks like I have to do it myself."

The more she talked, the more I noticed a faint accent—the same as Mammie's.

Also, the more she talked, the more time we had to formulate a plan. So I tried to keep her going.

"Who are you?" I asked, my gaze roaming the space, searching for any signs of a prepared spell or hex she could hit us with, but too much of the room lay beyond the flames' flickering light. "Why are you doing this? Why the grudge?"

She gave an evil smile. "I'm so glad you asked. I want you to know why I'm ending all of you." She paused for dramatic effect. "I am finally getting vengeance for my loved ones, who were slaughtered two hundred years ago outside a small town in Romania. Ring a bell?"

Oh, fuck, I thought as Xandru said the same words aloud.

She glanced at him, then focused back on me. "That's right. I descend from a line of mages who put your brothers and cousin down, but not before they murdered most of our coven. The witches who'd been part of creating the curse on all of you moroi." She jabbed a finger in my direction. "*You* shouldn't exist. Neither should he." She flipped her hand toward Gabe. "And I'll take care of your sister when we're done here, just to be sure her gene's never triggered. But first, I need the Eye of Valerian."

My gaze snapped back to her, my mouth gaping in disbelief. "Do you really think we'd hand it over after you just threatened to kill us all?"

"Oh, please. I know you don't have it. Tase knows where to come. But will he show? Will he give it up as long as he believes it'll benefit him? That artifact has the power to convince him that he can be king of the world. It did this to your little brother, because he exposed himself to its power for too long, then tried to deny it. See how the Eye fights back?" She glanced down at Gabe's still body, then up again, a gleam in her eye. "I wonder what it's doing to Tase right. Now."

Xandru growled.

"What do you know about the Eye?" Addie demanded.

"Enough."

"What do you want with it? It's a moroi artifact," Xandru bit out. "What can *you* do with it?"

"You want to make them go strigoi, don't you?" Addie accused. "That's how you'll end them?"

She tapped a finger to her cheek. "Good idea. But unfortunately, no. I'm just a buyer for someone else."

"Who?" all three of us asked.

She studied each of us in turn, a knowing glint in her eyes.

"The Collector," she said curtly. "And before you ask, I don't know who he is. Never met him. Don't care to. I only took the job because it meant taking all of you down, too. The joy of finally being able to destroy the Petrans and the Rocas is my payment."

The thrill in her voice sent chills down my spine, and my entire body tensed. Xandru also stiffened as he stood slightly in front of me, his hands curled into fists. Angry heat waves came off his body.

"A collector of what?" Addie remained calm compared to the two of us.

"*The* Collector," Magda corrected harshly, as though it mattered greatly to her, regardless of how much she tried to say otherwise. "Of magical artifacts—dark ones, cursed ones, powerful ones. He wants them all. Like the Blue Dragon Dagger, the necromancer's athame, a fae lantern, the Eye of Valerian . . . Your town is full of such objects . . . at least, what Tase and the Bishops haven't smuggled out. Of course, they smuggle just as many in, so maybe it's a wash. I don't know. I don't really care. I just want my payment."

"You're not getting it," Xandru growled, leaning toward her.

Magda rolled her eyes, dismissing his threat. Addie stepped up in the woman's face, crossed her arms, and stared her down. "He's right. You're not."

The older woman flinched, fear flickering in her eyes. Was she scared of Addie? Why?

Another plume of black smoke appeared, but Addie's hands shot out, dissipating it. Rather than vanishing this time, Magda hung in the air, a knife in her hands aimed at Addie's throat. The older woman spun away, producing more smoke as she did. Addie cast another spell.

Now Magda was on her knees in front of Gabe's body, the knife poised a foot over his chest.

"Come any closer, and I'll do it," she threatened. "Tase's time is almost up."

Desperation tainted her voice, the smell of fear pouring off her. She *was* afraid of Addie.

"But Tase won't come, will he?" The quaver in her voice faded as she mustered up some kind of bravado. She lifted her chin and squared her shoulders, glaring at Addie the whole time. "He thinks it will fix him. And he wants nothing more, does he? Now that he knows he has a son."

I blinked, shocked at this news, and glanced sideways at Addie. Her face paled, but she otherwise didn't respond. She wouldn't. Not right now. She wouldn't show weakness.

Xandru showed no surprise. Of course. He'd already known, hadn't he? He didn't deny or question the claim, so it must have been true.

And so much made sense now.

Magda smirked, her courage returning. "Oh, maybe that was supposed to be a secret. Oopsy." She rolled her eyes before her pale gaze returned to me. "So what do you think, Michaela? What is Atanase Roca willing to sacrifice? His life? His son's? Or a Petran? I think we already know the answer."

Grinning wickedly, she lifted the knife higher, and her hands flinched.

Then they plunged.

Addie shouted a spell.

Magda cried out.

The knife's point poked the fabric of Gabe's hoodie, but stopped.

I flicked my wrist, and the metal blade flew out of her hands.

She flicked her own, and a new one replaced it, its long, razor-sharp edge held at my brother's throat.

"My blades are laced with black magic. He won't be able to heal from even the smallest nick," she taunted.

Addie's head tilted, her eyes narrowed.

"I have what you want right here," a familiar voice called out from the darkness, stilling us all, even Magda.

Her gaze swept over the entrance, searching the shadows.

Tase emerged, sauntering into the room, flipping a round object between his fingers, the firelight bouncing off the silver and moonstone. At the same time, my throat felt like it caught on fire with a need for human blood. My mouth salivating, I swallowed, trying to calm the burn.

Was Magda doing that?

No.

The Eye of Valerian. It whispered to me, calling on my bloodlust.

Magda watched Tase like a hawk until he stopped a few yards in front of her.

"You won't give it up," she accused. "Not if it'll cure you."

Tase's green gaze passed over Xandru and me, lingered on Addie for a moment, then slid to Magda.

"So you're saying that I'm right. It *can* break my curse. I just want to be sure we're clear here," he said with a cocky flair, making me growl.

Magda swallowed slowly, seeming to delay her answer. What angle would she take? Truth or lie? I was riveted to her moving throat, my ache for blood growing.

"There are ways," she finally replied. "Give it to me, and I will help you."

Tase tapped his finger against his lip. "I don't believe you. It's a moroi artifact. *You* can't do shit with it."

"It's a tool. One with many powers. *I* know how to access the one you need. And you don't, do you? Otherwise, you would have done it already. Otherwise, you wouldn't be here. You *owe* me!" she yelled.

Her hand moved the slightest bit, the knife's blade ever closer to Gabe's throat. If I tried to move it, it could easily slice his skin. Even at the angle she held it, bending it could still scrape him.

I glanced at Addie. She glared at Magda, her eye scanning everything about the other woman, but she shared my dilemma. Any movement by Magda or the knife could end my brother's existence.

"We can work together," Magda offered to Tase. "Deliver it to me, like you've been paid to do, and I will help you."

One side of Tase's mouth curled up in a cocky smirk. "Nope, that's not how this works. You see, *you* don't get to give the ultimatums."

Are you fucking kidding me? She held a poisoned knife to my brother's throat, and Tase was being an arrogant ass!

Growling, I coiled to spring at him. Xandru was faster, though, wrapping his arms around me. I tried to elbow him in the ribs to break free, but he was too strong. Or I was too weak from the bloodlust shooting through my veins.

Magda was right.

Tase had proven over and over that he would always choose himself.

Especially over a Petran.

He didn't care about Gabe or me. I didn't even know if he cared about Addie or Xandru, the rest of his family, or even this son he supposedly had.

He cared about Tase and Tase only.

Right this very second, he was probably devising a way to sweeten the deal for himself.

As though reading my mind, Tase turned his green gaze to me.

Smiled.

Winked.

"I'll give it to you," he said to Magda while watching me. I fought harder against Xandru's hold, but to no avail. "But on one condition."

"I already said I'll show you how to use it," Magda snarled.

"That's not my condition." His stare pierced into me. My heart raced. "I'll give it to you . . . if you let the boy go."

And now my heart stopped.

"You'd trade your life for a *Petran's*?" Magda asked. "Now *I* don't believe *you!*"

Tase's gaze remained locked with mine.

"Yes, I trade my life for a Petran's." He flipped the pocket watch in the air, tossing it toward Magda. "Because we're family, and that's what family does."

CHAPTER 20

XANDRU

*M*ichaela fell still in my arms as we watched the Eye of Valerian soar through the air, glinting in the firelight as it arched upward.

I couldn't believe my eyes. I couldn't believe Tase had actually done that. I was surprised he'd shown up in the first place, but to hand over the one thing that could save his own life? Especially to save a Petran? Was this even my brother?

Magda jumped to her feet, and her arm flew up, her hand open to catch it, a wicked gleam in her eyes.

But then the timepiece suddenly changed direction, and Addie plucked it out of the air.

"I don't think so." She closed her hand around the artifact.

Immediately, the thirst for human blood that had been burning in my throat diminished for the first time since Tase had walked in with that thing.

"Addie," Michaela gasped.

"Trust me," she murmured quietly.

Magda screamed and lunged at Addie with the blade. Addie swiped her hand out, and Magda flew backwards as the knife clattered to the floor. The woman landed in a crouch, her eyes wide as she looked around, assessing her situation. Flicking her wrist, another blade appeared. But not by magic. It slipped out of the sleeve of her cloak. Holding it in one hand, she swept it back and forth at us, as she slowly backed up, until her ass pressed into the wall. I released Michaela from my hold, and we moved forward as a group, closing her in, watching for any sudden gestures that could be a spell.

"Wait!" She threw her other hand up in a "stop" gesture. We all froze. But no spell came. "You still need me. You don't know how to use it."

"I'll figure it out," Addie snarled.

"You don't have time," Magda insisted. "His exposure has made him worse. But I can help with that, too."

"How?" Tase growled.

Her gaze bounced between him and me. "Disperse it."

"What?" Addie demanded, her tone edged with disbelief.

Magda nodded frantically. "Tase can barely control the curse anymore, but if you disperse it, he'll be better able to. It'll buy you time."

"I have an idea," Addie said. "Why don't you just break the curse yourself? If you know so much about it."

Magda froze. Caught.

"You don't know, do you?" Tase asked.

"You claim to be from the mages who created the curse, but you can't break it?" Addie moved closer.

"I . . . I can figure out how. I have their books. I will help you." Magda's heart pounded. The tart smell of fear poured off of her. "Just don't kill me." Her wild eyes flew to me, her words coming fast. "If we don't remove the curse from your brother, he will die. You can take it. You can help him. If your brothers and sisters take it, too, spread it out, you'll all survive even longer. And then we'll have time to work on the Eye of Valerian together."

"No," Tase and Michaela said at the same time.

"No," I agreed. "Not our brothers and sisters. But I'll do it."

Magda bobbed her head in a violent nod. "Good, good. It will work."

Addie glared, eyes narrowed. "No, it won't."

"Yes, it will," Magda argued. "I have the books. I have the spells. I'll share them with you."

Addie cocked her head. "And you think you can remove the spell from Tase and give it to Xandru?"

"It's worth a try, is it not?" the older woman asked.

"Yes." I couldn't believe I agreed with her, but we had to at least try.

"The fuck it is," Tase said. He jabbed a finger at me. "You're not doing this."

I squared my shoulders and lifted my chin. "My choice, not yours."

Michaela spun on me, shaking her head. For the first time in a week, she looked at me with something other than hatred.

"You can't do this," she whispered.

"I have to." I brushed my thumb over the soft skin of her cheek. "He has a kid, Kales. His son deserves the chance to have a dad. I have . . . nothing."

"You have *me*." She blinked rapidly, tears pooling in her eyes. "What about us?"

I managed a small smile, but I really wanted to sweep her into my arms, bury my face in her neck, and cling to her forever. "We'll figure it out. You heard her. This will buy us all time. But I have to at least try. For my brother. For both of our families. For *all* of us."

She stared at me in silence, a million unsaid things flickering in her eyes.

"He's here, Kales. He came through. That means something. Now it's my turn to come through for him."

"You're always coming through for him," she muttered.

"And I always will. For all of you. That's what family does. Right?"

She pressed her lips together as a tear rolled down her cheek. I caught it with my thumb and brushed it away. Her chin trembled as she finally nodded, and then she threw herself at me. I caught her in my arms and pulled her into me, relieved to finally be holding her again. Her body shuddered against me as she fought to suppress a sob.

"Michaela, come here." Addie held out her hand. "It'll be okay. I promise."

Michaela hesitated before stepping out of my embrace, and I reluctantly let her go. She moved over to Addie, who laid her arm over Michaela's shoulders, giving her a squeeze. Addie leaned her head against Michaela's, and her lips moved, but if she spoke actual words, I couldn't hear them. She grasped Michaela's hand for a brief moment, and Michaela's eyes tightened. Then she dipped her chin before they both straightened.

"Let's see what you can do," Addie said to Magda, her tone challenging.

The other witch blinked, then nodded. She lifted both hands up, one palm facing me and the other facing Tase.

The knife wobbled and rattled on the floor, then rose into the air.

Her mouth curled up in a devious smile.

"I *will* end all of you," Magda threatened. "But not today. And not because I give a flying fuck about any of you. I will do it for the Collector. Everything else is Magda's story. Not mine."

Then everything happened in a second.

The blade flew through the air right at me.

I lifted my hand, and the knife stopped.

At the same time, Michaela flicked two fingers.

The knife rotated, pointing back at its thrower.

Magda shrieked and jerked forward as though to run, but couldn't.

Addie chanted softly with her hands splayed out in front of her, paralyzing Magda.

"*You* end today," Michaela said as the blade plunged into Magda's heart.

The woman exploded.

Literally.

Black smoke suddenly filled the room, blinding us. Wet, gooey gunk rained down, splatting on my head, my shoulders, the floor. A most horrific, yet familiar, odor brought me to my knees, gagging. The sound of vomit hitting the floor came from Tase's direction.

"Fuck," he choked out.

"Gross," Addie gasped.

The smoke began to clear.

I blinked and stared through it as I rose to my feet.

Magda was gone.

A pile of pink plasma-like substance was left where she'd been.

"Skinwalker," Michaela gasped, her voice muffled behind the glove she held to her face as she lifted from a crouch.

"Where the fuck did she go?" Tase demanded. He blurred around the room, looking for her.

"Who did she become?" Addie said. "That's the better question."

"Why the hell did you do that?" I shouted at her and Michaela. "She was our hope! And now we don't even know what the fuck she looks like!"

Addie snorted and gestured at the mess around us. "Open your eyes, Xandru. She wasn't a witch. I could barely sense any power in her diluted blood. Her little bit of magic couldn't do anything more than save her own ass with a parlor trick."

"She was bullshitting us," Michaela said, flicking a piece of Magda's old skin off of her.

Addie held up the Eye of Valerian, and Tase, Michaela, and I all groaned. Fire erupted in my throat again, but I couldn't tear my eyes away from the pocket watch.

It was a beautiful piece, the silver lid's intricate design embellished with slivers of moonstone.

It was an ugly piece, its darkness calling to me.

"This is our key to breaking Tase's curse," Addie declared. With her other hand, she held up a metal skull, about the size of my fist. One eye socket was closed off, covered with clock gears of various colors and sizes. The other was open, empty. I vaguely remembered noticing it at Dad's old shack a few weeks ago, when I'd been overcome with bloodlust. Addie had been inspecting it earlier when we'd gone there, looking for Tase. I didn't know she'd pocketed it. Now, she opened the skull's jaw, snapped the Eye of Valerian into the inside of the empty eye socket, and shut the jaw. "And this is the cage we keep it in until we figure it out."

She dropped the whole thing into her coat pocket.

The dark whispers in my head silenced. The burn in my throat vanished. Both Tase and Michaela moaned with relief. And Tase's bright green eyes faded as more gray bled into them.

A murmur came from the center of the room.

"Gabe!" Michaela shrieked, blurring for her stirring brother.

"Kaekae?" he whispered. "Where are we?"

She fell to her knees beside him and gathered his thin body into her arms, rocking him while she cried tears of relief. "Are you okay?"

"Yeah." He wriggled to free himself. "But you smell disgusting."

She threw her head back and laughed. "Oh, my god, you're okay!"

"We all smell disgusting," Tase said. "Can we get the fuck out of here?"

Michaela stood and faced him. "Thank you."

He shrugged. "I didn't really do anything."

"But you were willing. You stepped up, Tase, and I appreciate it."

"We're family, Michaela. Like it or not. If the time ever comes, I know you'd do the same for me and mine." He jerked his head in Addie's direction. "Smarty pants over there is the real hero, though. She was one step ahead of all of us."

Addie scowled at him. "Fuck off, Tase."

He opened his mouth, but must have realized saying anything was pointless. He had a lot of groveling to do if he ever wanted to be on her good side again.

"Well, you *were* one step ahead," Michaela said to her. "How did you know?"

"The real Magda had real magic." Addie shrugged. "I don't know what that thing was, but it wasn't her. It took me a while to figure it out, but I knew something wasn't right, so I called her bluff. See, the Luna Coven's spell on Tase ensures that it stays with him. That was the deal when we first cast it, remember? There's no way it can be dispersed unless one of us does it. But I wanted to see if she'd even try."

Tase rolled his head toward me. "And your dumb ass volunteered as tribute."

My turn to shrug. "It's what we do."

"What about the rest, though?" Michaela asked Addie. "How'd you know about the Eye and that skull cage thing?"

Addie gave her a pointed look. "That I'll tell you later."

"So, back to what Tase said first," Gabe said weakly. "Can we get the eff out of here? You guys stink, and I want to go home."

THAT EVENING, I rapped on Michaela's door, then fisted my hands in front of my mouth and blew on them as I waited for her to answer. After we'd returned through another portal this morning, she'd only had four words for me before shutting the door in my face.

She opened the door now, dressed in leggings and a long-sleeved, oversized T-shirt that I knew she wore as pajamas, her hair piled in a messy bun on top of her head. Her mouth fell open. "You came."

I offered her a smile. "You said, 'We need to talk.' So I'm here to talk."

"I know. I didn't think—"

"If there's one thing I've learned, it's not to ignore you when you say we need to talk."

She returned my smile and motioned me inside. "Is that all you've learned?"

I peeled my coat off and hung it on the coatrack before turning to face her. "Not even close."

Her smile remained as she walked by me, her arm brushing against mine. She curled up sideways on the couch and pulled a thick purple sherpa blanket onto her lap, then patted the cushion in front of her before using the remote to turn the TV off.

"I've learned a lot, too," she said as I sat down next to her, angling my body to face hers.

"You have?" I asked.

She gazed at her lap, her fingers picking nervously at the blanket. "I learned that you will do whatever is necessary to protect those you care about. Even if it means lying and keeping secrets from others you love."

I swallowed. "Kales—"

She looked up at me. "It's okay, Xandru. I understand. I didn't like being the one you lied to, but I get why you did." She blinked and looked away for a moment. "When you were willing to take Tase's place and accept that deadly curse into your body for him, for his kid . . . it hit me. You'd do *anything* for your family. Even die for them. And . . . to be honest . . . I both love and hate that about you."

"I'd do the same for you and your family."

"I know that now. I didn't believe it before, but I was wrecked with Gabe. He was all I could think about. But when you came with us to the mine, I knew. You could've insisted on finding Tase and then sent him off in the opposite direction to save himself. You could've left Addie and me alone to fend for Gabe ourselves."

"You two did it all anyway," I pointed out with a chuckle.

She snickered. "Yeah, we did. But you came. And that's what matters. Like Tase, you showed up when I needed you most."

"I was trying before then, too. I was doing everything I could think of on my end to fix things. To help you. Kales, I want to *always* show up when you need me most."

"Until you're needed by your family."

"No. Not anymore." Gnawing on my bottom lip, I mentally pulled together the right words to convince her. I tapped into the conversation Tase and I had today. "Look. In his own fucked-up way, Tase thought he was doing the right thing for everyone. He wants to break the curse so he can try to be a dad someday. And he thought if he could use the Eye of Valerian to do it, he'd also figure out how to use it to help Gabe, too. That's why he disappeared for so long—he was trying to figure it out, all the way up to the last minute. He thought if he turned it over, we'd never have a chance to fix everything. But he ran out of time."

"That's what he says . . ."

"But I believe him. You know why? Because the Eye's darkness had a hold on him, was digging into him, but he fought it. He overcame it to show up in that mine. And there's only one way to overcome darkness."

Michaela nodded, understanding. "Light. Love."

"Exactly. Tase just has a really weird way of showing it."

"And he always will. He'll always be doing something stupid that you'll have to bail him out of."

"Probably," I agreed. "But it will never again be against you or your family. He knows that from this point forward, you come first in my life. From now on, you and Gabe and Aurelia are part of our family. He made that vow, and in front of all of our siblings, so they know, too. And they'll follow Tase's lead. Even Adrian and Alina."

She tilted her head. "So no more tug-of-war between our families with us in the middle?"

"If there ever is, I will let go of them before I let go of you. That was the vow *I* made to them." I took her hand into mine and held it to my lips. "So, yes, I will always be there when you need me most."

Smiling, she cupped her hand against my jaw. "I need you to trust me, too, though. Because we still don't have that part right. If you'd told me about Tase having a son and everything else, we could have been working together all along instead of apart."

"It wasn't my secret to tell, and it would have put you in a bad situation with Addie."

Her thumb stroked my cheek. "I get it. Like I said, I know where you were coming from. But there's one thing I feel like I know about my parents and their secret to staying married for over two hundred years. And probably yours, too. They confided in each other, and they kept each other's secrets. They *trusted* each other. What they shared in private stayed that way, no matter who else it might affect. I think that's what husband and wife must do."

I lifted a brow. "Husband and wife, huh?"

She smiled shyly and lifted her shoulder in a slight shrug, her hand on my face brushing against my short beard. "Maybe someday?"

I turned my head enough to plant my lips into her palm. "Definitely someday."

She leaned forward, rocking up on her knees so our faces were inches apart, and brushed her lips against mine as her hands slipped behind my head. "I missed you."

"You have no fucking idea." I went in for a longer kiss, and the need to taste her, to please her, to claim her as mine again took over.

"Xandru," she murmured against my lips, "I need you most right now."

CHAPTER 21

MICHAELA

"So I put that Eye thing in the leather cuff thing and wore it before we went to Denver," Gabe was telling Aurelia as they prepared for the first day back to school after winter break. I thought I'd wake up early to see them off. I also had a date with one of my besties and a demon summoner.

"I never saw you wear it," Aurelia said.

"Duh. You would have made fun of me. Besides, it made me feel . . . weird." He shrugged, as though it were nothing, but I knew better.

He'd already told me how he'd found the Eye of Valerian in the metal skull in the conservatory and had taken the Eye out. He couldn't remember what he'd done with the skull, because the Eye had him so enamored, but evidently, he'd tossed it back in the conservatory, and Tase had found it.

Tase kept it because it was a skull—it looked cool.

Gabe wanted the timepiece for the leather cuff he'd found previously, having no idea that it was a dark artifact. Almost immediately he started to feel strange, but he didn't connect the feelings to the Eye until the afternoon we left for Denver. He hadn't wanted to leave it behind, in case someone else found it, so it'd been in his backpack, feeding him darkness, and that's why he freaked out in the car. Then in the hospital, it had called to my and Xandru's bloodlust when he opened the bag and grabbed it in relief that it wasn't lost. By the time we returned to his room, the darkness had already overcome him, and he attacked me again.

After Gabe awoke as a mature moroi, he buried the artifact, too afraid to tell anyone about it, even when Tase started harassing him for it. But even buried, it had called to him. Once Tase took possession, its power only became stronger, likely feeding off of Tase's curse while also returning the energy to him. Addie thought the longer Gabe denied its power, the more drained he became, until his body shut down his mind, putting him into the coma.

"Weird?" Aurelia snorted. "It almost killed you."

"Well, it didn't," I said. "We need to put all of this behind us. Not. One. Word. To anyone at school. Gabe had a virus. He's over it. That's all. Understood?"

"Of course," Aurelia said flippantly.

Yeah, that wasn't going to work. I hated memory spells, but there was too much at risk for anyone to know as much as they did about the Eye of Valerian. Especially two kids, who could easily let something slip to the wrong person without realizing it.

A horn honked outside.

"Gallad's here," Gabe said. "That's cool that he offered me a ride to school."

"You have all of your catch-up work?" I asked.

The Academy had actually returned to classes last week, but I'd kept Gabe home longer to ensure he was okay. He seemed to have fully recovered, but only time would tell. He'd been a little disappointed about having to go back to the Academy, but he understood now how easily things could go wrong. He didn't want to take any risks.

What he didn't know was that Gallad was ordered by the Court to give Gabe a ride to school today, and on the way, he'd be changing my brother's memory about the Eye of Valerian.

"I'll see you both tonight for the Festival of Lights, right?" I asked Aurelia and Gabe as they headed out the door. Neither answered, and Gabe was already on his way down the steps, Aurelia right behind him.

"Hey, hold on a sec." I took her by the shoulders and dipped my head to look into her eyes. "Thank you for not being a brat during all of this with Gabe."

She shrugged. "You had a lot going on. I didn't want to add to it."

Her kindness made me feel even worse as I made the connection with her mind and compelled her to forget about the Eye of Valerian and what it had done to Gabe.

"Gabe had a virus, but he's fine now," Aurelia repeated.

I nodded. "See you tonight."

"See ya, Kaekae," Gabe called before slipping into Gallad's car.

"Yeah, see ya, *Kaekae*," Aurelia echoed as she ran off down the drive to meet her ride at the street.

Sindi laughed from the front porch of the cottage next to ours. "I kind of like being an aunt. I get to teach them all kinds of fun stuff. Kaekae."

"Shut up," I growled, but then I smiled. "So does this mean you're staying for a while?"

She snorted. "Who else is going to run this inn? You're going to give me a raise, though, right?"

"Heh. Let's see how this ski season goes first."

She stared out at the snow-covered lawn and rocked on her boot heels. "Ah, well, I'd stay anyway. I still haven't bagged me a lumberjack." Giving me a sideways glance, she smirked. "Or a Roca."

She ran off for the inn, my only response a snowball to her back. Watching from an upper window, Mammie shook her head, smiling. She'd been able to return to our realm, but not as often as before or for as long.

"What is it about the Roca men that makes them so irresistible?" Addie asked, as she strode up the driveway Xandru had plowed overnight.

Giving her a pointed look, I descended the steps to meet her.

"There's only one I find irresistible. As far as your pick, I have no idea."

"Yeah, me, either." She sighed. "But you know, you can warn Sindi away all you want, but it'll never work. Look at me. I can't get past friendship and booty calls, but for some reason, I hold out hope for more."

"Well, if he's anything like Xandru in bed, it's definitely the booty calls that are irresistible."

"Yeah, those booty calls are pretty fucking awesome," she said on a sigh. She bumped my shoulder as we began walking toward the square. "Don't tell them that, though, or the next thing we know, one of them will be starting a booty call business."

We hit the corner of Main and Eleventh and continued north toward Into the Mystic New Age Books and Gifts on the east side of the square, where we were meeting Harper Sinclair.

I braced myself, before saying, "So Tase is okay."

As expected, Addie growled. "Like I care."

"I know you do. I also know you won't ask. But being your best friend, I will anticipate your questions: He's doing better. He's regained control, more like he was in the beginning. And . . ." I angled my head to look at her. "He misses you. He won't stop asking me about how you're doing."

We walked in silence for several strides, Addie pretending to ignore me.

"That Eye is a dangerous piece of incredible magic, in the wrong hands," she finally said.

Understanding, I went with the subject change. "Well, I'm glad it's in yours now. I don't think anybody else's would be more right. Definitely not Tase's."

"No shit. If he'd kept that thing much longer, he would have been way worse off than Gabe. We all would have." She suddenly growled again. "Hey! You made me talk about him."

"Sorry, not sorry. So are you going to tell me how you knew? About the Eye of Valerian and the cage and everything?"

We stopped in front of the new age shop, but Addie blocked the door for a moment. "That's why we're here."

"To meet with Harper."

"Yes."

"Because she has this new power to summon demons?"

Addie's nose scrunched. "No. And it's not a new power, but she's learning how to control it now. She can also summon and channel other spirits." She bit on her lip for a moment, making me tense with whatever she was about to say. "Michaela, she channeled your parents on New Year's."

I flinched. "What? Eloise said they're surrounded by darkness."

"Yeah, well, that's kind of Harper's thing. She can get past—or through—the darkness." She reached into her coat pocket and pulled out a crumpled piece of paper that she handed to me. "This is what she scribed."

I opened the ball of paper to find a message scrawled on it, the handwriting nice and neat at first but becoming harder to read as the message seemed to gain in urgency:

Atanase holds the Eye of Valerian. He covets the power for himself. Wants to harness it. Lacks understanding and respect. Just like our boys. History will repeat itself. Stop him Adelaide. Save our son. Save our daughters. Save our town from another massacre. Put the Eye in its cage. A skull in a shack on the side of the mountain.

I looked up to find Addie watching me. "This is how you knew?"

"Yes. And the message was right. I found the skull—the cage—in the Rocas' mountain shack when Xandru and I were hunting down Tase."

"Wow." I blinked as realization dawned on me. "Harper can communicate with my parents?"

"Apparently. And we think they have more to say." She pointed to the paper, at a place that I thought was just scribbles at first glance.

"It says *come back*."

She turned and opened the door. "So here we are. I thought you might want to join us this time."

We entered the warm shop that was stuffed full but artfully arranged and inviting. New age books lined the bookshelves, which were painted in an array of bright colors. Candles in all shapes and hues were on display on tables covered with colorful scarves. Glass cases showed off jewelry and crystals. A mauve and gold chaise lounge and stuffed blue-checked chairs sat near an herbal tea counter. All was surrounded by purple walls.

Eloise, Harper's aunt, came through the beaded curtain in the back, dressed, as always, in brightly colored leggings and a tunic.

"Good morning, girls," she greeted with a smile as she brushed back wisps of auburn hair from her face. "Harper is in the back room. Same place as before, Addie."

With a nod, Addie led me through the beaded curtain to a back room, dimly lit with a single table lamp. A petite woman with long brown hair, about our age, was sitting on the opposite side of the table with paper and pencils spread out before her. When we entered, she looked up at us with pretty green eyes, her bare face showing off a natural beauty, especially when she smiled.

I'd met Harper a few times in the past, but didn't really know her, except through Addie, who'd spent a lot of time after school at the Academy, where the other girl had gone. Socially, Harper had always kept to herself. Since I'd been on the Court, and with recent events involving her, I'd learned why. Now, she was trying to find her place with the rest of us, with Addie's help.

"Hi," Harper said with a hint of shyness. "Um . . . have a seat."

She motioned to the mismatched chairs on our side of the table. Addie and I peeled off our coats and hats, then sat down next to each other.

"Did Addie explain how this works?" Harper asked. I shook my head. "Well, you basically sit there, and I bring demon spirits to the party."

"They'll even fetch the booze," Addie added.

I looked back and forth between the two of them, trying to figure out if they were serious.

Harper snickered. "I'll try to leave the demons alone today. You want to talk to your parents?"

"You can really reach them?"

"I guess I did on New Year's. But in fair warning, I haven't done this much. I'm still learning."

I nodded. "Okay. Well, let's try. What can it hurt?"

Harper cringed. "Let's hope nothing. This time." She quieted for a moment, then said, "Mihail and Irina Petran, your daughter is here."

I held my breath, but nothing happened at first. Then the energy in the air shifted, and Harper's hand suddenly grabbed at a pencil and began writing:

We are here Irina and Mihail

"Oh, my god," I breathed. "Mom? Dad?"

Hello again dear daughter

Tears filled my eyes, but I didn't know what to do. I looked at the paper and writing instruments around me, wondering if I should write a note.

"You can talk to them," Harper said.

"Um . . . I miss you both," I started, feeling awkward.

Harper scribed: *We miss you Gabe Aurelia. We are sorry. So sorry.*

"Me, too," I blurted. "I wish you would have let me stay here. I didn't get to say goodbye to you."

We tried to do what we thought best. We were wrong. We should have never done that to you. We are sorry.

My throat tightened. I had so much to say to them, but now that I had the chance, words failed me. Maybe because of the lack of privacy, with Harper and Addie here. Or maybe because I knew discussion was pointless. They admitted they were wrong and apologized. We couldn't change anything. It was time to let go. At least now I could say goodbye, tell them I loved them one more time.

We love you so much, too. We are so

Harper's hand stopped moving.

My focus flew from the paper to her face. "What happened?"

She shook her head and whispered, "Something's with them."

"Mom, Dad, are you okay?" I asked, trying to suppress the panic in my voice. "Mammie can't find you. Eloise says there's darkness around you."

Harper's hand remained still.

"*Mom?*" My heart picked up speed at the thought of losing them already. "Dad?"

"Mr. and Mrs. Petran?" Addie said.

The room fell deathly still and quiet for several heartbeats. A sob leaped into my throat.

But then Harper's hand began to move frantically:

Need help. Infernum. Break the curse.

I gasped and looked at Addie. "They're in the Infernum? But how? Why?"

In Infernum. Part of curse. Adelaide. Eye of Valerian. Break the curse. Break us free.

Harper wrote the same message three times, then the pencil fell from her fingers and rolled across the table, as she slumped back in her chair.

"They're gone," she whispered, her hand trembling. "Something was trying to stop the message. I think it took them away."

I didn't know how long I sat there, stunned, staring at the papers.

"What do we know about the Infernum?" I finally asked.

"It's a place like a purgatory to trap supernaturals who can't be killed but should be," Addie said. "Immortals, demons, and the like."

"But moroi can be killed. We're mortal. They *died*. Right? So what are they doing there?"

"Dark magic could have sent their souls there," Harper said. "They said it was part of a curse?"

"And something with the Eye of Valerian," Addie said.

I stared at the paper Harper had been writing on.

"Break the curse. Break us free," I murmured.

"And my name." Addie pointed at it. "They were trying to tell me this. It must be why they said to come back last time." Addie grasped my hands and pulled them to her, twisting me in my seat until I faced her. She dipped her head to lock eyes with mine. "Which means they know I can do this, Michaela. That it *can* be done. I can end Tase's curse and break them free, too. I *will* do this, okay?" She stared at me, her brown eyes imploring as she waited for an answer. "I *can* do this."

I slowly nodded. "Okay. Yeah. I trust you."

"Okay." She gave me a small smile before turning back to Harper. "Again—this is badass, girl."

"I hope I can help," Harper offered. "Whatever you need. I don't know if I can get them back, but we can try another time."

Addie stood, taking me with her, since she still held my hand. "Sounds good. In the meantime, I have work to do. Lots of research. Maybe I can bring them questions, if we can reach them again."

Harper stood, too, and gave me a smile. "Are you sure you'll be okay?"

I nodded. "Um, yeah." I cleared my throat because my voice came out hoarse, then I tilted my head to the side, toward Addie. "My bestie is a powerful witch. You can apparently do some really cool shit that will help. And me—" I paused, thinking. "Well, I don't know what I have to offer, but we'll figure this out. Right?"

"Right." Harper's grin widened when I included her.

"Definitely." Addie released my hand, but looped her arm around mine.

She turned us and walked us toward the front of the store, but I stopped at the door, pausing for a moment.

I looked over my shoulder. "Harper, you should join us for girls' night sometime. Graysin and Callie won't mind. But you might have to be careful with Sindi. She has over a century's worth of dead family and friends she'll want you to channel."

Harper smiled. "That could be fun. Girls' night, I mean."

"I'll call you," Addie said as we stepped out into the cold, blustery January morning. The sun had made a showing, but they were calling for more snow tonight. At least the skiing would be good this weekend.

We walked back down Eleventh Street toward Main and our next destination.

"What do you think about the Collector?" I asked Addie as I stared at the pawn shop sign we walked toward. "Do you the skinwalker was telling the truth?"

"That's what you're thinking about right now?"

"It's what I want to think about right now."

She released my arm. "Okay, got it. Well, first of all, I forgot to tell you that we're pretty sure the skinwalker is the same one that had been at the inn last spring. I kept some goo from the mine to test, and it seems to have all the same traits as the other goo. But there's no way to know for certain. As far as the Collector . . ." She shrugged. "I don't know. Faux-Magda seemed to know a lot about our town's artifacts, so maybe. Maybe she or he or it *is* the Collector."

"Yeah, maybe." I tilted my head forward, toward the pawn shop. "Or it could be Old Man Mills. I mean, he's a dragon. Maybe artifacts are his treasure."

"I don't know if he's sinister enough to go as far as they did to obtain the Eye of Valerian."

"True, but I still don't trust him. With that logic, though, it could be Roman. Or Ada Daryn, leader of the Green Coven." Which, I'd learned since being on the Court, was the primary coven that took care of the Court's nastier business that the Lunas didn't want to dirty their hands with.

"Oh," Addie said. "They could be working together. They are a thing."

"Ew. Really?"

We stopped at the curb to cross Main Street, and Addie leaned in close to whisper in my ear. "Graysin and Callie caught Ada blowing him at last year's Moons in the Mist Bonfire."

"Oh, gross! I didn't need that image in my head."

She laughed. "You're welcome. So I guess that's another mystery we need to solve: Is the Collector real?"

"I think we should let the Court work on that one. You have a more important mystery to focus on." I'd tried to say it lightheartedly, because I knew she was attempting to cheer me up, but the subject was too heavy and fell flat.

We walked the rest of the way to Coffee Haven in silence, not breaking it until we sat in a corner seat with hot drinks in our hands.

"Are you sure you're okay?" Addie finally asked.

I huddled over my cup of nectar, staring at the table as I self-assessed. Then I looked up at her. "Yeah. I'm okay. Gabe's better. Aurelia's . . . Aurelia. Xandru has some kind of surprise date planned for us that he swears will be the best date ever. And my friends are awesome. So what if my parents are trapped in purgatory, fighting off demons and the worst kind of evil darkness there is that wants to eat their souls?" I snorted. "But I trust you, and I believe in us. I know that somehow, we'll all be okay."

She nodded. "Okay. Good."

"I mean, it's mostly on you," I added. "They actually gave *your* name. To break the curse and save Tase, and set them free from Hell. And all before Tase gets himself killed and Lucifer himself chomps on my parents' souls. No pressure or anything."

She rolled her eyes. "No pressure. I got this."

If only I didn't know her well enough to sense the uncertainty in her voice.

But I really did trust her. And I honestly believed if anyone could succeed at this task, it was Adelaide Beaumont.

I also knew she wouldn't have to do it alone.

After all, she, too, was family.

EPILOGUE

MICHAELA

*A*urelia and Gabe ditched me for the Festival of Lights. I'd even done my best mom-style guilt trip about it being our first one together to honor our parents and Mammie. After all, the Festival of Lights was about paying tribute to the town's fallen who'd protected the people and the town's secret during the Massacre of 1876, and ever since. Our parents and Mammie had played a role in protecting the people then and since then, and now they were gone, too.

But Aurelia preferred to do the whole thing with a group of friends, and Gabe just wanted to go to Cody's house so they could play video games right after.

"I told them it was a school night, so they'd better be home by nine, though," I told Xandru as we rode down Main Street in his truck, admiring the bright pink and purple streaks in the sky as the sun set behind Miles Mountain.

"Ech. You're such a mom," he teased. The hand that had been resting on my thigh gave a playful squeeze as he turned right on Eighth Street.

"Hey, where are you going? Addie, Sindi, and everyone are meeting us on the slopes. Other way." I pointed behind us.

"Remember that surprise date?"

"You mean, the best date ever?"

"Well . . . surprise." He looked over at me with a broad grin.

"Wait. Now? But everyone else is waiting on us. What about the Festival of Lights?"

He hitched his thumb toward the rear window. "I have lanterns in the back. Everyone else? Who the fuck cares?"

I turned to look out the back window, glancing at the lanterns and a bunch of other stuff piled up in the bed. My gaze slid up, though, toward the ski slopes behind us, where all of our friends were. Then I turned and slumped into my seat, although I was admittedly excited to see where he was taking me. Sindi and Addie might have been mad, but they'd get over it. Or, for all I knew, they were in on the whole thing.

I figured out the where pretty quickly. "You're taking us to our spot?"

He didn't answer, but drove in silence. And that was exactly where he went. But instead of parking us as usual, facing the town, he backed in.

"Stay here a minute," he said, before sliding out into the cold.

I turned in my seat and watched as he hopped into the bed of the truck, but then he hung a blanket over the rear window, blocking my view. I sighed as I turned back around and stared into the darkness that was quickly descending. Anyone who'd never been in the mountains in the middle of nowhere had no idea just how dark dark could be. Within minutes, only the snow, a faint glow, could be seen.

My door opened, startling me. Xandru held his gloved hand out. "My lady?"

He helped me out of the cab, then wrapped a thick blanket around me before leading me around to the tailgate.

"Oh. Wow," I breathed, taking in the sight he'd prepared.

He'd used his metal-working ability to create several candelabras that were somehow propped on the sides of the truck's bed. In the bed was a huge pile of blankets and pillows, as well as a thermos and picnic basket sitting in the corner. On the tailgate rested two large paper lanterns, ready to be lit. We leaned against the tailgate, Xandru's arm around me, taking in the view.

Down below us, the lights of town spread out, everything still decorated for Christmas. Town tradition kept all holiday lights on until January eighth, the night of the Festival of Lights. Then the town would go black as the lights were extinguished in memory of the blackness of the night of the massacre, when a band of supernatural hunters had attacked the settlement that became Havenwood Falls.

"It's almost time," Xandru said as he gave me a squeeze.

I tried to see if I could find our friends on the side of the mountain opposite us, where the slopes were brightly lit, but they were a popular place for launching lanterns. Several groups of people dotted the white expanses that weaved through the dark clumps of trees. My vampire vision wasn't quite good enough to pick them out.

Fat snowflakes began to fall, and our breaths plumed out in synch. Xandru pulled me closer, and I cuddled against him. A few moments later, the lights below began to blink out, block by block, and then the town square. The ski resort's lights were last, and when they went dark, the whole town was plunged into blackness.

This was the moment of silence.

I closed my eyes and silently sent word to Mom and Dad, hoping they knew we would do everything we could to free them. Thanking them for their love and sacrifice, even if I didn't agree with their decisions. Forgiving them for those decisions. I also paid my respects to the Rocas, because without them, there would be no Xandru.

"Ready?" he whispered a minute later.

I nodded, and we pulled apart. Lifting one of the lanterns, I held onto its frame as he lit it, then used one hand to help him with his. We turned to face town, lanterns held above our heads, watching as thousands more blinked to life. Then they began to rise from the bottom of the canyon. Then more from all four mountainsides. I looked up at mine, its orange flame glowing down at me.

"I love you, Mom and Dad," I whispered, releasing the lantern and watching it rise.

Xandru released his, then swooped his arm around me and pulled me into the bed of the pickup. We scooted back against the pillows, he piled the blankets on top of us, and then we lay back and watched thousands of lights rise from Havenwood Falls into the inky sky.

"It's so beautiful," I said, snuggling closer into Xandru. His arms tightened around me, but I was strangely not freezing, and not just because of the blankets. I wiggled my butt. "Do you have a heater *under* us?"

He chuckled. "I do. I rigged a way to heat the whole bed. I also have hot chocolate." He pointed toward the thermos. "And wine, if you prefer."

"You thought of everything."

"I tried."

I looked up at him and kissed his stubbly jaw. "You really do have a romantic bone in your body, Roca. My mom might be impressed."

He laughed, but the sound seemed a little off. "I hope so." He breathed out what sounded like a sigh, the heat fanning against my cheek.

"I love you always, Xandru Roca," I said.

"And you are my world, Michaela Petran," he whispered against my ear. Then he let go of me with one hand, reaching for something under the blankets. "But Kales?"

"Yeah?" I said as I gazed out at the lanterns.

"Will you be my world forever?"

I broke my gaze from the sky and turned to look at him. "What?"

He brought his hand out from under the blankets, holding a ring between his thumb and forefinger. "Will you be my world forever?"

My throat closed up with tears. Happy tears. All I could do was nod. He slipped the ring onto my finger, and I threw my arms around his neck.

"Yes, Xandru," I finally managed to say. "I will be your forever."

He pulled back to look into my eyes. "Mine."

"Yours."

He held my face in his hands and leaned in for the kiss.

"This really is the best date ever," I murmured, before he pulled me back for another.

Then we snuggled deep under the blankets and made love as the lanterns dotted the sky.

Honoring our past.

Celebrating our present.

Creating our future.

WE HOPE you enjoyed this story in the Havenwood Falls series featuring a variety of supernatural creatures. The series is a collaborative effort by multiple authors. Want to know more about the characters in this book and their stories?

- Find out what happened to Aster, Reeve, and the rest of the McCabes in *Fate, Love & Loyalty* by E.J. Fechenda.
- Read about the Kasun wolf pack in *Written in the Stars* by Kallie Ross.
- Find out what happened with Macy and Gallad in *Reawakened* by Morgan Wylie.
- Read about the black bear shifters in *Alpha's Queen* by Lila Felix.
- Learn more about Old Man Mills and the frost dragon shifters in *Somewhere Within* by Amy Hale.
- Discover Harper's story in *Ink & Fire* by R.K. Ryals.

OTHER CHARACTERS MENTIONED HERE HAVE COME from other books in the Havenwood Falls shared world, so be sure to read them all.

HAVENWOOD FALLS BOOKS by Kristie Cook:

Forget You Not
Lose You Not
Break Me Not
The Collector: Awakening
Savage Salvation
Sun & Moon Academy Book One: Fall Semester
Sun & Moon Academy Book Two: Spring Semester

IMMERSE YOURSELF IN the world of Havenwood Falls and stay up to date on news and announcements at www.HavenwoodFalls.com.

ABOUT THE AUTHOR

Kristie Cook is a lifelong, award-winning writer in various genres, primarily New Adult paranormal romance and contemporary fantasy. Her internationally bestselling Soul Savers series includes seven books, as well as several companion novellas. Over 1.2 million Soul Savers books have been downloaded, hitting Amazon's, B&N.com's, and Apple's Top 100 Paid lists.

She has also written the Book of Phoenix trilogy, a New Adult paranormal romance, and is the creator and publisher of and contributor of the Havenwood Falls multi-series shared world.

Besides writing, Kristie enjoys reading, cooking, traveling, getting her hippie on, and feeding her addictions to coffee, chocolate, cheese, The Walking Dead, Game of Thrones, and Supernatural. She has lived in ten states, but currently calls Florida home.

Email: kristie@kristiecook.com
Author's Website & Blog: http://www.KristieCook.com
Facebook: http://www.facebook.com/AuthorKristieCook
Twitter: http://twitter.com/kristiecookauth
Goodreads: https://www.goodreads.com/KristieCook
Instagram: http://instagram.com/kristiecookauth

ACKNOWLEDGMENTS

Firstly, thank the Creator—that this book is done!

Secondly, so much appreciation and love to all of the Havenwood Falls authors. We are family.

A very special thank you to Regina Ryals and Randi Cooley Wilson for helping me whip this story into shape, and, of course, for letting me use your lovely characters. Thanks to E.J. Fechenda, Kallie Ross, Amy Hale, Morgan Wylie, Lila Felix, Kristen Yard, Susan Burdorf, Michele G. Miller, Cameo Renae, Heather Hildenbrand, and Belinda Boring for the contribution of your characters and/or storylines.

Thirdly, I'm thankful always for my family, without whose support and love I could never create.

Also, much appreciation to Regina Wamba at MaeIDesign.com, our art director, for the gorgeous covers and graphics, and to Liz Ferry at Per Se Editing, for preventing embarrassing mistakes.

And finally, thank you, lovely reader, for giving up a sliver of your life to come into our world and read our stories. I hope I have made it worth it and that you'll continue to visit Havenwood Falls.

A Havenwood Falls New Adult Novella

HAVENWOOD FALLS

TRAGIC INK

HEATHER HILDENBRAND

Tragic Ink (A Havenwood Falls Novella) by Heather Hildenbrand

All's fair in war and unrequited love.

Tattoo artist Gwen Facharro prefers working alone in her Havenwood Falls shop. Coworkers want to be friends, and friends ask too many questions. The last thing Gwen wants to do is answer them. Especially when her inked images tend to take on lives of their own—and not everyone uses the fae magic for good. If the Court finds out, she'll be tossed in jail. Or worse, banished from town forever.

Although they grew up together, Seelie warrior Rhys Graywalk has been very careful to keep Gwen at a distance. Between the secrets he keeps *for* her and the ones he keeps *from* her, his plate is already full. Romance isn't on the menu. It can't be. He has his orders.

But when the people around her start turning up dead, Gwen's fears become reality. Someone has discovered her secret. Someone who wants Gwen's talents for themselves. And they won't stop until they get it.

To separate the truth from the lies she's been told about her fae heritage, Gwen is forced to work with the only friend she's ever really known. She's just not sure she can handle rejection a second time.

TRAGIC INK

AN EXCERPT

*T*he buzz of the tattoo gun vibrated against my skin until the bone in my hand ached from holding it steady. This was my third tattoo of the night—and the longest by at least two hours. I hadn't stopped to stretch, and now my neck and shoulders were paying for it. The way I hung over my work, hovering and squinting to get it just right, left me stiff and aching. It was a pain in the ass, really, the soreness that would inevitably follow tomorrow morning. But I loved it. The concentration required for the precision of the lines. Bringing an art piece to life on the canvas of someone's skin. It was a thrill every time, even if this one was so large and time-consuming. We were on our third and final session, but at least the patient was compliant. Strangely silent, actually. But it was better than when they complained.

When I was finally finished with the bright blues of the seascape, and the aqua scales of the mermaid's tail had been shaded in to the edge of the fine lines, I switched off the machine and set it aside. On the table before me, Sean stirred and sighed as if he'd just woken from a peaceful slumber.

"Is that a wrap, then?" His Irish accent was still thick despite the fact that he'd lived in Havenwood Falls for as long as I could remember. And I'd grown up here.

I nodded my head. Only Sean could sleep through a full-color back piece. "That's it," I confirmed.

He sat up slowly, his large back and broad shoulders probably just as stiff as mine. If the numbness had worn off enough to let the pain set in, he didn't show it as he swung easily to his feet from the table where he'd spent the last few hours facedown. His graying hair was disheveled, but then my short blond hair probably looked about the same. My own shirt clung to my back where the stuffiness in the room had left me coated in sweat. It wasn't something I minded. Not when it was the result of giving someone a fresh piece. A shower did sound heavenly right about now, though.

Sean stood and stretched and then fell still again, waiting for what we both knew came next. Standing behind him, I slathered a thick layer of Vaseline over the mural I'd given him and then wrapped it in plastic. When I tried reminding him of the care instructions, he waved me off. "Yeah, yeah, I got it. This ain't my first rodeo, girl."

He was right. This was his fourteenth, if I was counting correctly.

I let it go and slid my gloves off while he shrugged into his button-down. He left the buttons open on the top half, revealing a hairy chest and the edges of the older ink that covered his shoulders and flowed down his arms.

"You're catching up to me," I told him with a raised brow.

"Nah. None of mine are worth even half of those." He nodded to the various tattoos flowing up and out of my black tank. My arms were covered down to my wrists, and my chest was inked up to the edges of my collarbone. The only tattoo that I hadn't done myself was a small symbol on my left shoulder. Magical in its own way, but not like the rest. If the Court of the Sun and the Moon, our local leaders, only knew their mark wasn't the only one on my body that held spells . . . Thankfully, they didn't. Yet.

Sean studied the hawk on my forearm with sharp eyes. Something like fear jangled my gut at the way his attention caught on it. His words finally sank in, and I stiffened.

"What do you mean?" I asked.

Sean blinked, but the gleam in his eye remained. And the certainty in his tone was unmistakable. "Come on. You know what I mean, Gwen. They say your tattoos are more than just ink."

Motherfucker.

Fourteen times this guy had been in my chair, and he'd never once let on he knew about me. About what I could do. If he had, I damn sure wouldn't have inked him. Partly out of principle. Mostly, to avoid this exact conversation.

"Look, Sean," I began. "I think you're mistaken about what it—"

"No mistake. But don't worry, your secret's safe." He looked believable enough, and I had known Sean for a long time now, but even so, my gut roiled with fear and the guilt that always gnawed at the edges. "Honestly, I've just been hoping you'd pour a bit of that magic of yours into some of the ink you've put on me. I'd never tell a soul if you did."

And there it was.

The request that only the really plugged-in residents of this town bothered to make. They wanted the magic. Too bad for them I wasn't giving it out anymore. Not unless I was forced, but that was another issue altogether. And if the first thirteen pieces I'd done for him were any indication, Sean should have known that already.

I narrowed my eyes. Maybe he was sent here to test me. Maybe Ada was checking to be sure she was still my only customer when it came to the top-tier services Tragic Ink could provide.

"Look, you got what you paid for. That's all I'm offering," I said in a tone that left no room for argument—or more questions.

He shrugged and backed off, heading for the door. "Sure, no problem. Next time," he said.

The way the words hung there, even after he'd left and the door had clicked shut behind him, made it hard to tell what he meant. Did he mean he'd see me next time? Or that he'd expect the bonus package next time?

I made a mental note not to tattoo Sean, the Irish healer, ever again.

Then, shoving aside my anxiety, I straightened the studio and shut everything down for the night. I checked my phone, which had been set to silent while I worked, and read the five texts from Aelwyn, my foster mother. The first three were reminders about what time she was expecting me. The last two were warnings not to be late again. I texted her back to let her know I was on my way, hoping I wouldn't have to hear a lecture about how tardiness was a form of disrespect—Aelwyn wasn't strict, but on this she'd always been a dog with a bone—and hauled ass while I cleaned up. Hurrying as I shut off the lights and the neon "Open" sign, I locked up and took off into the frigid night for Aelwyn's house.

The few residents that were out walking on Main Street never even noticed me as I slipped out the front door of my second-floor tattoo shop and down the stairs, taking a hard right into the alley that ran between my shop's building and the next. From there, I cut through the back alleyway that ran behind Eighth Street until I reached the narrow space where I parked my truck.

Sliding in, I fired it up and slid my palms together to warm them while I waited for the engine to heat to something warmer than the frigid temperature outside. Winter in the mountains of Colorado was not exactly tropical. To ward off the chill, I let some of my human glamour slip. In the shadows of my truck, I felt my ears lengthen and come to a point at the top and the shape of my face narrow.

My human glamour made me appear shorter than I was, so without it my head brushed the roof of the truck. My suddenly longer legs bent more sharply at the knees, too cramped for the seat, but I dealt with it just long enough to let the fae blood inside me heat my skin. Between that and the heating vents, it was enough.

I waited until my hands and toes had warmed. Then, just as quickly as I'd let it fall away, I called my glamour back up, and by the time I blinked, I looked human again. Blonde, slender, and covered in ink, though that last part never changed, glamour or not. The tattooed star tingled a bit as the magic it was laced with settled back into place. I'd had it since I was a kid, a requirement for all the permanent supernatural residents of Havenwood Falls. It was also the symbol that housed my glamour and logged me with the Court of the Sun and the Moon so they could keep track of who was supposed to be here—and who wasn't human. It also helped lessen my weakness to iron, which was a nice benefit considering the stuff was literally everywhere these days, and all fae were sensitive to it.

As I'd grown older, the fact that I'd chosen such a common symbol had irritated me, but I knew if I had to choose all over again, I would still pick it. The stars had always called to me, even as a little girl. In fact, when Ethan had sprung to life that first time, it had almost made sense to me that I'd conjured a creature with wings. My heart had always craved flight.

Almost as if he knew I was thinking of him, the gray hawk inked on my arm seemed to twitch impatiently. "Easy, boy," I muttered and shoved the truck into gear, rumbling out into the empty alley and from there to the outskirts of town.

The drive wasn't long, but it was just treacherous enough this time of year to slow me down even more.

Aelwyn had always been supportive of my tattoo business. She'd been the one to encourage my art and to help me discover what sort of magic I was capable of using with it. She'd also been there to see Ethan come to life. And because of her support, I knew, once a week, she willingly ate dinner late just so we could have this time together after my work was finished. Still, keeping her waiting was a good way to be greeted with a lecture. I wanted to avoid that part if possible. A hot meal settled better when it wasn't preceded by a tongue-lashing.

My stomach twisted as I wondered if I would be the only dinner guest. Just as quickly as I thought it, I shoved it away. He hadn't been there in months, thanks to the bar he'd bought last year taking up so much time. And even when he did show, we barely spoke. It had been like that for years now. What was one more awkward dinner?

Nothing, I told myself. It was nothing. *He* was nothing.
***

It was utterly dark when I parked in front of the old Victorian where I'd grown up. Trees surrounded it, with only the winding drive ribboning in from the mountain road providing a view of the place. My headlights cast a narrow beam over the front entry, and I frowned as I pulled to a stop directly in front rather than off to the side where I usually parked. Something wasn't right. Trying to figure it out, I looked around to check the solar-powered lanterns that led the way across the lawn to the front door. None of them were lit. The porch light wasn't either. I looked closer and frowned. Even the lights inside were off.

Something anxious curled in my gut.

I left my headlights on and the engine running as I got out. Taking care to keep to the shadows, I crept around the shrubs as the gray hawk on my arm stirred and scratched. This time, I didn't hold back. The darkness would shield any prying eyes, and besides, I might need him. Despite the cold, I peeled my jacket away, revealing my tank top and bare arm underneath.

With silent permission, I let the magic call him forth. On a sigh, he raised his beak, already on alert, and in the next blink, the hawk had peeled itself away from my skin, its body filling in with form and feathers until it was much more than the ink outline I'd drawn on myself years ago.

With a sharp keening sound, my familiar took to the skies, soaring up and over the rooftop, doing a quick loop to investigate. I slid my jacket back into place and took a shallow breath, my eyes half-closed as I concentrated on the magic that allowed me to see the world through Ethan's eyes. I rarely allowed him loose like this so close to town where humans might see, but the darkness and the slithering unease that raced up my spine left me too anxious to resist.

When Ethan had done a full loop and found nothing out of the ordinary, I blinked, clearing my sight and refocusing on the yard in front of me. Slowly, with a silent stealth inherent to fae, I crept toward the front door.

I tried glancing in through the darkened window as I passed. Nothing moved inside.

My heart beat faster.

Aelwyn had been old when I'd been brought to her as a baby. Even by fae standards, which was saying something, because of how slowly we aged compared to humans. If she'd lost her balance and fallen . . .

But that still didn't explain the dark house.

With a steadying breath, I tried the knob, twisting it in my hand and shoving inside. The hinges creaked, and I waited, listening. The scent of mistletoe hit me first. Not unusual. Aelwyn had an affinity for the stuff, and her garden out back was covered in it. But something was off. I just didn't know what.

Somewhere in the back of the house, there was the tiniest creak of a floorboard.

I flew into motion.

Racing for the kitchen, I tore down the narrow hall, skipping the living and dining rooms as I passed them on my right and left. It was dark as hell, but I knew my way around this house, lights or no.

When I reached the kitchen, I flipped the switch and was a little surprised to see the overhead light come on so easily. It washed the room in a yellowish tone, and I blinked at the sudden change. The back door stood wide open, the yawning darkness of the backyard beckoning me. I almost obeyed, but something out of the corner of my eye stopped me.

I whirled, searching.

A pot stood simmering on the stove, red sauce bubbling up the sides. Another pot sat in the sink. Spaghetti. She'd been making my favorite. When I caught sight of a chunk of white hair peeking out from behind the stove, I closed the distance, curving around the pantry and pulling up short.

My lips parted, but no sound came.

I dropped to my knees.

My mother lay on the floor, her legs curled at an awkward angle. Her white hair was splayed around her face, fanning out around her so that the ends were mixing with the pool of blood that was leaking fast from her abdomen and chest onto the floor underneath her.

"Ma," I choked out, my hands hovering over her uncertainly.

All I wanted to do was help her. But I had no idea how.

At the sound of my voice, her lids fluttered and then her blue eyes opened, squinting as if in pain. They widened when she saw me. "Gwenllian."

"What happened?" My voice cracked as I struggled to hold back a sob. "What can I do?"

"Nothing. It is too late to help me." She pressed her lips together, and her face contorted sharply.

A sob escaped. "Ma, please. You can't—"

I broke off, unable to say the word.

Die. She couldn't die. Not yet. Not like this.

"Listen to me now," she said quietly. "Hush and listen. I have kept this from you solely for your own safety. I thought I would have more time, but . . ."

"More time for what?" I asked through tears that blurred her face until I could barely make her out.

She drew a slow, pained breath. I squeezed her hand, willing her to go on. Part of me wanted to tell her to save her breath. To hang on while I ran for help. But something held me there. Something that knew these were our last moments, and I wasn't willing to waste them on pointless efforts. I blinked until I could see her weathered cheeks and light eyes once more.

"Gwen, you are special. Important. I've done all I can, but they have never stopped hunting you. You must not let them find you. Leave this house. Don't come back. Find Rhys. He will know what to do."

"What are you talking about, Aelwyn? Who is hunting me? Who did this to you?" Her words jumbled against each other in my mind —all of them taking a backseat to the puddle of blood I was now sitting in, while still more leaked from the fresh wounds on her chest. The horror of watching her bleed out this way overrode any sense I might have made of whatever secrets she was trying to spill.

She clutched my hand much too weakly, her eyes pleading with mine. "You are a bright star, Gwenllian. Much too bright to conceal.

But you can't hide anymore. They have come for you. And you must not run from that. You must not run from who you are."

"I don't understand what you're saying," I sobbed. "Who am I hiding from?"

Aelwyn didn't answer, and for a terrifying moment, I thought she was already gone. My head bowed, and I leaned in to lay my head on her shoulder, my cries filling the silence.

"You will," she whispered, so low I might have missed it if I hadn't been lying so close to her lips. "Rhys will protect you. He always has."

"Rhys?" I sat up, confused and heartsick at the thought of asking him for anything.

"Promise me," she said, because Aelwyn knew. She'd always known. Somehow. "Please."

"I promise," I said, my voice breaking. My heart ached, because it was a promise I would keep no matter how much I didn't want to. The first stirrings of rage began in my gut. Even now, I could see the life fading in her, and I knew that when she was gone, I would have nothing else stopping me from my revenge. "Now tell me who did this."

"I love you, *nighean*."

Daughter.

It was what she called me when she was trying to comfort or reassure me, usually when my magic had gone awry or my heart had felt broken. And it was absolutely broken now. "I love you too, Ma. Don't go."

She didn't answer.

My shoulders shook as I lay with my cheek against her shoulder and my hand still squeezing hers. A coldness had seeped into her skin, and now, it felt odd, like I was holding onto a stranger. Thinking that only made me cry harder.

Outside, Ethan gave a sharp call, and I jerked my head up, blinking away the tears that blurred the kitchen cabinets as I looked toward the open door. For a split second, it all slid into place. The reality hit me that Aelwyn was gone and someone had taken her from me. And that someone might still be close by. For a moment, that was enough to dull the grief and sharpen my thoughts.

I looked down at Aelwyn. Her blue eyes were closed, and her chest no longer moved with the rise and fall of labored breaths. I swallowed back a scream as I searched for a pulse. I found none.

And just like that, my helplessness vanished. Instead, I had purpose. Not once in my life had I chosen violence to solve something. In fact, the only time violence had occurred at my hands, I'd spent the next few years punishing myself for it. But now, tonight, violence called to me. The idea of avenging Aelwyn made my blood sing.

No longer frozen in shock, I rose slowly to my feet. When I heard Ethan call again, I sucked in a breath and twisted toward the door. It was a battle cry. The call he used to let me know when he'd found his prey. Sometimes, when I loosed him in the woods behind the house, we'd hunt together. Him with his talons and sharp eyes as he soared overhead. Me with the bow and quiver I kept in my old room upstairs. Tonight, though, I had a feeling he wasn't signaling dinner.

I wiped my bloody palms on my dark jeans and ran to the knife block, yanking free the largest of the blades. I clutched it tight in my stained hand before racing out into the darkness in the direction of Ethan's call. If Aelwyn's murderer was still out there, I was going to find them. And when I did, I was going to kill them.

PURCHASE *TRAGIC INK* at your favorite book retailer.

www.ingramcontent.com/pod-product-compliance
Lightning Source LLC
Chambersburg PA
CBHW021007260626
47169CB00006B/1981